TEMPTED BY DECEPTION

RINA KENT

To villains.

AUTHOR NOTE

Hello reader friend,

If you haven't read my books before, you might not know this,
but I write darker stories that can be upsetting and disturbing.
My books and main characters aren't for the faint of heart.

Tempted by Deception is the second book of a trilogy and is not
standalone.

Deception Trilogy:
#0 Dark Deception (Free Prequel)
#1 Vow of Deception
#2 Tempted by Deception
#3 Consumed by Deception

Sign up to Rina Kent's Newsletter for news about future
releases and an exclusive gift.

My husband. My villain.

We started with death and blood.

We started with games and carnal pleasure.

Adrian and I shouldn't have been together.

He's wrong.

I'm wrong.

What we have is the epitome disaster.

Yet, it's impossible to stop.

My husband will either destroy me or I'll destroy him.

PLAYLIST

Hate Myself—NF

Peace of mind—Villain of the Story

Drown—Bring Me The Horizon

M.I.N.E—Five Finger Death Punch

How to Save a Life—The Fray

Gasoline—Halsey

Worlds Apart—The Faim

I'll Be Good—Jaymes Young

I Know How to Speak—Manchester Orchestra

Sorry for Now—Linkin Park

The Light Behind Your Eyes—My Chemical Romance

Fake Your Death—My Chemical Romance

Roses—Awaken I Am

Follow Your Fire—Kodaline

Lion—Hollywood Undead

Only Us—DYLYN

Choke—Royal & the Serpent

You can find the complete playlist on Spotify.

PROLOGUE

Adrian

Age seven

"Y**OU'LL DO AS YOU'RE TOLD.**"

I nod once.

It's better to be obedient when my mother is in this state—or any state, really.

She's been pacing the length of our small apartment for a few minutes, staring at her phone one second and typing on it the next.

My feet dangle as I sit on the tall chair in our living room that smells of burnt food because Mom hates cooking and she's terrible at it. My book, *The Nutcracker*, lies on my lap, although I haven't been able to read due to Mom's mood. It's snowing, the window covered with a dusting of white, like in the Christmas movies, but the fireplace offers some warmth from the outside cold.

My mother, who's tall and slender, always goes to the gym, leaving me alone at home, so she can keep her 'shape' after 'I ruined it' when I was born. I don't know what that means, but she says things like that all the time. She's wearing a tight blouse with an elegant skirt, and her blonde hair is pulled up in a bun.

Her lips are blood red and her earrings are long and dangle to her neck like tinsel at Christmas, which I celebrated with my father and his wife, Aunt Annika, this year. Mom spent the entire month after throwing things at me, but it was worth it.

Mom hates Aunt Annika. She does and says stuff that hurts her, like how she can't even have a baby. My stepmom says nothing in front of Mom, and sometimes even smiles, which makes my mother more furious. But I often see Aunt Annika crying alone in her room. I stand beside her and pat her hand. Sometimes that's enough to make her stop.

Mom doesn't let up, though. She even asks me to search for things when I'm at Dad's house that she can use to hurt Aunt Annika.

I don't want Aunt Annika in pain. She bakes cakes for me and gives me sips of her tea. She takes me outside for walks and buys me gloves and scarves to protect 'my little body,' as she says, from the cold. She hugs me, too, and kisses my cheeks.

Mom never does that.

Because of her job at the hospital, Mom isn't home much. But I am. After I get in from school, I spend a lot of time all alone. It's scary at night because I think the monster under my bed will come out.

Mom says that's nonsense and the real monster is Aunt Annika. Because of that 'bitch,' she can't be with Dad.

Over time, I've given Mom false information since I don't want Aunt Annika hurt. When Mom found out, she slapped me, and once, she smeared my face with red pepper powder. It burned so much that I saw stars, but I didn't cry. Mom and Dad don't like it when I cry.

Mom says Dad is a powerful man and that I need to listen to him and her. But Aunt Annika told me it's better not to listen to everything Dad says.

"Is it because he's powerful?" I asked while she was reading a book to me after helping with my homework.

A shadow passed over her features as she smiled. Her smile is always sad, not like Mom's which looks like a cartoon bad guy's. "Because he's dangerous, *malyshonuk*."

"Like the bad guy in the cartoon?"

"Mm-hmm."

"But Mommy says he's powerful."

"In a bad way." She wrapped her arms around me. "I wish I could take you and leave, my sweet pie."

I wished that, too. I also wished she was my mother. At least she never hurts me and she makes me feel comfortable. At least she likes me.

Mom doesn't.

"What did that whore tell you?" Mom asks me with a harsh tone and I flinch. I don't like it when she calls Aunt Annika that.

"Nothing." My voice is small.

She stomps toward me and I tighten my hold on the book, waiting for the slap, as usual. No matter how much she hits me, I'll never get used to it. I hate the pain that comes with it, but most of all, I hate that she doesn't treat me like most mothers treat their children.

Sometimes, I ask Aunt Annika why she's not my mother instead, and she just smiles in that sad way.

Mom doesn't slap me this time, but she bunches her fingers in my shirt and lifts me up by it. Up close, she's pretty in a scary kind of way. Like witches from cartoons. "Tell me what she said, you little fucker!"

I can't breathe.

It's not the first time I haven't been able to breathe. Mom used to place a pillow over my face when she caught me crying to make me stop.

That's why I don't do it anymore. That's why I want to get used to pain, so I won't need to cry.

The book that Aunt Annika bought me falls to the floor with a thud as I grab Mom's hands with my smaller ones, trying to remove them.

"M-Mom..."

Her expression doesn't change as she stares down at me. "You think you're in pain, you fucking bastard? How about the pain I went through to give birth to you? Do you believe I wanted an illegitimate child? I'm Dominika Alekseev, first in my class at Harvard Medical School, and yet, I sacrificed myself. Instead of aborting your bastard existence, I gave birth to your father's fucking spawn so he'd leave that bitch. But did he? No. She's some fucking nobility, after all, and holds more value to him, even childless. So don't sit there thinking you mean anything except to serve as a bridge between me and your father. You are *my* son, as unwanted as you are, and you will not take that bitch's side over mine or I will fucking kill you. I will finish the life I gave you. Understand?"

She shoves me against the chair and I suck in a long gulp of air, gasping and wheezing. The wood digs against my side and a stray splinter stabs into my arm. Tiny droplets of blood appear on the surface of my skin before sliding down onto the book.

I rush forward, falling to my knees on the wood floor, and wipe the cover of *The Nutcracker* with the back of my hand.

Mom yanks the book from my fingers.

"Mom, no!"

Her head tilts to the side. "She gave you this, didn't she?"

I shake my head once.

"Don't lie to me. She's the only idiot who loves this trash." A sly smile paints her lips as she opens it and positions her hands to tear it. "Are you going to tell me what she said?"

"I...she..."

"What?"

I don't want her to rip my book, but I also don't want to tell her about Aunt Annika.

"Fine, then, you little bastard."

"No!" I lunge toward her. "She...she said we'd go on a vacation."

She raises a brow. "Vacation? Where?"

"Russia."

She laughs, her perfect white teeth showing under the red lipstick. The sound is so loud that I want to place both hands on my ears and not listen to her anymore.

"Well, well. The model good girl plans on leaving." Still clutching the book, she retrieves her phone and walks to the fireplace.

Mom stares at the book and mutters, "Trash," and throws it into the burning flames.

I spring forward, trying to get it back, but the fire has already eaten it. Tears sting my eyes and I hit Mom's leg. "You said you'd leave my book alone!"

"I lied. Now, hush." She pushes me away and I fall on my butt on the floor beside her. The sting makes me wince, but I learned to mask it quickly.

Mom places the phone to her ear and a hand on her hip. "There's a change of plans... Yes...an accident...tonight..."

After she hangs up, she turns around to face me with a triumphant smile, the one that looks like the bad guy. "You finally proved your worth, tiny bastard."

"Are you going to let me go to see Aunt Annika this weekend?"

"Nope."

"But Dad said..."

"Your dad won't be taking her side anymore, Adrian. Because no matter how long he stays with her and no matter how much Bitch Annika and I worship at his feet, only one person matters to him. The one person who will carry on his legacy." She tilts her head to the side. "*You*."

I stand up, meeting her head-on. "Dad said I could spend the weekend with Aunt Annika."

"You won't be able to anymore."

"Why not?"

She leans in to whisper in my face. "Because your beloved Annika is finally going to disappear."

"No…" Tears stream down my cheeks. All I can think about is her smile, even the sad one, the hugs, and how much she cares about me. She can't disappear and leave me with Mom and Dad.

"Yes. It's about time she does." Her phone rings again and she smiles. "That was faster than I expected."

I watch her as she listens to someone on the other end. Her brows draw together and her red lips twist. The weight in my chest lifts as if it were never there. When Mom is mad, it means Aunt Annika is safe.

"No, Georgy can't suspect anything… Yes…I will think of a way to keep him preoccupied."

After she hangs up, she stares at the fireplace, hand back on her hip and her fingers balled around the phone.

"Is Aunt Annika all right?" I ask in a low voice.

She turns around abruptly, as if she's forgotten I was there. I don't like the spark in her eyes or the slight smirk on her lips. "How could I not think of this? The best way to keep Georgy occupied is you, my little bastard."

When she slowly approaches me, I stumble, stepping back, not wanting her to hit me again. My legs bump against the coffee table and I end up landing on my butt.

Mom stops in front of me, her shadow falling over me and blocking the light from the fire. "Why are you running away from me?"

She glides her nails over my cheek, then into my hair, but she's not caressing it like Aunt Annika does when putting me to sleep. Mom's hand is cold like the look on her face.

It's like being in Russia during the freezing winter.

Mom grabs my arm and I remain still as a stone, unable

to move. She dials a number on her phone and sniffles a little before she puts it to her ear. "Oh, Georgy! What to do about Adrian?"

She pauses and I can hear Dad's frantic curses in Russian from the other end.

Tears slide down Mom's cheeks. She always cries when talking to Dad, even though her expression right now is still like the bad guy's.

"He…he fell down and broke his arm…I don't know what to do! Please come over, please!"

More curses from my father. More Russian.

"Oh, my baby!!" Mom shrieks and hangs up, sniffling, then just like that, her expression turns to normal. "Now, Adrian, you wouldn't mind making a little sacrifice for your mother's happily ever after, would you?"

Before I can say anything, she closes her hand around my arm and twists it in the opposite direction, hard.

An ugly pop echoes in the air and I shriek.

ONE

Lia

Age twenty-four

NOTHING GOOD EVER COMES WITHOUT PAIN.

Since I was a little girl, that fact has been cemented into my head with bloodstained fingers.

I was born from pain, raised by pain, and eventually embraced it.

However, no matter how much pain I've had to endure, I've never managed to become numb to it. Not even when I went out of my way to train my body for it.

Pain is real, suffocating, and with the right amount of pressure, it's bound to break my every last barrier.

My endurance is stronger, though.

Loud cheers fill the hall long after the curtains fall for the finale of *The Nutcracker*. I remain on pointe, hands poised in my salute even after we're out of the public eye.

My ankles scream to be put out of their misery, as they have repeatedly over these last couple of months. Long rehearsals and endless tours have dulled my senses, almost bleeding into one another.

I give it a few seconds, catching my breath before I softly land on the soles of my feet. My ballet shoes are inaudible in the midst of the fuss backstage.

Other dancers release relieved breaths as they either pat each other on the back or simply stand there dumbfounded. We might belong to the New York City Ballet, one of the most prestigious dance companies in the world, but that doesn't lessen the pressure. If anything, it makes it tenfold worse.

We're expected to be our absolute best whenever we go on stage. When the company handpicked its dancers, the only rule was: no mistakes are allowed.

The roaring applause at the end of our performance isn't something we hope for, it's something we're expected to accomplish.

The director, Philippe, a tall, slim man with a bald head and thick white moustache, walks over, accompanied by our choreography director, Stephanie.

Philippe smiles, his moustache tipping with the movement, and all of us release a collective breath. He's not the type to smile after a show unless we've done a perfect performance.

"You were marvelous. Bravo!" he speaks with a pronounced French accent, and claps. His entire body joins in the motion, his colorful scarf flying and his tight blazer straining against his body.

Everyone else follows his lead, clapping and congratulating each other.

Everyone except me, the lead male dancer, Ryan, and the second female lead, Hannah.

Some dancers attempt to start small talk with Philippe, but he brazenly ignores them as he walks to me and lifts my hand to his mouth, brushing his lips and moustache against my knuckles. "My most beautiful prima ballerina. You were a work of art tonight, Lia *chérie*."

"Thank you, Philippe." I pull my hand back as swiftly as I can and wince when a tendon aches in my left leg. I need to get a pain patch on that as soon as possible.

"Do not thank me. I'm the one who's honored to have a muse like you."

That makes me smile. Philippe is definitely the best director I've worked with. He understands me better than anyone ever has.

"Ryan." He nods at the male lead, rolling the *R* dramatically. "You were perfect."

"As expected." Ryan raises an arrogant brow. He has those all-American good looks with a square face, deep blue eyes, and a cleft chin.

"You, too, Hannah," Philippe says dismissively to her. "You'll need to work on your pointe for *Giselle*."

Her expression lights up as she smirks at me, then clears her throat. Hannah is blonde, a bit taller than me, and has cat eyes that she always accentuates with thick, shadowy makeup. "Does that mean we'll be auditioning for the lead role?"

Stephanie steps up beside Philippe. She has deep black skin and naturally curly hair that she's gathered into a pink band. As a former prima ballerina in the NYC Ballet, she has a reputation that precedes her and is as tenacious as Philippe, but they work surprisingly well as a team. "There will be an audition, but not for the lead."

"But why—" Hannah stops herself from snapping at the last second.

Stephanie motions her head at me. "The producers already picked Lia to be Giselle."

Hannah's gaze meets mine with nothing short of malice. I give her a cool one in return. Being in ballet since I was five has taught me to rise above their petty jealousy and catfights. I'm here because I love to dance and play characters that I'm not in real life. Everything else is white noise.

That's probably why I have no friends. Some kiss my ass for their own benefit, then stab me in the back, and others are malicious about everything.

Everyone here is just a colleague. And as Grandma used to say, it's lonely at the top.

My tendons start aching again and I hide my wince. I overwork myself during these marathon shows and I need aftercare.

Now.

I tip my head at Philippe and Stephanie. "If you'll excuse me."

"*Quoi?* You're not going to join us for the celebration party?" the director exclaims. "The producers won't like this."

"I need aftercare, Philippe."

"So do it, and then join us, *chérie.*"

"I'm afraid I can't. I'm exhausted and need downtime. Please relay my apologies."

Philippe and Stephanie seem displeased, but they nod. It's unheard of for a prima ballerina not to attend celebration parties, but they know how much I hate the limelight outside of dancing. Besides, most of those producers are sexist, perverted assholes. I'd rather not meet them unless I absolutely have to.

The dancers slowly trickle into the dressing room, chatting among each other.

Hannah leans over to whisper, "Maybe the producers will finally realize how much of a fucking talentless bitch you actually are."

I stare at her. Thankfully, she's not tall enough to look down on me. "If you rehearsed as hard as you run your mouth, you'd probably have a chance at taking some lead roles from me."

She clicks her tongue and her face contorts, highlighting the bold makeup that gives her a witchy appearance. "How many of the producers did you fuck, Lia? Because we all know you wouldn't get this many lead roles if it wasn't for whoring yourself out."

Her words don't sting. Not only are they untrue, but I've also heard such jabs from the entire ballet troupe over the years. In the beginning, I wanted to prove I'm no whore and that I got this far by torturing myself, but I soon realized it was pointless. People will think what they want to think.

So now I've grown accustomed to them, but at the same time, I won't allow Hannah or anyone else to walk all over me. Squaring my shoulders, I say with mocking calm, "Until then, you'll have to remain Miss Number Two."

She raises her hand to slap me, but Ryan clutches her wrist and pulls her against him. "Now, Hannah, don't get worked up over people who mean nothing."

He lowers his head and kisses her, open-mouthed, harshly, but his eyes remain fixed on me. The lust in them and in his tight pants is visible from my position.

I turn around and make my way to my private dressing room backstage, but I'm not going to bother with changing. After they put something itchy in my clothes one time, I make sure to check everything before I shower, but I'm in no mood tonight, so I'll just do it at home.

My feet come to a halt once I'm inside. Countless bouquets from admirers and the producers stuff the room, barely allowing me to move.

I comb through them until I find a bouquet of white roses. My lips curve in the first genuine smile of tonight as I hug them my chest and lower my head to take a deep inhale. They smell like home and happiness.

They smell like Mom, Dad, and bright memories.

I refuse to associate them with the day when everything ended. I place the roses back on the table and take the card, grinning as I read it.

You're the most beautiful flower on earth, Duchess. You not only grew on the harsh pavement, but you also flourished. Keep growing. I'm proud of my little Duchess.

Love,

L.

Luca.

We might not see each other often, but my friendship with him will always be there.

My smile pauses when I lift my head to look in the mirror. I'm in a soft pink tutu with a muslin bodice and a tulle skirt. It's tight around my breasts and waist but is wide at the bottom.

My hair is pulled up and my face is full of glitter and layers of makeup. I don't have the time to remove it, because if I don't leave right now, one of the producers will corner me and force me to attend their show-off party. They'll parade me from one of their associates to the next as if I'm livestock for sale.

I take out the pins and release my hair, then remove my ballet shoes. I wince at the droplets of blood marring my big toe and massage it. It's nothing to worry about.

Pain means I did my best.

After slipping into my comfy flats, I put on my long cashmere coat and wrap a scarf around my neck and half of my face.

I make sure no one is outside my room before I hug Luca's flowers to my chest, snatch my bag, and hurry to the parking lot.

A long breath leaves my chest when I'm on the road with the flowers in the passenger seat as my lone companion.

I wish I could call Luca and talk to him right now. But the fact that he didn't come to meet me backstage means he's keeping a low profile.

Ever since we met as kids, his entire life has been about being in the shadow of action and dealing with the wrong crowd.

I'm not an idiot. I know that as much as he took care of me, Luca didn't get his money legally, but as he says, the less I know, the better. He doesn't want to put me in danger and neither do I.

So we kind of look out for each other from afar.

But I miss him.

I want to tell him all about today's show and how the pain in my ankle kept me on the edge. I want to tell him about the blood because he'd understand what it means to be in pain.

He's the only person I can call both family and a friend. And it's been months since I last saw him. I had hoped he'd make an exception today and come out of the shadows, but apparently, that wasn't the case.

I arrive at the parking garage of my building in less than thirty minutes. It's located in a quiet suburban neighborhood in New York City and has excellent security that makes me feel safe at home.

My ankle is throbbing when I exit my car. I lean against the door to catch my breath and a cramp tries to break the surface. After taking a few deep breaths, I beep the locks, then remember my bouquet. I might not get Luca in the flesh, but I can at least feel his presence through the flowers.

I'm about to get them when a loud sound of screeching tires fills the garage. I duck down and remain in place when another screech follows.

Usually, I wouldn't stop for any commotion, but hearing disturbing noises late at night at an apartment building like mine is rare. In fact, it should be almost impossible.

I stare up at the cameras blinking red in every corner and release a shaking breath.

I'm safe.

But for some reason, I don't come out of my hiding spot beside my car. It seems vital at this moment, and if I get up, I feel like something disastrous will happen.

The ache in my ankle pulses harder, as if it's sensing my stress and participating in it.

A black Mercedes comes to a shrill stop in my direct view, its tires leaving angry black marks in its wake.

No one gets out, though.

Another black car, a van this time, brakes behind it. Then I watch in horror as its window lowers and bullets fly in the direction of the Mercedes.

I jump, placing both hands over my ears to block out the loud gunshots. Inching back, I find myself crouched between my car and the wall. Thank God I always leave some space.

The gunshots go on and on like a crescendo of a musical, up and up, faster and harder and *louder*. For a second, I think it'll never end. That it'll keep going for an eternity.

But it does stop.

My heart beats in my throat, nearly spilling my guts on the ground as I hear some rustling and then curses in a foreign language.

Could I be trapped in a nightmare?

I dig my nails into my wrist and squeeze until pain explodes on my skin. No. It's not a nightmare. This is reality.

The voices are now high-pitched, angry, and not holding back. I probably shouldn't look, but how am I going to escape this horrible *Black Mirror* episode if I don't see what's going on?

Making sure my body is still hidden behind the car, I grab the hood and peer around it. The Mercedes that was shot at has multiple bullet holes in the windshield, but the glass didn't break.

All its doors are open, and while I was fully prepared to find dead people, the car is empty. Instead, three men dressed in dark clothing are outside, all holding guns. Two of them are wearing suits. One is bulky and blond with a scowling face; the other is lean and has long brown hair tied at his nape. They're forcing a chubby man to his knees in front of their third companion.

He's wearing a simple black shirt and pants. His sleeves are rolled to above his wrists, exposing a hint of tattoos. One of his hands rests by his side and the other holds a gun to the chubby man's head.

I only get the view of his side profile, but it's enough to tell me he's the one in charge.

The bossman.

From this distance, I can't tell what he looks like except that he has dark hair and light stubble. He's tall, too. So tall that I feel his superior height even from my hiding position.

I glimpse at the van that stopped behind them and wish I hadn't. Two men are sprawled over each other on the floor, unmoving, blood covering their unrecognizable features.

Bile rises to my throat and I inhale deeply to stop myself from retching and giving away my existence.

I'm distracted from the view and illogically drawn back to the scene in front of me when that foreign language starts up again. The two men are talking to the bossman in a language I don't recognize. I think it's Eastern European.

"Who sent you?" Bossman asks with a Russian accent, and I swallow at the calm power behind his words. He doesn't shout, doesn't kick or punch, but it sounds like the worst threat of all.

"Fuck you, Volkov," Chubby Man snarls in an accented voice—Italian.

"That's not the right answer. Are you going to give me one or should I go after your family once I'm finished with you?"

Sweat breaks out on the chubby man's temples and he curses in Italian, which I do recognize. It's the only other language I somehow speak besides English.

"What's it to you?" Chubby Man is twitching badly.

"That's not the answer. I assume you would rather I go after your family."

"No. Wait!"

"Final chance."

"Boss wanted to keep an eye on—" Chubby Man doesn't finish his sentence before the bossman pulls the trigger.

The shot rings in the air with haunting finality.

I slap both hands on my mouth to stop myself from shrieking. My stomach churns, about to throw up the apple I had for dinner.

The man's vacant eyes roll to the back of his lifeless head as he drops to the ground. Bossman lets his hand that's holding the gun fall inert at his side. His bland eyes are focused on the corpse as if it's dust on his leather shoe. His expression remains the same—a bit focused, a bit bored, and absolutely monstrous.

He just executed a man in cold blood and has no reaction to it.

That's even more terrifying than the act itself.

Just when I'm about to throw up my dinner, his head tilts to the side.

Toward me.

TWO

Lia

I'M FROZEN.

My limbs have turned to stone and my body doesn't follow my brain's command to move.

Flee.

Survive.

Tentacles of fear wrap around my rib cage, keeping me imprisoned in place.

And that's not even the strangest part.

To say I'm not scared of the gun in his hand would be a lie. I haven't been this close to a weapon since I moved to New York and adopted a completely different lifestyle. However, that's not what robs my breath and burns my lungs.

That's not what digs rusty daggers in my chest and forbids my body from acting on my brain's commands.

It's the deep ice in his gray eyes.

They're as harsh and unforgiving as the winter, as cold, too, with the sole purpose to eradicate any life in his way.

He stares at me with silent apprehension. He's not glaring or scowling, but the threat is right there.

In his silence.

In the fact that he knew to look straight in my direction as if he were aware I was there all along.

Paralyzing fear loosens my limbs and a shot of survival instinct bursts into my ribcage. It's like I'm back in that black box, locked, left all alone, and the only way to remain alive is if I dig my way out.

I've always used that childhood memory as my darkest time, the one moment that I compare everything to. The jabs, the behind-my-back talks, the harassment. All of it.

But I feel like this situation will put that moment to shame. I survived the other time, but my chances of getting out of this alive are slim to none.

Still, I stand on shaky legs and dart behind the cars, hoping to get to the elevator and—

I'm not even two steps in before a harsh grip wraps around my upper arm and I'm yanked back with a hand to my mouth.

I don't stop to look at who it is.

A rush of life bubbles in my veins and I squirm, hitting and biting at the hand. My movements are frantic and far from calculated. I doubt that I'm doing any damage, but I don't stop to think about that. I don't stop to let them hurt me.

In my attempt to get free, the bulky blond guy drags me to where the murder took place. My insides lurch at the view of the dead man with a hole in his forehead, sprawled on the ground. My struggles increase in volume and I kick and scratch, mumbling my cries for help that merely come out like an ugly horror movie sound.

Cold metal meets my forehead and my whole body goes slack. I'm standing in front of their bossman with the impenetrable gaze of his, freezing ash eyes boring into me. My heart thumps and my lips tremble beneath the hand that's muting my voice.

This close, he's even more striking, but in a quiet kind of way, like the rare attractive people who don't want to stand out in a crowd.

Is he going to kill me now as he did that man? If I have any doubt, the complete disregard in his blank stare erases it.

This man is capable of killing countless people without a second thought. He's capable of ending lives and walking away as if nothing happened.

"Kolya is going to remove his hand and you're going to be quiet," he says ever so casually as if he's inviting me for tea. "If you don't, I'll have to shut you up using other methods."

My face must be as pale as the white neon lights overhead. All I keep thinking about is the metal that's now connected to my forehead and that I will soon meet the same fate as the Italian man.

"Nod if you understand," he continues in his unperturbed tone.

What choice do I have except to agree? I certainly don't want to find out what his 'other methods' are.

I nod, but he looks at me for a beat too long, stealing all the air from my lungs. I think he hasn't seen me nod or something, but then he tilts his head at the man standing behind me. Kolya, he said his name is.

The man releases me, just like that, and leaves me in front of his boss. I massage the spot where he grabbed me, sensing a bruise already forming. I try my damnedest not to glance sideways, because if I catch a glimpse of the corpses, I'll start vomiting.

The bossman studies me for a long second, his gaze sliding from my face to my arm. I drop my hand, forcing it to stay still by my side.

"Fight or scream and you won't like the consequences." He digs the gun deeper into my forehead, driving the point home.

"O-okay." I sound like a scared kitten.

And I am.

These men just killed people. Why would my fate be any different?

He drags his gun down the hollow of my cheek. I swallow, and it's not only because of the deadly weapon. The way he watches as the metal slides down appears to be nothing short of anticipation.

The observation is burning—invasive, even—as if he's sizing me up, and contemplating whether he should waste a bullet on me.

If I want to get out of this alive, I need to be smart about it. I need to bargain my way out of this situation as best I can.

"I'll pretend I saw nothing." My voice quivers, even though I try to sound as confident and neutral as possible.

"Will you now?" His tone isn't mocking, but it suggests he doesn't believe a word I say. "Are you sure you won't call 911 as soon as you round the corner?"

My lips part. I should've realized he'd figure that out. I mean, yes, of course I'm calling the police. Who in their right mind would witness a murder—a triple one, at that—and remain quiet about it?

At the reminder of the dead men, my stomach coils, rippling with tension, and I bite down the taste of nausea.

"Yes," I whisper.

"How come I don't believe you?" The slow tempo of his voice implies that he not only thinks I'm lying, but he also finds the idea that I thought I could fool him ridiculous.

You know what? Screw justice right now. I just need to save myself. Justice won't be able to do it for me.

"I really won't," I say it like I mean it this time, because I truly have no plans to scheme against him considering that the possibility of being shot is hanging between us like a guillotine.

"What's your name?" he asks out of the blue, taking me completely by surprise.

I think of a fake name to give him, because the less he knows about me, the better. But before I can open my mouth, he lifts my chin with the gun. "And do not lie to me. I have my ways of finding the truth, and if I catch you in a lie, it'll be your first and final strike."

"Lia," I blurt out, fear getting the better of me. "My name is Lia."

"Lia…" he rolls my name off his tongue with his accent, as if that will give it meaning. "So you'll pretend you saw nothing tonight, Lia?"

I nod more times than needed, my chin hitting the gun with every movement, and nausea recoils in my belly.

"How will I make sure of it?"

"You…you can trust me."

His lips twitch and I find myself holding my breath, waiting for the smile to break free, but it never does. It seems trapped somewhere out of reach, just like the rest of his emotions. "Trust you? Surely even you realize how absurd that sounds."

"There are surveillance cameras," I blurt again. I want to tell him that the police will find out about the murders—and mine—if he decides to go through with it.

"Don't worry about those. They're not flesh and bone and, therefore, can be dealt with expeditiously. The current topic of discussion is *you*."

A human. Flesh and bone he can hurt.

His underlying threat mounts in the air and swiftly pierces through my jumbled nerves.

I rack my brain before I finally whisper, "I…I have money. It's not much, but…"

"Do I look like someone who needs your money?"

I stare at him then, *really* stare at him. At his pressed pants and elegant shirt. At his leather shoes and the expensive watch strapped to his wrist. He definitely doesn't look like someone who needs money. However, he specified it. He said he doesn't need *my* money, as if that has a category on its own.

He glides the tip of his gun to my mouth and I shudder, recalling exactly where that muzzle was only seconds before.

"You'll keep these lips shut. You'll forget all of our faces."

I nod meekly. My only focus is to escape his swirling orbit that's more freezing than the winter outside.

"If you let even a single word out, I'll know, and believe me, you won't like what happens, Lia. In fact, you won't like it in the slightest."

A burst of fear snaps my shoulder blades together and I stare at him, dumbfounded. How will he know? How is that going to be possible?

"Is that clear?" he speaks slowly, unhurriedly, cementing his words.

I nod.

He pulls his gun away and I let out a long sigh.

"Use your words, Lia."

"Yes." My voice is barely a whisper.

"Say, 'yes, I understand.'"

"Yes…I understand."

He reaches for me with his other hand and I freeze as his fingers replace his gun, gently gliding over my lips. Flames erupt across my skin, even though his touch is like crossing paths with death. Literally and figuratively.

"These lips will stay shut."

My throat clogs and I'm unable to make a sound or even nod my head.

He releases me as fast as he grabbed me and a cold wave washes over the earlier fire, dousing it in one harsh sweep.

The bossman tilts his head toward the elevator. "Go."

For a second, I don't believe what he's said, that he's simply letting me go. I take a tentative step backward, fully expecting him to pounce on me.

He doesn't make a move to follow.

I back away another two steps, not breaking eye contact. When he doesn't move, I run to the elevator and punch the call button.

My frantic gaze is still on *him*.

The stranger.

The scary fucking stranger.

He remains as I left him, his gun motionless at his side and his attention on me as if he's contemplating whether or not he should shoot me in the face anyway.

The elevator finally opens and I dash inside, holding my breath and shaking uncontrollably as I hit my floor's number and code. I miss the first time because of my trembling fingers and scattered thoughts. I have to try again before my passcode is accepted.

As the door finally closes, I slide down to the floor and empty my stomach in the middle of the elevator.

He didn't kill me. He didn't put a bullet in my head.

So why do I feel like I just signed my death certificate?

THREE

Lia

IT'S BEEN A WEEK SINCE THE DAY I WITNESSED THREE people getting killed, and somehow ended up intact.

A whole damn week of biting my nails, watching my windows, and having an unhealthy obsession with the rear-view mirror whenever I'm driving.

I was supposed to take some downtime before I got back to rehearsing the upcoming ballet, but I've been on a rollercoaster ride worse than if we'd had consecutive shows.

On the surface, it might appear to be foolish paranoia. After he let me go, it may seem that I'm only obsessing over it because of the surge of adrenaline I experienced that night.

It's not paranoia.

Far from it.

I'm not an idiot. I'm well aware that night wasn't the end of it. If anything, it's the beginning of something ugly I have no control over.

I debated with myself about telling the police, but I quickly shooed that idea away. I believed him when he said he'd know if I talked. I believed him when he said the consequences will be dire.

After all, I saw him murder a man in cold blood and not bat an eyelash about it. That sort of person is capable of doing worse.

To cement my theories, the following day, I rushed to the reception area after spending a sleepless night tossing and turning in bed. I asked the receptionist if something had happened in the parking garage, but he only stared at me as if I were a crazy old hag. I begged him to go down there with me, and when we arrived, there was nothing. Nada.

I didn't expect the car or the bodies to stay there, but I at least thought there would be some blood, some bullets, some *evidence* of what I had witnessed.

However, the place was wiped clean.

The only thing that remained was a hint of the black tire marks, and even those weren't fully visible.

I considered that my mind might have been playing a sick game on me. That's what it does when everything gets to be too much. My demons come out to play and my subconscious goes to war with my conscious, torturing me with my own head.

But that couldn't be possible in this situation.

I tested my pain receptors back then. I know it wasn't a hallucination.

Point is, someone who can hide triple murders overnight can surely find out if I talked to the police.

And I wasn't ready to sacrifice myself for justice.

I called Luca, though. Since I suspect the stranger and his men run in some sort of a crime organization, I thought he'd know something and tell me how to protect myself.

But even Luca has been MIA.

While it's not strange for him to disappear off the face of the earth for months at a time, the fact that he's not answering my calls or emails has only managed to escalate my paranoia and anxiety levels.

I can count on one hand the number of hours I've been

able to sleep this past week, even with the aid of pills. My nightmares have been magnifying and spiraling out of control, and I had sleep paralysis and the fear of it left me in tears all day long.

If this goes on, I'll backpedal sooner than I expected.

Inhaling a deep breath, I walk backstage. While everything else is out of control, there's one thing that isn't.

Ballet.

I'm wearing a snap-closure soft pink leotard and a short black skirt as well as my broken-in ivory pointe shoes. I usually wear them at home for weeks on end before I rehearse with them or use them in an official show.

They become more flexible with time and help me with going up on pointe, especially when I have a rigorous rehearsal— like today.

All of the dancers are on stage as Philippe and Stephanie talk about the choreography. Other dancers hate Philippe's perfectionist nature, but I love it. He respects the art too much to let them slack off. Besides, *Giselle* was recently done by The Royal Ballet, gaining international recognition, and he will stop at nothing to top it.

That makes two of us.

Playing Giselle has been my dream since I first watched it as a little girl. I found magic and heartbreak in her story. Hope and despair. Love and death. I thought it was the most beautiful thing a ballerina could dance.

I had a chance to play in *Giselle* in my teens, but only as part of the corps de ballet. I didn't get to experience that despair and live in the head of a woman so betrayed that she escaped in her mind.

That story hit so close to home and I need to experience it, to feel it in the very marrow of my bones.

I was the prima ballerina in *Romeo and Juliet, Swan Lake,* and recently, *The Nutcracker.* But *Giselle? Giselle* will be the peak of my career. Something I will tell my grandchildren about someday.

"Needless to say"—Philippe fixes all of us with one of his custom glares, his celebration mode long over—"I need complete and utter discipline. No gaining weight. No hangover faces. No breathing the wrong way. Slouch, and you're out of my performance. I want to see *des jolis postures* all the time or I will bring dancers who will show it to me. *Faite vite, allez-y!*"

Everyone scatters to warm up, their professional faces on display. Ryan stands beside me as he stretches his long legs. "Another love affair between you and me. Don't you think it's fate?"

I keep my attention ahead as I slowly do a *plié*. My ankles haven't been throbbing as badly as that night, but I still feel that cramp lurking in my tendon, waiting to rip it.

"I thought your fate was with Hannah, Ryan."

"Do I hear jealousy, my dear Lia?"

This time, I stare at him. "That's the difference between you and me, Ryan. You hear jealousy. I hear, leave me alone."

I don't wait for him to reply and walk to Stephanie so I can ask her about a part of the choreography. Her posture is refined and elegant, still having the grace of a queen despite being in her early fifties.

She sends one of the staff away when I approach her and folds her frail arms across her chest. "Tell me."

"Do you have the finalized choreography for the last part of act one?"

"Why are you asking?" Her voice is deep due to the number of cigarettes she smokes on a daily basis.

"I was watching the performances of—"

She cuts me off with a finger. "Didn't I say not to watch other performances? Are you a copycat, Lia?"

"No. I watch them so I can get inspired before I put my own spin on it."

"Why? Are you stuck somewhere?"

"A little."

"Which part?"

"At the end of act one, right before Giselle dies, how do I convey the emotions without being melodramatic?"

"First of all, you need to stop addressing Giselle in third person. She's *you* now. If you don't live inside her, she won't live inside you." She places a hand on my chest. "If you don't allow her to consume your heart and soul, you'll only go down in history as another ballerina who portrayed Giselle well enough."

Stephanie's words hit harder than I expect them to. I'm vaguely aware of my surroundings when the door to the theater opens and the producers waltz inside, accompanied by their associates. They often watch us rehearse, even though Philippe dislikes it with a passion.

"Just know this." Stephanie takes my hand in hers. "In order to be Giselle, you have to be a whole ballerina and a whole person. No one denies you're a whole ballerina with perfect technique and elegance that's spoken about in all the ballet circuits, but are you a whole person, Lia?"

She releases me and summons the staff over, unaware of the shackle she just snapped around my ankle.

My insecurities bubble to the surface, attempting to suffocate me and pull me under.

Turning around, I stuff all those emotions to the bottom of my gut. Luca once said that I have to face my past to live on, but I declined, stubbornly burying that black hole and its dark box and going on with my life. I've been doing great and I will continue to do so, no matter what he or Stephanie says about it.

After the warm-up, we go through the opening scene. I don't stop moving or take any breaks. I feel like if I do, my ankle will act up. I need to see Dr. Kim about it. He's been taking care of my legs since I had enough money to hire him as my attending physician. He's the best orthopedist around, and as someone whose daughter wants to become a ballerina, he understands how much we fuss about the slightest pain in our ankles. But I'm sure he'll shoo me away with some muscle ointment, as usual.

When it's time for my entrance, I step into Giselle's shoes. I'm the timid maid who loves to dance with no care for the world. I leap, then twirl, letting the symphonic music flow through my veins.

Since it's a somewhat solo scene, I'm pulled from my surroundings and living in my head, a poor maid who has nothing on her mind but dancing. Not knowing that in her innocence, she's attracting a wolf in sheep's clothing.

That's when I sense it. I'm about to jump when a sharp presence wrenches me from the confines of my fragile Giselle.

For the first time during a rehearsal, I stare at the audience. The producers are there, animatedly chatting among each other.

One isn't a producer, though.

Far from it.

His dark gray eyes lock with mine and I lose my footing. But I save it at the last second, landing on my feet instead of on pointe as per the choreography.

He's here.

The stranger has come back.

FOUR

Lia

I CEASE BREATHING.

I blink once, twice, desperately trying to chalk this up to another play of my imagination, a manifestation of my demons and hallucinations.

Maybe I've exhausted my mind so much that it's started to fabricate things.

Raising a shaky hand to my wrist, I sink my nails into it. Pain explodes on my tender skin and my mouth parts.

This is real.

I'm not dreaming or hallucinating. I'm not waking up from this nightmare in a cold sweat. This is the actual world.

A few rows ahead, the stranger who held a gun to my head a week ago is sitting with the producers. He's wearing a gray cashmere coat over his black shirt and his hair is styled, neat, looking like a CEO who's just been to a meeting. His demeanor is composed—normal, even.

But there's nothing normal about him.

Even from this distance, I can feel the danger emanating off him in waves and aiming daggers straight at my chest. His expression is neutral, but it wouldn't be more terrifying if he were scowling. Because I know what that façade hides, what actually lurks beneath the surface.

A killer.

A lethal, cold-hearted one at that, who wouldn't hesitate to pull the trigger.

Did he change his mind and come to kill me after all?

Is this my last dance before I meet the fate of the men from that night?

My legs tremble and I'm a second away from collapsing on my face or vomiting the salad I had for lunch.

"Lia!" Philippe's impatient voice echoes through the air, yanking me back to the present. In my stupor, I forgot that I stopped mid-movement.

What the hell? That's a first and it doesn't go unnoticed. The other dancers scowl at me as if I personally hurt them. Philippe and Stephanie watch me, puzzled, because they know I'm not the type to lose focus or get distracted.

Not when it comes to ballet.

"I'm sorry." I release a long breath. "Let's go again, please."

I don't trust myself to not break down here and now if I keep staring at him or imagining his gun pointed at my head. So I take refuge in the one thing that gives me joy—dancing.

My movements aren't as fluid as I like, but it's impossible to force myself into that headspace. Not when dread and fear like I've never felt before continue to shoot at me from every direction.

When I was trapped in that black box, I believed I knew what fear felt like. It was dark and tight and made me wet myself.

But that was far from what I'm experiencing right now. Fear has evolved into a tall, dark-haired stranger with terrifying gray eyes and a lethal weapon.

I try my hardest to ignore the spectators, like I always

have, but it's damn near impossible when I know he's there, watching, contemplating, biding his time until he decides to pounce on me.

I never pay attention to the audience, because they interfere with my performance and my interpretation of the character's emotions. The only time I look at them is once I'm done and everything is finished.

Now is different.

Now, I can feel his intense cold eyes piercing into me and peering inside my head. In a way, it feels like everyone else has disappeared and he's the only presence I can sense. The only person who's watching me. Just like Albrecht was watching Giselle that day and became infatuated with her.

That thought sends a chill to my bones, but my feet don't falter. I don't lose my footing again. If anything, I become one with the music, and as Stephanie said, I let Giselle take over me. I let her be a naive fool who's dancing in the forest. The lone difference is that I'm well aware of who's watching me—more than aware. I know his eyes are taking in my every movement.

Instead of deterring me, the thought allows me to completely let go. I'm free-falling like a feather, boneless and suspended from my body's physical reality.

I stand on pointe more than specified in the choreography and give my performance of the year. I don't even know what's come over me. Is it the fact that this could be my last dance? Or do I want to show him my passion for what I do, hoping that he'll have mercy and let me go?

Either way, I don't stop or hold back. I give it my all, pushing my muscles to their limit.

When I'm finished, I stand in place in fourth position, catching my breath. A round of applause comes from Philippe and I'm immediately wrenched to the present. The spell breaks, the world and people filtering back in with a symphony of sounds and chatter. For some strange reason, I miss the state where it was only me. I turn around to find the director ready for a hug.

"Bravo, *chérie*! This is my Lia." He points at his forearm. "You give me chills."

"Thanks," I murmur.

Stephanie rubs my arm. "You became one with her, didn't you?"

"I think so." I keep talking in a low tone, not wanting a certain someone from the audience to hear.

I chance a glance around the theater and find the stranger's seat beside our producer, Matt, empty. I search for him in case he's changed places, but he's nowhere to be seen.

A long breath heaves out of my lungs. Maybe he didn't come for me after all. Or maybe my plan worked and he saw how much I love ballet? Though I doubt it.

He's the type who destroys things instead of preserving them. Why would my passion be any different?

After we finish rehearsal, I head to my dressing room to have a hot shower before I leave. I could use a cup of tea and some mindless television right now.

My limbs are still shaking from the stranger's sudden reappearance and I'm lightheaded, as if I'm walking on the clouds.

My mind is somewhere else when I open my dressing room door and close it behind me. That's when I sense something is wrong.

Cautiously, I turn around and gasp, hands flying to my mouth, when I find *him* standing next to my dressing table, running his fingers over the jewelry and makeup products scattered by the mirror.

If I thought he was intimidating when sitting several rows away in the audience, he's damn terrifying up close. I can almost feel the muzzle of his cold gun nestled against my forehead, ready to fire and tear me to pieces.

Without thinking twice, I turn to flee, my sweaty hands grabbing the doorknob.

"I wouldn't recommend it," he says casually. "That will make me use violence, and I would rather not bruise that fair skin, Lia."

The sound of my name coming off his tongue sends new tendrils of fear through me. It's like he's making it his mission to up the intensity of such emotions in me.

My chin quivers as I release the doorknob and slowly spin around, my ballet shoes skittering against the floor. I know I should run, but at the same time, I'm well aware that his threats aren't idle. He killed someone—or three—what's one more addition to his list?

He's still in front of my dressing table, but he's stopped going through my things and is standing upright now, one hand in the pocket of his black pants and the other by his side. I almost forgot how tall and broad he is, how his physique can eat up all the atmosphere and any oxygen that comes with it.

The scariest thing about him isn't his gun—that I'm sure is hidden somewhere. It's the absolute calm etched in his handsome features when he's about to use that gun. It's his complete composure right now while I'm trembling like a leaf in a hurricane.

He is that hurricane, wrecking people's lives without being affected in the least.

"How did you get in here?" I'm thankful my voice doesn't betray my scattered emotions.

"I don't think that's the question you want to ask, Lia. Shouldn't you be more worried about *why* I'm here?"

"Are you going to kill me?" I whisper, choking on the words.

"Why? Have you been talking?"

"No. I swear."

"I'm aware you haven't, or we wouldn't be standing here."

He knows I've kept my mouth shut, but he's still using the

intimidation factor to corner me. I'm so thankful that I didn't decide to play detective. While those men's deaths shouldn't go unnoticed and I haven't stopped having nightmares about them, I also don't want to die. I still have so many things to do and I refuse to be an indispensable pawn in someone else's chess game.

However, the fact that he's here while knowing I didn't talk means he's not done with me.

Not even close.

And that realization, although I've been contemplating it all this time, snaps my spine into a painful line.

"Are you going to hurt me?" My voice is small, divulging my erratic heartbeat.

"Depends."

"On what?"

"On your ability to follow orders."

"W-what orders?"

"Have dinner with me, Lia."

"What?" I mean to snap, but it comes out as a bewildered murmur. Did this killer/stranger/the one who threatened and continues to threaten my life just asked me to have dinner with him?

His face remains the same, caught in that eternal calm that only monks should be allowed to have. "Dinner, something where people eat and talk."

"I know what dinner is. I just…I just don't know why the hell you're asking that of me."

"I already answered that question. To talk."

"About what?"

"You'll know once we have dinner."

"Can't we talk here?"

"No."

It's a single word, but it's so closed off that I know he's done entertaining my questions.

Still, I have to ask this, "What if I don't want to?"

"As I said, your safety depends on your ability to follow orders, Lia."

I swallow at the subtle threat in his tone. His message is clear. If I don't have dinner with him, he'll act on that threat. Worse, he might even finish what he started a week ago.

"It would've been easier to take you to an unfinished construction site or ambush you in your apartment building, but I'm offering you dinner in a restaurant with people around. You're smart enough to realize the difference, aren't you?"

The difference between getting hurt and not. My ability to stay alive and the complete opposite.

While everything in me revolts against the idea of going anywhere with him, my survival instinct rushes forward.

Dinner is definitely much better than being killed in a parking garage and having all traces gone in the morning.

Besides, he awakened something inside me earlier by merely sitting in the audience. I chalked it up to coincidence, but now that he's standing in front of me, my legs tingle with the need to move, to do something, anything.

If I have to do this, I might as well find out why someone like him, a dangerous criminal, was able to draw that reaction out of me.

"I need to change," I say, tactfully avoiding his gaze, not only because of its intensity, but also because he seems to peer into me whenever we make eye contact.

"Then change."

"You need to leave for me to do that."

"And allow you to call for help or escape? I don't think so."

"I won't call for help. If that was an option, I would've done it already."

"You would've done it already," he repeats, rolling the words over his tongue with that sinful accent.

"Yes, and I won't escape either. There's just one door."

"There's a window in the bathroom that you can climb through."

God. He already went over this entire place, didn't he?

"I won't escape. Just go. Wait outside the door."

He pulls the chair and sits down, his long legs stretching in front of him before he crosses them at the ankles.

"I'm going nowhere, Lia. Now, change."

FIVE

Lia

MY KNEE-JERK REACTION IS TO YELL OR SOMEHOW run from him.

But I'm logical enough to know that won't deter him. If anything, it could—and would—put me in danger.

However, if he thinks I'm changing in front of him, he has another thing coming. He may be a terrifying monster, but I won't be his willing prey.

I loosen the pins in my hair, then remove them and throw them on the dressing table beside him not so gently. I'm sweaty from rehearsal and in desperate need of a shower, but that will have to wait because there's no way in hell this stranger and my naked body will exist in the same room.

My dark locks loosen, falling to my shoulders, and I resist the need to sigh in relief.

He's watching my every movement like he did when he sat in the audience. His gaze zeroes in on my actions instead of my body in a mechanical kind of way, and although he doesn't seem to be weighing me up sexually, I'm suddenly self-conscious about my skirt that barely covers the crack of my ass and my leotard, which molds against the curve of my breasts.

I open my locker with unsteady hands and retrieve one of the dresses I keep here, then throw it on over my clothes. He raises a brow when the material falls to my knees. It's tight at the top with a full skirt.

I give him what I'm sure appears to be a smug look as I reach back to close the zipper. The pervert must've believed he'd see me naked and even sat down for the show, but I just abolished his plan.

He stands and I jerk against the locker, my victory dance coming to a screeching halt.

"I thought you said you were going to change." He stops a foot away.

He's so close, like that day when he held the gun to my forehead, and even though the weapon is currently absent, it's as if its cold muzzle is there again.

My senses are so heightened that I feel every intake of air and the goosebumps breaking out over my bare arms. His smell shoots straight to my head and nothing prepares me for the subtle mixture of woods and leather. On the surface, it's a harmless scent, but on him, it's a translation of his lethality.

Despite my need to cower, I lift my chin. "I did change."

"That you did." He grabs me by the shoulder and spins me around. Then he holds my hand that's still on the zipper, sending a shiver down my spine.

I expect him to pull it down and force me to get out of the dress, but he uses my fingers to zip it up. The sound reverberates in the silence of the room and I gulp as his lips lower to the shell of my ear. "It'd be wise to not provoke me. I dislike it and I'll make sure you dislike it, too."

He releases my hand and swiftly turns me back around to face him. It's completely unfair that a devil like him has such an intimidating physique and a handsome face to go with it.

"Shall we?" He motions at the door.

After changing into flats, I grab my coat and bag, then follow him.

Thankfully, almost everyone has left. I don't want them to see me in the company of this stranger. But I need to know why the hell he was allowed entrance into our rehearsal. Only producers and their selected associates can attend. Not even our family and friends are allowed in.

Though he was sitting beside Matt, our executive producer. Does that mean he knows him?

I stay one step behind him, feeling like I need to watch him and get a read on when he'll make his next move.

He stops abruptly and I crash into him, my head colliding against a wall of muscle. I wince, taking a step back.

The stranger tilts his head to the side. "Walk beside me."

When I don't make a move to comply, he continues, "Or I can hold you with an arm around your waist."

"I'll do it," I blurt, falling in step at his side. I don't look at him the entire way until we reach the parking lot.

A black Mercedes waits for us there. It's the spitting image of the one I saw that night, but there are no bullet holes anywhere.

The passenger door opens and the lean man with long hair steps out and opens the back door.

Seeing him brings back memories from last week and it takes everything in me not to give in to nausea.

"I have my car," I whisper.

"Give me your keys and it'll be at your apartment building."

"No, thanks." There's no way in hell I'm letting him—or his men—near me more than need be.

He watches me for a beat before he continues guiding me to his car. He gently ushers me inside and follows after me. The man with long hair slides into the front seat, and the other man, the bulky blond, Kolya, is behind the wheel.

Are they his guards or something? Just what type of man is he if he needs guards?

The car leaves the parking lot and I keep a careful eye on the city through the window, trying to memorize as many twists and turns as possible. If I somehow end up getting kidnapped, I need to know where the hell he's taking me.

"How come you haven't asked about my name?"

The stranger's calmly spoken words pull me out of my observation. He's watching me with a particular interest that makes my skin crawl.

"Does it make a difference whether I know it or not?" I try to keep the venom out of my voice.

"I suppose it doesn't, but I'll tell you anyway. It's Adrian Volkov."

I briefly close my eyes to rein in the pain. Now that I know his name, he'll never let me go. For some reason, I feel like I've signed my fate.

First, my death certificate, and now, my fate.

Just what more is he going to take from me?

The car comes to a halt in front of a cozy-looking diner. I don't know why I expected him to take me to some high-end restaurant with a waiting list. This is surprising, and not in a good way.

He gets out first and offers me his hand. I'm about to ignore it, but he grabs my palm and pulls me out. We step into the restaurant, and the guards remain outside in the car.

The inside of the restaurant is as cozy as the exterior. The soft yellow lighting casts a warm hue on the red banquettes. The tables are dark wood and there are multiple creative quotes about eating for the soul hanging on the walls. A few people are scattered throughout, chatting joyfully. I wonder if they'll help me if I say the man holding my clammy hand is a serial killer or if they will be killed themselves.

The stranger, Adrian, leads me to a back table that's

separate from other people and away from doors and windows. I realize it's on purpose when he pushes me to the end of the booth that's near the wall.

He settles opposite me, and when the waiter comes, he doesn't even touch the menu as he says, "An unopened bottle of your best wine."

"Salad," I whisper, opting not to check the menu myself. The sooner I'm out of here, the better.

"What type, miss?"

"The simplest one you have."

The waiter nods and leaves.

I'm acutely aware of Adrian watching me, his fingers casually interlaced on the table. They're lean, masculine, and have veins etched across the surface.

And now I'm ogling them.

I can't believe I'm ogling the same fingers that held a gun to my forehead. Or maybe I'm watching them because of that fact. I know people like him exist, but I've always wondered how they could so easily end lives. Do they not feel, or have they become desensitized to it like I have to haters?

However, when I had that question, I never thought I'd ever be this close to one of his kind.

Adrian taps his finger once against the wooden surface. "You have an expressive face. Did you know that, Lia?"

"No, I don't."

"Yes, you do. Maybe it's not visible to others, but it's almost impossible for you to hide your emotions."

"Is that why you brought me here? To tell me I have an expressive face?"

"I told you why I brought you here. To talk."

"Then talk."

"I would rather you do the talking. Tell me more about yourself."

"Why would I do that?"

"Because it'll determine whether you get to walk out of this restaurant breathing or not."

My chest jolts and I bunch a napkin in my fists to stop my hands from shaking. "Why are you doing this? You already let me go."

The dark depth of his gray eyes is similar to deep cloudy skies—blank, composed, and cold. "I only let you go until further notice. Now is the time for that notice. Are you going to tell me about yourself?"

There's no winning with this asshole, is there? He's already come with a purpose and he won't stop until it's met.

"What do you want to know?" I snap so he'll get it over with and let me go.

"I don't want to know anything in that tone. Repeat the question without the anger part."

"Do you enjoy this?"

"What?"

"Being the Grim Reaper over others' lives."

"Not if I can help it, no. Being the Grim Reaper doesn't actually give me answers...just bodies."

A lump rises in my throat and I stiffen at his unspoken threat.

The waiter returns with a bottle of wine and my salad. Adrian motions at him to leave when he opts to open the bottle.

As soon as the waiter is gone, he does it with sure movements. He doesn't hurry or get flustered, like a typical person who's confident about himself and his surroundings. While I'm usually the same in my own world, I seem to lose all my confidence in his company.

Being held at gunpoint will do that, I guess.

Adrian pours me a glass and one for himself, and although I wasn't planning on drinking, I need some liquid courage right now.

I take a long sip, then sigh. "What do you want to know?"

"What's your last name?"

"I'm sure you could've figured it out on your own. It's all over the rehearsal hall."

"Or I could easily run a background check on you to find out everything."

My head tips up at that. He's telling me without stating it that he's powerful enough to figure out whatever he wants about me.

I take another sip of wine. "Does that mean you haven't already?"

"It wouldn't make a difference to you whether I have or not."

"Of course it would."

"No, it wouldn't. It makes a difference to me because I would acquire information. You, however, have nothing to lose or gain."

"I have everything to lose with you."

He taps his forefinger against the table, lips twitching, but like the other time, he doesn't smile. "You're smart enough to recognize that. Continue being smart and answer my question."

"Morelli." I stab my fork into the salad and bring it to my mouth, chewing with aggressiveness.

"Lia Morelli. Were you born in the States or in Italy?"

"Italy."

"Both parents Italian?"

"Mom was American. Dad was Italian."

"Both dead?"

"Yes," I snap, gulping what remains in the glass in one go. "Is your questioning over?"

"That's one." He takes a leisurely sip of his wine.

"One?"

"One strike. I told you not to speak to me in that tone."

"What tone should I speak in then? Is there a fucking

manual on how to talk to a *murderer?*" I hiss the last word under my breath.

"Two. And while there's no manual, you ought to use that clever head of yours and not provoke me."

I snatch the bottle and pour until the glass almost overflows. Some surrounding tables gawk at my lack of manners, but I'm past the point of caring. I'm fuming, and the more he probes about my past, the faster the wounds I've kept hidden sting, ripping at the stitches so I'll set them free.

"How did your parents die?" he asks ever so languidly, obviously not reading my mood. Or maybe he asks in spite of it.

He's probably taking pleasure in this.

Sighing, I say, "An accident."

"What type of accident?"

"Gas asphyxiation." The words leave my throat in a pained whisper. My fingers tremble around the wine glass as I bring it to my lips. I don't want to think about that time, but my demons swirl from the background, wrapping their tentacles tightly around my throat.

"Breathe, Lia." A hand flattens against mine, pulling it and the glass down to rest on the table.

That's when I realize I'm balling my other hand and moisture is stinging my lids.

I stare at him, at the eternal calm that's in his eyes despite the chaos he's inflicted with merely a few questions. "Why are you doing this?"

"To get to know you."

"You can't force someone to talk about their life. That's not getting to know them."

"It is for me."

"Then shouldn't I get to know you, too?"

He pulls his hand from mine. "If you want."

"Does this mean I can ask you questions?"

"Sure."

"What do you do exactly?" I probably shouldn't try to find out more about him, but I already know his name. If I want to survive him, I need to look further into who he is and what he does.

"I'm a strategist."

"A strategist who kills?" I lower my voice.

His lips curve in a small smirk as he tips his glass at me. "Exactly."

"A strategist for whom?"

"I don't think it would make a difference if you knew."

"You said I could ask questions."

"I never said I would answer them all."

"That's not fair."

"Fair is for weak people, Lia. You've been in a monstrous world long enough to realize fairness doesn't really exist."

"It does exist, even if people like you are doing their best to erase it."

He lifts a brow as he swirls his wine. "People like me?"

"You know."

"No, not really. Why don't you enlighten me?"

"Criminals."

"Criminals. Interesting analogy."

"It's not an analogy when it's true." I push back against my faux leather seat, giving up on the salad and sipping the wine. It's helping to loosen the nerves that have been on high alert since I first met this man.

"According to you, perhaps."

"According to the world. You *killed* people."

"People like me, *criminals* per your words."

"That doesn't make you a hero."

"A hero is the last thing I want to be. Selflessness has never been my thing."

"So you would rather be the villain?"

"A villain is the hero in his own story, so why not?"

"The villain always loses."

"In Disney films. In your ballet performances, perhaps. In real life, however, the villain is the one who always wins."

This man has absolutely no regard for morality or societal standards. While I'm not shocked such people exist, I've only met them in ballet. The spiteful mean girls—and boys. I've never met a person with a destructive mindset who wouldn't hesitate to use a gun.

It makes him even more dangerous.

I lift my chin. "But wouldn't you eventually be killed by a villain just like yourself?"

"Probably. Until then, I'll do what I do best."

"Which is?"

"Nothing you should worry about. *Yet*. Now, back to you, prima ballerina, when did you come to the States?"

I empty half the glass, needing more loosening of my nerves. "When I was five."

"With whom?"

"My grandmother raised me."

"The American one, I assume."

"Yes."

"Is she still alive?"

"She passed away a few years ago."

"I'm sorry." He doesn't sound sorry at all. It's more like those apathetic condolences people offer.

"If you were sorry, you'd stop asking me these questions."

"Any other family members?" he continues as if I said nothing.

"None."

"Friends?"

"No." I finish the wine, refusing to tell him about Luca. That's my secret from the world.

He slides his glass across the table, and I'm once again drawn to the masculine fingers and how they casually wrap around it, how his nonchalance is as breathtaking as his actions. "I understand now."

I pour more wine to stop myself from ogling him. "Understand what?"

"The loneliness in your eyes. You managed to transform it and translate it with your body language on the stage. That is very creative."

"I'm not lonely." My voice lowers at the end, betraying my defensiveness.

"If you say so."

"I'm *not*. I have…I have three million followers on Instagram."

"Wow. Impressive."

"Stop mocking me."

"Wasn't that the reaction you were hoping for? Validation by showcasing your fake followers?"

"They're not fake. They're real people."

"What do they know about you aside from your pre-performance and workout selfies?"

"Have you been stalking me?"

"Your Instagram is public. There was no stalking involved. But yes, Lia, I've been through it, and I think it's rather…dull."

My blood boils, bubbling to the surface, but I mutter, "I don't care what you think."

"But you care about what others think. That's why you keep that page. Be it because of the need for some sort of twisted validation or for attention. Though I don't think you're consciously pursuing the latter."

How does this man read so much into details? How does he go to depths even I haven't thought about? Consciously, at least.

"Are you trying to prove how much you have a hold on me? Is that it?"

"I'm not trying to prove anything. As I said, I'm just getting to know you, Lia."

"And then what? After you get to know me, what are you planning to do with me?"

"What makes you believe I plan to do something?"

"I'm not an idiot. I know this is only a phase before you move on to the next step."

He pauses with his glass of wine halfway to his lips. "What do you think I'll do?"

"Fuck me?"

"Eventually."

The single word, though calmly spoken, crashes my world and splinters it into a million bloody pieces. My stomach sinks with a mixture of feelings. There's the sharp tang of disappointment, but that's not all. Malevolent butterflies claw at my skin with a dark sense of enthrallment.

All the nightmares I had after that night start to scroll through my mind's eye. The shadowy, blurry images morph into two figures on a bed as one of them rams into the other.

I never wanted to identify them, but now, one of them is as clear as the face in front of me.

Him.

His strong body is pounding what seems to be both pleasure and pain into the person lying beneath him.

One of them is still faceless, and I desperately want it to be me.

"Even if I say no?" I murmur.

"If I were a rapist, I would've broken into your apartment in the middle of the night and taken what I wanted. I would not have asked you to dinner."

"Am I supposed to appreciate the gesture?" There's a slight slur at the end of my speech. This is probably my third glass of wine.

Shit.

In my attempt to loosen my nerves, I went ahead and got drunk in the company of a monster who wouldn't hesitate to use it against me.

This is the absolute worst. I not only have a low alcohol tolerance, but I also lose my inhibitions in all senses possible even when slightly intoxicated.

Adrian raises his glass to his mouth, barely sipping. He hasn't poured himself anything aside from his first. "It's not obligatory, no."

"I...I want to go home." I stand on unsteady feet, then fall back on the seat. I'm still catching my breath when a large presence appears by my side.

He clutches my arm and gently pulls the glass of wine from my fingers. "I believe you've had enough to drink for one night."

"I want to leave."

"Then let's leave." He places a few bills on the table and wraps a strong arm around my waist as he leads me out of the restaurant.

I don't know if it's the alcohol or everything that's transpired tonight, but I feel like I'm levitating. My nostrils fill with his masculine scent and his firm hold on me only heightens it.

But somewhere at the back of my mind, I still recognize that he's dangerous. That he's a monster hidden under a composed façade and gentlemen's clothes.

I wiggle away from him. "I can walk on my own."

He releases me, and before I can be relieved, I stumble. Adrian holds me by the elbow and pulls me to him so that my front is flat against his hard chest.

I'm so small compared to him, barely reaching his broad shoulders. I'm thin and tiny in contrast to his large physique and monstrous aura. As if the asshole could use another thing to intimidate me with—aside from my life.

We're standing at what I assume is the back entrance of the restaurant, because it's not the same one we used when coming in. The place is empty except for a few cars in the parking lot.

Only a single streetlight is in view. Even in the semi-darkness, Adrian's eyes are intense but have that sheen of utter calmness. I wonder what it'd take to disturb that look.

To disturb *him*.

"Why did you wait a week to find me?" I murmur.

"I was busy."

"Busy gathering information about me?"

"Probably. Why? Have you been thinking about me, Lenochka?" His voice drops with the last word.

I don't tell him he's the only one I've been thinking about, in the most terrifying way possible, and that when I saw him again in the audience, something inside me unlocked. That I think I had my best performance yet, just because I knew he was there.

Instead, I say, "Everyone thinks about their Grim Reaper."

He strokes a strand of hair behind my ear. The gesture is gentle, but the undertone is far from it. If anything, it's charged, dark, *stifling*.

"Then don't make me into yours."

"How—Mmmm." My question is interrupted when he crashes his lips to mine.

His hand holds my face in place as his tongue forces its way inside my mouth. I place my palms on his chest, intent on pushing him, on slapping him, but instead, my fingers curl into his coat as a helpless sound escapes my throat. His tongue invades my mouth, conquering it, then swirls against mine with a feral need.

The man kisses as confidently as he walks and talks, but there's none of his calm behind it. Nothing to hold his stoic face in place. He gives as hard as he takes, tilting my head back so he can deepen the full invasion.

I'm no virgin. But this kiss alone is more intense than any sex I've ever had.

More claiming, too.

When he pulls back, a desperate moan echoes in the air.

Mine.

Staring into his shadowed eyes in the dark, I'm fully aware that things have shifted between us after that kiss.

I just signed away something else. No idea what, but it's now in his hands and there's no way I'll be able to get it back.

Just like my fate and my death.

SIX

Adrian

LIA TRIES TO REMAIN AWAKE.

She fights tooth and nail for it by shaking her head, pinching herself, and eventually tapping her cheeks.

But it's useless.

She falls asleep against the car door because, in her attempt to remain awake, she was also religious about keeping her distance from me.

I watched her entire struggle from my position with my forefinger tapping against my thigh. I didn't have to do anything except wait for the inevitable.

People, in general, think they can change things with the sheer force of their determination. That the danger signals would push their brain and it's enough to propel their system forward. What they fail to understand is that the brain can contradict itself and send different signals. After all, the body's exhaustion can and will overrule the brain's plots.

I grab Lia by the elbow and pull her close. She doesn't even stir as her head lolls down on her chest in what has to be an uncomfortable position. I maneuver her so that her head is resting against my thigh.

The scent of roses fills my nostrils. She doesn't only smell like them, she feels like them, too. Beautiful, small, and able to be plucked away by any passer-by. They bloom fast and die just as fast.

Unlucky for her, this passer-by is none other than her worst nightmare.

A small sigh leaves her lips and I want to reach out to my guards, Kolya and Yan, and erase that sound from their heads. I don't like that they can hear or see her like this.

Though I shouldn't particularly care, something has changed. I don't know whether it started when I saw her that night or after her performance today, or if the deal was sealed when she moaned in my mouth as I devoured her lips.

They're red now, a bit bruised, a bit broken, just like her.

Lia Morelli is a lot more than what her file contains. The pictures in it show a petite woman with angelic features, but none of them display the haunting look in her blue eyes or the loneliness eating at her soul.

There's a certain fractured quality about her, a wound she's hiding away from watchful eyes. But she's been blinded to the reality that untreated wounds decay and rot.

Taking advantage of people's wounds is my specialty. Smashing them in is what I do best.

My parents' son through and through.

However, I shouldn't want to get involved with Lia. Could it be because we share a trait? Or because she's hiding her broken nature with a fragile façade?

When I watched her dance, shining under the spotlight, I didn't see her ethereal beauty or angelic face. I didn't see her elegance or her perfect technique.

I saw darkness attempting to fester in light. I saw a person trying their hardest to escape who they truly are.

And that's what led to a chain of consecutive events.

"Are you sure you want to go to her place, sir?" Kolya meets my gaze from the driver's seat, speaking in Russian.

"Wouldn't it be better to take her with us?" Yan agrees.

"And do what? Torture her?" I speak in the same language.

I stroke a stray strand out of her face and keep my fingers in her soft hair that's the color of dark honey. She shivers as if feeling the impact of my words.

Yes, it would be easier to torture her, but that won't get me the answers I need and it's for a simple reason.

"She knows nothing," I say to my guards.

Kolya lifts a shoulder. "She could be faking it."

"She doesn't have what it takes to fool me, so no." I inhale her rose scent and recall how she tasted, a bit like fear but a lot like surrender.

Will she submit to me or will I have to...resort to other methods?

I glide my finger over her bruised lips and they part, allowing my thumb to nestle between them. Dark desire coils around my gut with a desperate need to have these same lips wrapped around my dick as I ram it inside her tight little mouth.

"Then what are you planning to do with her?" Kolya asks the million-dollar question.

"Depends."

"On what?"

"On her worth."

Truth is, I should've used her by now, whether she knows or not doesn't matter. However, a rebellious part of me wants to see where she'll go.

How *far* she'll go.

I have a feeling I'll come to regret my decision either way, so I might as well indulge my curiosity first.

The car comes to a halt in the parking garage of Lia's building.

Yan opens the door and I step out with Lia in my arms. She's light, tiny, and too soft. Her head drops against my chest, arm falling lifelessly to the side.

"Get some rest," I tell my men and stride to the elevator. I tap in the code for her floor and after we reach her apartment, I enter a few other digits until a beeping sound fills the hall.

There isn't a code my hackers can't get me. We've dealt with more hardcore situations than her fancy building.

An automatic light goes off in the entrance as soon as I step inside. I stand with her nestled into me. Her weight—or lack thereof—strikes me again. She's feather-light, almost like a child's, and sometimes, when she dances, it looks as if she has no bones, or as few as possible compared to normal people.

Holding her tight, I take note of her apartment. It's spacious and has a direct view over the city with its glinting lights. The shining flooring is spotless and she has soft pink sofas.

Countless ballerinas' pictures hang on the walls, but their faces are either shadowed or invisible.

My gaze searches every wall and every surface, but there are no pictures of her.

Not a single one.

Several awards are displayed on glass shelves, but there's no trace of her face.

Hmm. This engraves a few theories in my mind. The most prominent of all is that she doesn't like being trapped with herself.

It doesn't take me long to find her bedroom. I place her on the bed and slide her coat down her arms. Her cheeks are flushed red and her lips are parted.

When I rid her of the coat, she mumbles something unintelligible in her sleep before her breathing evens out. I watch her for a beat before my gaze flits to the rest of the room. This one is spacious, too, even though the furniture is minimal.

Two pill bottles on her nightstand catch my attention.

According to her medical reports, she takes sleeping pills and antidepressants. While her depression comes and goes on a whim, as she told her supervising psychotherapist, her insomnia is persistent.

What she paid a shitload of money to hide from her reports, however, is her consumption of something a lot stronger than her antidepressants.

My attention strays back to her. She sleeps completely still and in a straight position. Her feet are parallel and her arms are on either side of her.

This woman is still alive but already sleeps like the dead.

Her eyes move behind her lids and her lips and chin tremble. A pained moan slips from her mouth as she bunches both hands in the duvet on either side of her.

There.

The reason she paid money to erase her record and even resorted to morphine a few years back.

Her body arches off the bed at an uncomfortable-looking angle before she flops back in her earlier position. Her moans of pain escalate in volume, gaining a turbulent edge.

This is why she lives in a soundproof apartment.

Though I have every intention of watching her, I don't think it adds anything to what I already know.

Usually, I want to experience what I've learned firsthand in order to have a better grasp of the situation, but her broken moans and tears don't bring me the desired effect.

What I'm seeing is different from the angelic face she commemorates on Instagram or the characters she fuses herself with when she's on stage.

This is her, uncensored.

The real Lia Morelli, who ran from her past yet allows it to continue to haunt her.

I touch her shoulder to wake her up and her hands shoot up and grab my wrist.

Her eyes open, bleak at first, like a gloomy sky, but then she focuses on me, and although her hold slackens, she doesn't let me go.

"You," she murmurs with that slight slur.

"Me."

"Are you going to fuck me now?"

I raise a brow. "Is that an offer?"

"Do you need one?" Her eyes are half-droopy and I have no doubt that she'll probably remember nothing of this conversation come morning.

"No, Lenochka. I don't."

"Then why don't you take what you planned all along, Adrian Volkov?"

The sound of my name coming from her soft lips makes me want to stuff them with my dick and see what type of other sounds she'll make.

"Don't tempt me." There's nothing I want more than to rip off her dress and the clothes underneath and sink inside her. If I get her out of my system, my vision will be a lot clearer.

She sits up, releasing my wrist, and reaches to the back of her dress and lowers the zipper. Her process is messy at best as she shimmies out of it and throws it on the floor.

Lia kicks away her flimsy skirt that she wore during rehearsal, leaving her in a tight thing that barely covers her pussy and the crack of her ass.

Her nipples peak against the pink material and I'm tempted to pull on them to see if they get harder. Better yet, suck them into my mouth and feel them tighten against my tongue.

She lies back on the bed, her hair cascading on the pillow and her bare fair legs slightly parted. When she speaks, her voice is husky with arousal, "I'm tempting you then."

"Is that so?"

"You're going to take me, anyway. So do it and leave me alone."

"Why do you want me to leave you alone, Lia?" Unable to resist, I grab her nipple over the cloth, brushing the tip of my thumb over the bud. It does tighten, poking against the fabric, demanding more.

"Because...ahhh..." She arches off the bed, pushing into my hand.

Her moan of pleasure is the most erotic thing I've ever heard and a straight stimulation to my dick that's currently straining against my pants.

"Because what?" I probe, twisting both of her nipples in opposite directions.

"Because you...ahh...you..." She reaches a hand down between us and snaps open the thin piece of fabric covering her pussy. I watch with a growing hard-on as she rubs her clit in circles. Her rhythm matches mine on her nipples, falling in synergy with me.

She's barely looking at me with the way her lids are half-drooping, but she naturally follows my lead without me having to order her to.

"You...make me d-do things I don't...usually do... ohhh..." Her body convulses on the bed, eyes rolling back and her lip trapped between her teeth.

Seeing her orgasm is a piece of art, even better than her performance on stage. Her whole body comes alive and she completely lets go.

And fuck if that's not a turn-on.

It takes her a few moments to come down from her high, but she continues her slow rubbing, eyes darkening with lust so tangible, I can taste it in the air.

"Aren't you going to fuck me?"

I raise a brow. "Didn't you just orgasm?"

"Mmmm," she moans softly as I pinch her nipples one last time before I release her.

Her gaze sobers up. "What... Why?"

"Because I'm not a rapist, Lenochka." I brush a stray strand of hair from her eyes. "Sleep. I'll deal with you in the morning."

She shakes her head. "It's not rape if I want to."

"You want to? I thought you only wanted to get rid of me."

"That, too. If you fuck me, it'll be over."

"Who says it will?"

Her brow furrows, but I don't elaborate on my words.

She said that I make her do things she doesn't usually do. That makes two of us.

SEVEN

Lia

STRONG HANDS WRAP AROUND ME, CARRYING ME, holding me.

I'm about to fall into a feeling, something I've never experienced before. Something that I had in my little girl fantasies.

But then, my wrists are held above my head in a steel-like hold. My eyes snap open and I find a shadowy figure hovering over me, pinning me to the mattress.

It's dark, but I can make out the contours of his face.

Those hard features and that calm façade. Those intense eyes and the set of his jaw.

My dark stranger. The killer. The tormentor.

Adrian.

My body goes completely slack underneath him as he kicks my legs apart with his knee. His free hand tears my underwear and then he slams inside me with a feral force. I cry out, my back arching off the bed.

He rams into me as if he's intent on hurting me, as if he's punishing me with every ruthless thrust. His groin slaps against my flesh with the savage power of his hips, filling the air with ominous intention and crashing against my chest.

"You like that, don't you, Lia?" His voice is like velvet but with a hidden undertone. "You like being taken hard like a dirty little slut."

I shake my head, opening my mouth to speak, but he flattens a palm over it, muffling my words.

"Yes, you do. You were touching yourself to me just now. Look at how your cunt is strangling my dick."

I shake my head again, tears stinging my eyes. I refuse to think I'm that type of person. I refuse to think of myself as someone who gets off on such perverse acts.

But with every word out of his sinful mouth, my core tingles and my head turns dizzy. Being immobilized like this adds a scary type of anticipation. Any sounds I make come out muffled, haunting.

But he doesn't release me.

If anything, his hold turns rigid and his rhythm takes on a feral momentum. He fucks me like he's owned me since the moment we met. Like he's taking what was his all along.

My walls clench and an electric shock starts in my core and shoots all the way to my spine before submerging my entire body.

"Mmm…" I moan.

"There." Dark sadism coats his words. "Your true colors are showing. You like being taken and owned. You like being fucked like it's your first and last. That's what you strive to feel on the stage, too, isn't it?" He leans down and traps the lobe of my ear between his teeth and whispers hot words, "To completely let go."

My back arches off the bed in preparation for the orgasm.

The detonating pleasure is within my grasp. Just a little more and I'm about to reach it.

I startle awake.

For a second, I don't know what just happened. Adrian isn't on top of me and my fingers are rubbing against my aching pussy.

Holy shit.

Was that…a dream?

My hair sticks to my temples with sweat, and my heart beats so erratically, I'm surprised it doesn't leap out of my chest.

It's not news that my dreams are visceral. I used to hallucinate about them, too. That's why I had to come up with a coping mechanism and test my pain threshold to know if they were real or not.

My cheeks heat at the fact that I was touching myself to that dream.

I remove my hand from my most intimate part with a jerk, the act shaming me to my bones.

"It must be uncomfortable to stop right before an orgasm."

I freeze, my eyes widening as I slowly turn my head to the side. There's no way in hell what I heard is correct. It must be some play of my imagination. Maybe I'm associating this with my dream.

Maybe I'm trapped in that dream again.

Because nothing could explain the scene in front of me.

Adrian sits on the chair at my vanity, beside the bed, his legs crossed at the ankles. His coat is lying on the armrest and both of his shirtsleeves are rolled to his elbows, revealing taut forearms fully covered with black ink.

Soft morning light comes from the balcony, but it doesn't make his features less harsh or consuming. It takes nothing away from the face I was just dreaming about.

He taps his index finger on his thigh at a moderate pace. The look in his eyes is dark, focused, and says a thousand words without him having to utter a sound.

But no, this isn't real.

I reach a hand down and pinch my thigh. Pain explodes on my skin and I wince.

Adrian doesn't disappear.

Oh, God. Why is he not disappearing?

His gaze zeroes in on my hand that's still on my thigh and something passes in it before he slides it back to my face.

"What are you doing here?" My voice is barely a whisper while I struggle to process the scene.

"I drove you home after you got drunk last night."

I sit up and groan when a headache nearly splits my temples open. Memories of last night slowly filter back in, like I'm watching myself through a snow globe.

My eyes widen.

I kissed him.

Well, he kissed me, but I kissed him back. Then we got into his car, and then…black.

I stare at myself under the duvet, and I'm mortified to find that I'm in only my leotard and its snaps are open, revealing my aching pussy. My clothes are scattered by the side of the bed.

Pulling the cover to my chin, I fight the heat in my cheeks as my gaze flits back to him.

Adrian. The devil who found his way into my apartment.

He remains calm—nonchalant, even—as if he didn't just witness me in that state or watch me orgasm.

I pause, my heart thundering.

Wait.

He watched me orgasm? That was also a dream—it must've been. There's no way in hell I orgasmed in front of him.

Right?

"You were here all along?" I ask cautiously, almost fearfully.

"Correct."

"How did you get in?"

"You told me the code."

Why can't I remember that? And why the hell did I get

drunk in the first place? I already know why—to loosen up, but was it worth this price?

"Did something else happen?"

He raises a brow. "Such as?"

"Like... Like..."

"Asking me to fuck you and touching yourself to orgasm when I didn't?"

I can feel the color drain from my face, and I wish I could become one with the floor.

Adrian rises to his feet and my head snaps up when he stands beside me. "Now that you're not drunk, I can oblige."

"I didn't mean it," I blurt.

"Didn't mean it?"

"Yes, those words were meaningless."

"Do you often touch yourself and orgasm to meaningless words, Lia?" He takes my hand in his, the same one that was between my legs, and lifts it to his face.

Shame heats my cheeks when he inhales my scent deeply into his lungs. "Isn't that the ultimate contradiction?"

I pull my hand from his, fast and rushed, as if I'm saving it from catching fire.

His arm falls to his side with infinite carelessness, but he doesn't move, doesn't leave. He remains there, watching, *looming*.

My feelings disperse all over the place; my heart is still buzzing, thundering, with nothing to anchor it in its ribcage.

"I don't want this," I mutter.

"Seems that the drunk you is more honest than the sober you."

"Are you going to make me participate in sexual activities with you?"

"*Make* you?" he repeats, slight amusement shining in his eyes. "Do you remember what I said last night?"

I rack my brain over what he might have mentioned, and

my cheeks burn further with every recollection of my lustful acts. I can't believe I asked him if he'd fuck me.

God, I nearly begged him for it.

Where was my survival perimeter? If he'd complied, would I have let him screw me?

I shoo the answer to that question away. I really don't want to know what I would've done in that situation.

"Do you remember?" he insists with that calm that I don't believe for a second. This man is able to wreck lives without blinking an eye.

I nod.

"Use your words, Lia."

"I remember," I murmur.

"What did I say?"

"You're not a rapist."

"Correct. What else did I say?"

I stare at him, confused.

"After that, what did I say? I know you remember."

"That you'd deal with me in the morning." The words leave my mouth in a whisper.

"It's morning." He grabs the blanket and I tighten my hold around it. If I let it go, if I fall into his carefully spun web, I'll never find a way out.

I can smell the scent of his luring, the way he's carefully bringing me into the midst of his lethal world. First, I saw him kill someone in cold blood, then he allowed me to leave, but even that was calculated. It was a ploy to have me think about him all week long, looking under my bed and out my windows. Locking my doors and checking them several times after. Staring through my damn rear-view mirror, searching for his shadow.

Appearing during a private rehearsal was his way of telling me that he can get anywhere he wants. Find me anywhere I go.

The dinner was also a calculated move to have me loosen up so he could get closer without scaring me shitless. To show me that he's a normal man who can have dinners and dates.

But there's nothing normal about him. I never thought he was normal—and I never will. This man is the type who will, without any hesitation, go after what he wants.

And right now, that's me.

My chin trembles as I keep my solid hold on the blanket. I'm not a fool, I know he could yank it away at any second. Not only is he twice my size, he's also a killer, someone who's used to brute force while I'm accustomed to elegance and finesse.

"Did you do all that to fuck me?" I murmur.

"All that?"

"Giving me time. The dinner, the kiss. Not touching me when I was drunk?"

"The dinner was, as I said, to get to know you. The kiss was because I wanted to taste your lips. I didn't touch you when you were drunk, because I need you present when I'm fucking you. As for your first question, I gave you time to let you cope with the fact that I'm coming for you."

"I thought you let me go."

"You're smart enough to not believe that. During the entire week, you were jumpy, waiting, biding your time until I came back into your life again."

"You…you were watching me?"

"Yes."

"Are you a stalker?"

"I'm worse, Lenochka, but you already knew that when you touched yourself, showing me a side of you no one has seen."

"I wasn't lucid enough to realize what I was doing." My cheeks heat even as I say the words.

He tsks and I freeze as a muscle ticks in his jaw. "Don't lie. Not to me."

My knuckles hurt from how much I'm clenching my fists

and I can feel my insides dissolving into itself. There's nothing, absolutely nothing, I can do that will stop him.

If I fight, he'll overpower me.

If I try to escape, he'll catch me and probably hurt me.

My only possible option to not get hurt is to play into his hand, to let him have his way and hope that he'll leave me in peace. That after he gets me, he'll realize, like everyone else has, that I'm not a keeper.

I'm a diamond others admire from afar, but once they dig into it, all they find is black stone.

Adrian tugs on the blanket. "Let go."

I dig my nails into it, self-conscious about releasing my only lifeline.

"I'm not going to fuck you." He pauses. "Yet."

That doesn't relieve me as much as it should. If anything, it creates a hollow pit at the bottom of my stomach.

I wish he'd fuck me and get it over with. And since I'm not drunk, I can't ask that of him.

So I do the one thing I can in my situation.

I let go.

EIGHT

Lia

I LIE IN BED IN NOTHING BUT MY LEOTARD THAT'S unsnapped at my most intimate part.

Adrian watches me, mechanically at first, as if he has no interest in what he sees. As if I'm a mere object that's landed in his path.

But if that were the case, why would he want me? Why is he insistent on taking me?

"Do you do this to everyone who witnesses you killing?" I ask to dispel the tension that's brewing in the air and slamming against my chest.

"This?" His gaze slides to my face for a brief second.

"You know."

"Are you too much of a prude to name it, Lia?"

"*Fucking*," I mutter. "I'm not too much of a prude to speak up when necessary."

"I'm not fucking you, though."

"Then what do you plan to do?"

"Something similar."

"Do you do something similar to fucking with everyone who witnesses your murders?"

"No. I kill them."

My throat closes at his apathetic tone. He really has no regard for human life, does he? He must think of everyone as collateral pieces of a chessboard that he can get rid of as he sees fit.

He hooks his fingers on the décolletage of my top and pulls it down in one swift go, revealing my naked breasts.

I'm breathing heavily, my fists clenching into the mattress on either side of me. He reaches a large hand toward me, a hand that can throttle me or snap me in two.

I don't think as I grab it, my smaller palms cradling his in a desperate attempt to stop him from acting on his objective.

It could be because of the feral way he's staring at my breasts. I don't like it. But what I dislike the most is how my nipples have instantly peaked into tight buds under his merciless gaze.

Adrian raises a brow but doesn't force me to let him go, even though he could overpower me in a beat. My hands are wrapped around his, keeping them an inch away from my skin. As we watch each other in a dance of back and forth, I don't know if I'm fighting him or myself.

Or maybe I'm fighting my terrifying reaction to him. He's not touching me, but his warmth is creeping under my skin. He's merely looking at my breasts, but he elicited a shudder from my bones. One that I don't want to acknowledge, but it's there, tucked between my heart and ribcage.

All I can think about is how I came while he stroked my nipples over my leotard or how I dreamt about him plunging inside me with increasing roughness.

I don't want to know what will happen if he actually touches me. That thought is like acid on my nerves—melting, paralyzing, and damn frightening.

But at the same time, I want all of this to end, and the more I deny him, the longer I'll have to suffer.

With a deep breath, I release his hand, letting my arms fall to my sides.

His long, masculine fingers wrap around a taut nipple and twist, gently at first, then harshly with the intent to hurt. I inhale through my nose and exhale through my mouth to keep from feeling it.

But it's pointless.

My nipples send a zap of pleasure straight to my core. It's so strong that my entire body feels it. My every nerve ending comes alive under his ministrations and there's no way to stop the assault, even if I wanted to. It doesn't help that my nipples are sensitive, prone to easy stimulation.

I've always liked nipple play, but have hardly gotten any because of my small breasts. However, Adrian doesn't seem to care. He's stimulating them in a maddening way, as if he's been touching them for a lifetime.

"Was that a little rebellion just now, Lia?" He pinches both nipples hard and I arch off the bed, yelping.

"Mmm…"

"That's not an answer."

I shake my head.

"Use your words." His voice, although low, is firm and controlled with no room to be disobeyed.

"N-no."

He twists again, more forcefully this time, as if he's planning to break the skin, and I release an anguished cry mixed with a moan. "I said not to lie to me. Another strike and I'll have to deal with your disobedience."

"Yes, yes…ahhh…" I whimper when he massages the aching nipples with the pads of his thumbs.

His message is clear. If I obey him, I'll be rewarded. If I don't, he'll make sure I suffer.

He continues twisting and pinching my nipples, then runs the pad of his thumb over the tips as if soothing them, giving them a slight reprieve before he goes back to torturing them again.

I'm so stimulated that I think I'll orgasm with just nipple play. It'd be a first, and for some reason, I believe he'd be able to do it. My core throbs with bursts of arousal that match the rhythm of his fingers. Sometimes hard and fast, other times slow and agonizing.

He releases my left breast and it aches, tingling with the loss of his fingers.

Adrian lifts the leotard up to my stomach, tracing his fingers along my belly. I flinch, a whole body shiver going through me.

"Are you always this sensitive?"

I purse my lips and he flattens his palm on my stomach, pinching my nipple hard. "Ahh…that hurts."

"Then it'd be best to answer me when I ask a question."

"No," I whisper.

A feral gleam takes refuge in his stormy gray eyes. "No one's touched you properly to make you sensitive?"

"I'm not a virgin…ahhh…" I moan when he runs the tip of his thumb over the aching peak.

"That doesn't answer my question." His tone hardens and so does his touch, as if his mood has soured. "If I wanted to know about the loser who tore through your cunt and soaked his dick with your virginal blood, I would've found out and taught him how to truly touch you. Though I'd probably kill him soon after since…well, you know how I feel about witnesses. So tell me, Lia, has anyone touched you properly before? Has anyone pushed your buttons the way you wish?"

I'm shivering and flat out trembling, both at the threat behind his words and the calm in them. My thighs rub against each other due to the unfathomable effect he's having on me.

When I speak, my voice is barely audible through my moan, "No."

"But you wished for it, didn't you? When they were handling you gently like a porcelain doll, you wished for the roughness, for the sting of pain."

I shake my head violently against the pillow, mortification eating at my insides.

He pinches my nipple hard enough to elicit a whimper of pain. "What did I say about lying to me?"

"I'm not sick like you," I manage between throaty sounds.

"Oh, but you are." He trails his hand downward and cups my most intimate part. "Mmm. You're soaked, Lenochka."

Heat rises to my ears and I turn my head, trying to hide my face and my utter shame in the pillow.

"Look at me."

I don't, refusing to let him see parts of me he has no business seeing.

Adrian twists my nipple at the same time as he runs two fingers through my folds. "I said, look at me."

The pure authority in his tone, coupled with the pleasure and pain, make me peek at him, lips parted in a wordless cry— or a scream. I have no clue which sound will come out if I let it loose.

"You don't hide from me when I'm touching you, Lia."

"I'm not...ahhh..." My voice ends on a whimper-moan when he shoves those two fingers inside me.

"Don't finish that lie."

"Mmm..." My back arches off the bed at the sensation of being filled by him. It's been a long time since I was touched this intimately. Though I'm not simply being touched now; I'm being completely and utterly owned. Just like when he kissed me, Adrian holds me to him by an invisible thread. He's pulling on it, tugging and dragging me to his side as if I'm a marionette doll.

"You're so fucking tight. Do you feel your walls clenching around my fingers?"

I want to look away from the controlled lust shining in his eyes, but I can't. And it's not only because of his command. Something in me unlocked when his fingers went inside me. It's feral and harsh and out of control. It's as unforgiving as the marionette strings pulling me along with no clear direction or landing site.

I'm falling into that web; I can feel the strings digging into my skin, sinking deep with each of his merciless pounds.

He thrusts into me and I moan. He pinches my nipple and I gasp.

The rhythm is overwhelming, savage, but not messy. It's measured and with clear intent. Just like everything about Adrian.

He twists my nipples over and over again as he powers into my pussy. The heel of his palm slaps against my clit with every move and I see white stars.

"Do you hear your arousal, Lenochka? Do you hear how much you crave this? How your body is coming undone?" He rams his fingers in a few more times, as if driving the point home. I should be ashamed by the sound of my pleasure, the sound of his palm hitting my clit at an increasing pace.

But I rise to it. My back pushes off the mattress, meeting his fingers on my nipples and inside me.

My heart is nearly breaking out of my skin to match his rhythm, to somehow be equal in this fucked-up situation.

Somewhere in my brain, I know this is wrong. I know I shouldn't be trying to reach that peak, but that part is buried too deep to float to the surface.

Adrian rubs the heel of his palm against my clit while twisting my nipple and curling his fingers inside my tight walls.

The triple assault undoes me.

I cry out as I embrace the fall. I don't shy away from it as I let my voice express the ecstasy hitting me from all possible directions.

"Ahhh…I'm…I'm…ahhh!" My mouth remains open as a halo submerges me and transports me in an out-of-body experience. It's like I'm flying through the roof and watching myself tremble in Adrian's hold. His fingers are inside me, all over me, and I raise my hips so I can ride the wave.

Ride *him*.

I think I'll remain suspended like this for eternity. Maybe I've died and my soul is looking down at my body. The body that's caught in a web with no way out.

But Adrian wrenches me back to the land of the living when he pulls his fingers from me and places them at my mouth.

"Suck them clean."

"W-what?"

"You heard me."

"But—Mmm…" My words are interrupted when he shoves his fingers inside my mouth. The same fingers that were just in me. The same fingers that he brought me pleasure with.

My face burns with shame. Not only at tasting myself but also at how much of my arousal there is. How much I let go when it should've been the last thing I'd do in his company.

"Move your tongue, Lia." His tone is tender but with a firm edge meant to be obeyed.

I lap at his fingers, my face burning and my thighs clenching. The orgasm I just had doesn't seem to have finished. It rises to the surface, probing and holding on to the belief that there will be something else. Something more intense. Something that will keep me in that suspended halo longer.

A halo where I don't have to think about anything. A halo where I can only *feel*.

Adrian's penetrating gray eyes never leave mine as I slowly lick his fingers, curling my tongue around them. They're a work of art and are as masculine and lean as they look.

"Do you feel your abandon, Lenochka? Do you now see why you can't lie to me?"

I continue licking and sucking because, even though it started as an order, a part of me is perversely enjoying this act. And that part wants more of it.

And *him*.

Adrian pulls his fingers out and I release them with a pop, a line of saliva sticking to them. He then proceeds to use them to part my lips.

The gesture is more possessive than anything he's just done. More than the orgasm or the nipple play. More than his orders and his non-negotiable demands.

"Answer me."

"Y-yes..."

He glides his thumb across my bottom lip before mashing it against my teeth. A strange look passes over his features. It's fleeting but manages to send a shudder through my bones.

I expect him to thrust his fingers back inside my mouth or climb atop me and fuck me. But he releases my nipple and mouth at the same time, then slides the duvet up to cover me.

I watch with utter bewilderment as he heads to the chair, grabs his coat, and walks out.

I remain there, motionless, my body and heart on high alert until I hear the soft click of the front door.

Did he...leave?

I stay still for a few minutes, thinking that it must be a distasteful joke. That he will come back and either finish what he started or tell me what the hell he's planning.

He doesn't return.

I should be feeling relieved, and I *am*—I finally got rid of the asshole.

And yet, the marionette strings tighten at my nape and an empty sound echoes in my chest.

NINE

Adrian

FUCK.

Make that double fuck.

Kolya and Yan are standing in front of my car. The younger guard is running his hand through his long hair as he smokes a cigarette. He offers it to Kolya, but he shakes his head and scolds him in Russian, "Smoking is bad for your health."

"What are you, my father?"

"I would've beaten that habit out of you if I were."

Yan scoffs since he has absolutely no respect for those older than him. He's nineteen, reckless to a fault, and Kolya has to clean up after him so that he doesn't get himself killed by the other senior guards. Especially those my father left behind.

Upon seeing me, Kolya moves to open the door, but I beat him to it. I slide into the back seat and undo the top buttons of my shirt.

Kolya and Yan are inside before I can blink.

"Where to?" my second-in-command asks.

"The *Pakhan*'s house."

He nods and kicks the car into gear without asking questions.

While I don't make it a habit to attend breakfasts at Sergei's. I need a distraction from the woman I just left upstairs.

A part of me wants to stop the car, open the door, and go back. That part wants to finish what I started, to hear her erotic voice as she comes undone all over my dick.

That part also wants to erase the memory of any fucker who touched her in the past so that her body only remembers me.

But that part isn't keeping its sights on the reason why I'm doing this in the first place. I'm not getting under Lia's skin to fuck her. I'm getting under her skin for information.

In my dictionary, information is deadlier than any gun. It's a weapon of mass destruction, and if there's anything I learned from my psycho mother, it's that I need to grab the bull by the horns.

People think whoever has the largest and better equipped battalion wins. What they fail to understand is that if a battalion doesn't gather enough information about the enemy, they will never get far. They might win a battle or two. They might kill a thousand or a few, but the one with more intel is the winner of the war.

Being raised to never accept any losses has turned me into a master of acquiring information. I'm even better than both my monster parents combined.

I internally scoff at that. Why would I call them monsters when I've become worse than them?

But then again, monsters might recognize each other, but they don't necessarily like one another.

They're more interested in digging each other's graves.

In winning.

That's what I should be focused on—winning. My main

mission with Lia Morelli is to acquire information. But the lines blurred somewhere between her erotic moans and the way she looked at me while she came apart around my fingers, and then once again when she licked them as if she's been doing it for eternity.

I've never been as hard as I was in that moment. I've lost sight of my mission, like I did when she parted her lips and completely let go.

That's why I left. I need to play my cards right and that won't happen as long as I'm in her vicinity.

"Did you find out anything?" Yan asks. He always has a terrible way of broaching subjects.

Kolya shakes his head at him.

"What? That's what you wanted to ask, too."

"Shut it, Yan," my senior guard scolds.

"I don't see why I should."

"Yan…" I release a long sigh. "I told you to read the atmosphere before asking. Have you ever learned anything from me and Kolya?"

"I learned that you're too silent. If I don't talk, no one will."

Kolya glares at him.

"What?" Yan retrieves a cigarette and lights it. "You've been boring me since birth."

Usually, I'd tell him to put the cigarette out, but I couldn't give a fuck right now.

"Then why are you still here?" Kolya asks.

Yan taps a fist to his chest. "I was personally handpicked to guard Boss. That honor doesn't come easily."

"Obviously an error on the part of whoever picked you," Kolya mutters under his breath.

Yan gets worked up and starts enumerating 'all the shit' he recently went through in the Spetsnaz Special Forces so that he could come back to serve me. Kolya meets that with cold indifference because Yan only spent two years there, which is nothing compared to the time my second-in-command served.

I let their back-and-forth go in one ear and out the other. I try to use that time to implement my next plan, but all I keep thinking about are plump lips, perky tits, and a soft, pink cunt.

But that's not all. It's the way she moaned. The way she stared, dazed after she orgasmed. I want that sight in my brain, not as a spur-of-the-moment thing, but as a constant that I can revisit again and again until she's completely out of my system.

Kolya and Yan grow silent when we arrive at Sergei's mansion. I step out, doing the first button of my shirt. Since I spent last night watching and exploring Lia's apartment, I didn't get any sleep.

That's not a first.

I've spent all-nighters watching my screens and emailing my hackers, back and forth until I got the information I needed.

My abnormal sleeping schedules started after that day—the day my own mother broke my arm because it would help her get my father to her side. I didn't trust that she wouldn't do it again, that to become Georgy Volkov's wife, she wouldn't use me, over and over, to get in his favor.

She did succeed and became the lady of the house, even when most of my father's guards loathed her.

Since that night, though, I've always slept with one eye open in case she shows up at my door and takes the life she gave as she promised.

Yan stays by the entrance with several other high-ranked guards of the other brigade leaders. He's offering Mikhail's sol-dier a smoke and teasing Kirill's guard. Yan sometimes acts like a clown, jabbing and teas-ing, but his sole purpose is to get deets from them.

He might be reckless, but he understands my philosophy well and plots accordingly. It's one of the few reasons I keep him close.

Kolya follows me inside the *Pakhan*'s dining room and it's clear that we're the last to arrive.

Sergei sits at the head of the table, Vladimir on his left, while my chair on his right is empty. Mikhail, Igor, Kirill, and Damien occupy the rest of the seats. Their senior guards stand behind them like sturdy walls, all scowling, sometimes at nothing, other times at each other, depending on whether their bosses are making a fuss.

"Adrian." Sergei doesn't hide his bewilderment upon seeing me. "What a pleasant surprise."

"I thought I should have breakfast with you, *Pakhan*."

"Yes, yes. Come."

"Very benevolent of you to show us your noble face, Sir Volkov," Damien mumbles.

"It's a surprise, indeed." Kirill takes a sip of his coffee, watching me from beneath his glasses. I can feel his head spinning in a thousand directions to analyze why I showed up today.

I ignore them both and take my seat. Soon after, a maid rushes in with a cup of black coffee and places it in front of me before leaving.

There are different pastries, along with eggs, ham, and bacon on the table, and I have no doubt it's to appease Damien's gluttony, because his mouth is chewing something as we speak.

"Where were we?" Igor continues, ignoring my cutting him off. He's a pillar of the brotherhood and has been around since my father's time.

He has some of my father's traits—namely, ruthlessness—but unlike Georgy Volkov, Igor Petrov is wiser and knows which cards to play and which to keep hidden. He, Kirill, and Vladimir are the ones I watch the most. They're calm on the surface, but when they hit, no one sees it coming.

"Strengthening our alliance with the Italians," Mikhail grumbles with clear impatience.

"I think we should watch some more before making any decisions," Kirill says casually.

Damien points his fork at him. "Watching is for losers, Kirill."

"Watching allows us to read others," the latter shoots back.

"Action lets us take care of them." Damien's eyes gleam with the promise of violence.

"Leave your fists out of the equation for once, Orlov," Igor reprimands him.

"My fists brought us new territories, so how about you take my example and awaken your own fists, old man. You, too, Mikhail. You're pussy-whipped by your whoring business."

"You fucking—"

"Orlov," Sergei scolds, cutting Mikhail off.

"What?" Damien swallows his mouthful of pastry and licks his fingers. "Just stating facts, *Pakhan*."

"Learn some respect."

"Respect is earned, not learned." He grabs a muffin and points at me with it. "Look at Volkov here being a mute little princess, but everyone at this table will stop and listen when he actually speaks."

I lift my coffee to my lips and take a sip, paying him no attention. Maybe showing up here was a mistake after all. I could've worked out with Kolya, Yan, and the rest of my guards to ward off the tension. Now, I'm forced to participate in their endless—and as usual, useless—fights.

"Do you have anything to say, Adrian?" Kirill asks in his suave voice.

"About?"

"The Italians. You've been looking into them, haven't you?"

"I'm getting to know the Luciano family's dynamics, yes, but I'm not close enough to make any statements." I stare at Sergei. "The *Pakhan* will know if I make any progress."

"I don't like to rush you," the Vor says. "But we need the Lucianos, Adrian."

"They're making deals with the Colombian cartel and we need in," Vladimir elaborates as if I don't know that already.

Just because I don't attend morning meetings, doesn't mean I'm not privy to the brotherhood's affairs. I have a direct line with Sergei, as I previously did with his brother, Nikolai. Nothing is discussed at this table before the *Pakhan* asks for my opinion about it.

Igor interlaces his fingers in front of him, meeting my gaze as if I'm the only one in the room that he cares about. "If the Lucianos have all access to the South American cartels, they will have more power. They already cleaned their territory by wiping out the other families from New York, except a few Rozettis scattered about. Lazlo Luciano is power-hungry enough to come at us to ensure no one breathes in their presence."

Damien slams his fist on the table, rattling the coffee cups. "Let him come and I'll erase him and his little fucking soldiers."

Kirill releases an exasperated breath. "War is the last thing to think about, not the first."

"Maybe we should kill them all before the Colombians get involved." Damien widens his eyes as if he's come up with the most genius idea.

"Declaring war on our allies is a sure way to have everyone riot against us," Vladimir explains calmly, slowly, as if he's speaking to a kid.

"We'll kill them, too." Damien grins.

"Shut the fuck up, Orlov," Mikhail snarls.

"Or what? You'll unleash your pussy-whipped soldiers on me?"

"My pussy-whipped soldiers, and even my whores, have more common sense than you."

"Point is," Igor cuts off Damien and Mikhail's quarrel. "We need that partnership with the Italians."

"I'll have something for you soon, *Pakhan*," I say.

"How soon?" Sergei doesn't hide his pleasure.

"Before the deal with the Colombians."

"Now we're talking." Kirill smirks. "What's your method?"

I take my time sipping from my coffee, letting its bitter edge coat my throat. "That doesn't matter. The results I bring do."

"As usual." Sergei raises his glass of juice in my direction and I raise my cup.

Kirill is still watching me, no doubt wanting to figure out my method, but no one will know my in with the Italians.

If it were a few days ago, I would've told them all about Lia Morelli, but after today, she'll remain locked between me and myself.

She's now my secret.

Dirty.

Dangerous.

And entirely fucked-up.

TEN

Lia

MY LIFE GOES ON.

Or at least that's what I'd like to believe a week later. In my attempt to gather myself together, I pretend that my life does go on. That I didn't witness a murder, didn't kiss the murderer, then fantasize about fucking him and come by his stimulations. Twice.

Because that orgasm when I was drunk? Yeah that wasn't entirely me. I was merely adding a little friction to the avalanche he'd already caused by playing with my nipples.

I can blame all that on how sensitive they are or how drunk I was, but the fact remains that I was turned on by him, by his presence and calm savageness.

But that wasn't all. I asked him to fuck me.

In my drunken state, I nearly begged him to take what he wanted. Yes, I thought it'd hasten the process for him to leave me alone, but a hidden part of me craved that depravity.

Maybe too much so.

I suck in a deep breath as I land in Ryan's arms. It's our last move for today's rehearsal and I'm ready to go home, snuggle up in a blanket, and listen to some music. Hopefully, I'll fall asleep without my pills.

And without having any nightmares.

Ryan's fingers slide up my hip, feeling me up as he puts me down.

He always does shit like this, touching me when he shouldn't. Stroking me as if my body belongs to some sort of exotic animal he wants to study.

"Let me go," I grit under my breath.

"It's part of the choreography, sweetness."

"No, it's not." I push him away, but he digs his fingers into my hipbone.

"We're supposed to act as if we're in love, so how about you become a bit more cooperative?"

"It's called acting, Ryan. It's not real."

"True acting is derived from real life." He licks his lips, subtly grinding his erection against my belly. "You should try it sometime, *life*."

I elbow him, disgust coiling at the bottom of my stomach. I'm such a hypocrite. I've been dreaming about a damn killer since he left my apartment a week ago, yet I feel nothing but disgust for my dance partner.

But Ryan has serious behavioral problems. No matter how much I push him away, he takes it as an invitation to come back for more.

While I respect him as a dancer for his flawless posture and technique, I loathe him as a human being.

He leans in to whisper in my ear, "You're supposed to trust me since I always catch you, sweetness."

"While *acting*." I try to push him away again.

"What's going on here?" Hannah, his latest acquisition, barges between us, glaring at me.

Ryan lets me go with a smirk. "I told you we're only acting, Lia. No need to feel it so much."

Everyone's attention slides to me, some snickering and others horrified, while Hannah looks like she wants to strangle me.

I point at Ryan's semi hard-on that's visible through his tights. "I think it's obvious who was *feeling* it."

I turn around to leave, catching Stephanie shaking her head at Ryan. I told her the other day that I'm growing uncomfortable leading with Ryan, and she promised to talk to the producers and Philippe so that we're not paired for the next performance.

But I have to put up with him for *Giselle* and consider it a sacrifice for the sake of art.

"Where do you think you're going, *chérie?*" Philippe, who was too busy with the staff to pay attention to what happened, loops his arm in mine.

"Home."

"*Non, non.* Not tonight. We promised we'd go out for drinks for team spirit."

"I'm tired and I need some aftercare." Because as much as I hate to admit it, my ankle still throbs. Dr. Kim said it's fatigue and gave me muscle relaxers, but I'm paranoid as hell about using my legs when it's not for the purpose of ballet.

"Do the aftercare here and then join us."

"Philippe…"

"I'm not taking no for an answer. We miss having you among us outside of rehearsal."

He's the only one who thinks that. And maybe Stephanie, because she rocks.

I peek at all the glares shooting my way because of Philippe's obvious favoritism. He calls me his star, his muse, and the lead of his every masterpiece. Something that has dug the hole deeper between me and the other dancers.

If he wasn't openly gay and happily married, they'd say I'm sleeping with him like they do about the producers.

"Come on, change the mood." Stephanie takes my other arm. "You're stressed. I can feel it."

She can say that again. I haven't been able to sleep, probably since…well, since Adrian walked into my life.

Not that my sleeping patterns were better before him.

"*Oui, oui.* Stress is not good for my muse." Philippe clutches my chin between his fingers and gently shakes it as if I'm a baby.

You know what? A night out is better than overthinking until I collapse in my empty apartment. All I have to do is stay with Philippe and Stephanie.

"Fine." I smile a little. "I'm in."

"You won't regret it." Philippe rolls the *R* exaggeratingly with his accent.

I go to my dressing room, making sure to lock both doors, then I take a quick shower and place bandages on my ankles as I sit down to blow-dry my hair and put on makeup. I opt for a soft glittery eyeshadow. It's been a stupid obsession of mine since I was a little girl. Glitter and beautiful things. They signify hope, I guess. That's what I've wanted all along and the only thing that's kept me going.

I paint my lips in a nude color and apply some mascara. The makeup is a lot tamer than what I'm used to for official performances, but it still gives me that confidence. The hope.

To say my life has gotten back on course would be a lie. I've been watching my apartment door since that day Adrian walked out, waiting for him to come back. I've watched the audience, too, but he hasn't shown up in my rehearsals again. Not even once.

A part of my brain, the logical part, is somehow glad he's left me alone, but the other part knows, it just knows that's not the end of it.

Far from it.

If anything, that encounter might as well have been the

beginning. I know he'll come back, and this time, my life will be blown to pieces.

The cruelty of leaving me on the edge is too much. I want to scream and yell, but that won't bring a different result. It will just happen as he planned all along.

I need to find a way to get rid of him, to purge him out of my life once and for all, because in the small time he was in it, he disordered everything. Including my damn dreams.

After putting on a simple black dress with a plunging neckline, I throw on my coat and wear my flats, then go to find Stephanie and Philippe. The others have already headed to the club, and those two waited for me.

The director drives the three of us to a club downtown, French music with a soft melody playing on the stereo. Stephanie sits beside him while I'm in the back alone.

"Wait and see, *chérie*. I booked the entire VIP lounge for us."

"What are we celebrating?" Stephanie asks.

"Lia being the Giselle of my dreams, *bien sûr*. The producers went nuts after seeing your demonstration that first day."

I tuck an imaginary strand of hair behind my ear. "Speaking of the producers, who was the new face?"

"The new face?" Philippe meets my gaze in the mirror.

"That tall man," I speak casually, trying not to betray my need for information. In one of my sleepless nights, I googled Adrian Volkov and found some Russian dude's Instagram and Twitter accounts, but they looked nothing like the Adrian I met.

It could be a false name he gave me, but I highly doubt it. Most likely, people like him hide their presence from the internet because it can expose or implicate them.

"Ah." A light bulb seems to go off in Philippe's head. "The Russian."

"Yes," I blurt, which gets me a look from Stephanie, who's

perceptive to a fault. I hope it's not written all over my face or I'm not blushing to my ears.

Philippe pauses for a bit, lost in thought. "He's one of the executive producer's associates or business partners or whatever. Matt brought him in, if I remember correctly. Those with money have a lot of friends with money who have absolutely no appreciation for art."

So even Philippe doesn't know much about him.

"I heard he's from the mafia," Stephanie whispers as if not wanting anyone to hear.

My heart pulses harder as I murmur back, "He is?"

"I think so. Seemed like Matt was more scared of him than actually considering him a business partner."

I let the information swirl in my head, thankful for Stephanie's observations. I was too focused on Adrian to notice Matt's behavior—or anyone else's. "How do you know that?"

"Matt and his wife's expensive tastes have been landing them in trouble. But to be involved with the mafia is something else. I heard life is worth absolutely nothing to them."

She can say that again. Adrian certainly didn't hesitate when he finished that man off.

"Now, hush, Stephanie," Philippe scolds.

"Just saying." She changes the music to Tchaikovsky's Piano Concerto no. 2, ignoring Philippe's sounds of displeasure.

I sink further into my seat, absorbing the information I just learned. So Adrian is from the mafia. It could be another rumor, but for some reason, I believe it.

The part that bugs me the most is his relation to Matt. I don't think it's a coincidence. But what else could it be?

We arrive at the club before I can find answers to my questions, not that they've been forthcoming when it's about Adrian.

Stephanie and I loop an arm through each of Philippe's as he makes a grand entry into the club called Blue Diamond.

Thumping music greets us once we're inside. The place is packed with people drinking and grinding against each other. Blue lights cast a fantasy-like hue over them as the DJ works his magic with the latest trendy hits. Some of the ballet dancers are on the floor, too, dancing and shaking their asses. While many of us prefer classical music, others are chameleons and listen and dance to anything.

Philippe sways, twirling both Stephanie and me around, then shouts over the music, "*Alors*, smile a little. We have all night. Open bar, my treat."

More like his husband's treat since Blue Diamond is his. Which is why Philippe manages to book the VIP lounge whenever he wishes.

Steve, his husband, welcomes us with an exasperated sigh, probably because of Philippe's show-off attitude. As much as the director is a drama queen sometimes, Steve is anything but.

He's a big man with a trimmed beard and bulging muscles under his short-sleeved T-shirt from which tattoos of snakes peek through. He's self-made and rose from underground fighting to owning this club and a few other chains across the States.

"Miss me, *mon amour?*" Philippe coos, tickling his husband's beard.

Steve pats his hand, then motions for us to follow him upstairs. "I told you to stop attracting attention."

"Romance is really dead with you, *mon amour*. I should've gotten myself a French lover."

Steve grunts. "As if anyone in the world would put up with your antics."

"You do."

"Begrudgingly."

"I'm also putting up with your grumpiness, aren't I?" He levels him with a stare as he hugs me to his side. "Anyway, I brought my muse. Take care of us."

"Good to have you, Lia." Steve's words are warm, but his expression is the same as usual. It's been a few years since I've seen him and he's always been caring, even if it's in a distanced kind of way. I just love his and Philippe's old couple banter.

After he makes sure we're comfy in the private VIP lounge upstairs, Steve leaves us to take care of management business. I sit with Stephanie and Philippe on a sofa that's isolated from the others, which offers a direct view to the dancefloor below. The two of them order one shot after the other, but I only allow myself a glass of tequila because there's no way in hell I'm getting drunk again.

It's been a week, but I made more mistakes than I can count the last time I allowed the liquor to rule me.

I actively avoid the other dancers while I listen to my two companions' conversation. The others know not to join Philippe's table unless he invites them, so I'm somewhat safe. As soon as Philippe goes to the bathroom, or for a 'quickie with Steve' as Stephanie says with a scoff, Ryan comes over, dressed in trendy Italian slacks and a purple T-shirt. He sways on his legs a little, his focus on me. "Come dance with us, Lia."

"No, thanks."

"Come on, it'll be fun."

"She said no thanks, Ryan. Which part of that do you not understand?" Stephanie tells him with a smile.

His lips twist as he huffs and leaves.

I give Stephanie a thankful glance that she answers with a nod, obviously knowing that my complaints weren't in vain. We continue watching the dancing crowd until Philippe comes back, practically jumping and with his eyes gleaming. He definitely got laid or got high. Or both.

"Let's dance, *mes belles*."

Stephanie stands. "I'm always game for some twerking."

Philippe teasingly slaps her ass. "Work it, *bébé*."

"I'll just watch from here." I smile.

"No way. You didn't come all the way here to sit like a statue, *chérie*." Philippe says as he and Stephanie drag me downstairs despite my protests. I move slowly, trying not to put pressure on my foot.

Philippe twirls me, then Stephanie, and then they both shake their asses, inviting me to join. I just laugh at the scene, feeling a bit lighthearted by simply watching them. They can be so fun together. No wonder they've had such perfect chemistry working with each other all these years.

I'm still not comfortable with the dancing, however, so I shout over the music, "I'm going to grab a drink!"

"Hurry back!" Philippe calls out.

I nod, even though I actually intend to go back upstairs and watch them make fools out of themselves. But as soon as I get there, I regret it.

The place is empty except for two ballerinas who are making out in the back booth, groping each other's breasts. But that's not what makes me want to bolt.

It's Ryan.

He's waiting for me at the sofa where we were seated when we got here.

His eyes are wrong. I don't know what is it about them, but I dislike what I see in there. I turn to go downstairs and rejoin Philippe and Stephanie, but he grabs me by the arm and pulls me back so hard, I slam against his chest.

"What the hell, Ryan?"

"I thought you didn't want to dance, but you did it so well just now."

I try to wiggle my wrist from his hold. "Let me go."

"Or what?"

"Or I'll scream."

He covers my mouth with his palm and pulls me to him, rubbing his erection against my stomach as he forces me to move with him. "Now, you won't."

"Mfahhm…" I attempt to scream against his hand.

"It's just a fucking dance, Lia. Stop being a goddamn snob and do it."

I don't want to do it, because the way he's looking at me doesn't seem like it's just a dance. The feel of his hard-on is even more disturbing than earlier.

"You're such a fucking cocktease. Did you know that?"

"Mmmfop!" He's still keeping me from talking, so I try to kick him, but he pulls away at the last second and steps on my foot, the sole of his shoe nearly crushing my bones.

"Ahhhhh!" I scream into his palm. *No, no, no…*

"Do that again and I will break your fucking legs, Lia. You'll be good, won't you?"

I nod, tears of both desperation and pain clinging to my lids.

"You're going to come with me, nice and easy."

I'm about to nod, just so he'll get off my foot. Anything to protect it.

But before I can do anything, a shadow appears behind Ryan. Strong fingers wrap around his face and neck.

Fingers that only appear in my dreams these days. Fingers I would recognize anywhere.

If not for the searing pain from Ryan's shoe, I'd think this is another dream, but it's far from it.

The blue lights cast a scary glow on his face as he rips Ryan from me.

Adrian.

ELEVEN

Lia

ADRIAN IS HERE.

That thought isn't fully implemented in my mind when the reality of what's happening slams into me.

I don't even focus on the fact that my throbbing foot is free from Ryan's shoe.

The view in front of me is more shocking. More demanding of my attention.

Adrian stands behind Ryan, wrapping both of his strong hands around his neck and jaw. His fingers are sure and confident with no show of any hesitation or second thoughts whatsoever. Under the blue light, his eyes are blank, emotionless, just like that day he shot that man in the head as if he were killing a fly.

"What is this?" Ryan struggles back against Adrian, trying to elbow him, but it's no use. "Do you know who I am—"

His words are cut off when Adrian tightens his hold on his neck and speaks with a neutral Russian accent, "I'd shut up if I were you unless you want your neck snapped in the next second."

Ryan's face reddens as he struggles for breath. The wide look in his sleazy eyes is proof enough that he understands what type of clusterfuck he's gotten himself into. I have no doubt in my mind that Adrian would break his neck or his jaw without a single blink.

As much as I hate Ryan and his behavior, I don't wish him—or anyone—death. Especially not by the hands of a callous man like Adrian.

Ryan's eyes meet mine, pleading, imploring. His lips are blue, and his thrashes and attempts to pry Adrian's hold away are futile. If anything, the more he struggles, the faster his body loses oxygen.

"Adrian..." I whisper, trying to sound normal despite my escalating nerves. "Let him go."

"It appears he put his hand on you." Though his tone is calm, matching the blankness in his eyes, his actions are anything but. They're ruthless with the intention of finishing a life. "In fact, he didn't only put his hands on you, but also his feet and his cock, which I will cut off and feed to him."

He hits the back of Ryan's leg and I gasp as my dance partner falls to his knees in front of me, wheezing as if the air has been knocked out of his lungs.

"We'll start with breaking the legs first." Adrian steps on Ryan's calves and an ugly, haunted sob leaves the dancer's lips.

I'm wrenched back from my dizzy state as I rush to Adrian and grab his muscled arm, shaking my head frantically. "Don't do that."

He doesn't pay attention to me as he yanks Ryan's head back using his hands on his face. "He tried to crush your foot just now."

"I'm not him. Adrian, please. You...you don't understand what our legs mean to us."

"The only thing I understand is that he has a strike and needs to be taken care of."

My stomach churns at those words, *taken care of.* As in, killed.

I dig my nails into his shirt and pull, knowing full well that my strength doesn't match up to his, but it's the only way I can think of to make him release Ryan.

"Don't…please," I murmur.

Adrian's head tilts to the side, meeting my gaze for the first time since he appeared behind Ryan like the Grim Reaper. His face is still expressionless, but a muscle clenches under his stubbled jaw.

"Why are you defending him after what he did to you?"

"I'm not defending him. I just don't want to be the reason behind someone losing their career."

"He was ready to endanger yours."

"I told you, I'm not him." I pause before adding in a low voice, "Or you."

Adrian doesn't comment on that, keeping his merciless hold on Ryan, as if he plans to break his leg and snap his neck at the same time.

"Please…" I pull on his arm. I have no clue why I think I'd have any type of effect on Adrian when he made it blatantly clear that he's the one who calls the shots, but a part of me wants to believe that I can make a difference.

That I can prevent killing a dancer's legs.

Playing my last card, I rise on my tiptoes and press a kiss to Adrian's jaw. It's supposed to be a gesture to lower his guard, but I end up being the one with my guard down.

All the emotions I've experienced since I first met him rush to the surface. The frustration, the unknown, and the damn longing that I don't want to admit to.

All those feelings have been there, biding their time, waiting for this exact moment when my mouth meets his skin. My lips quiver for a second too long before I pull back, my heart hammering so loud, I'm almost sure he hears it.

Adrian's hold loosens from around Ryan's neck and my dance

partner uses the chance to try and scurry away, but his leg is still trapped underneath Adrian's leather shoes.

"P-please…" It's Ryan who's begging now, tears shining in his eyes as he struggles for air while trying to pull his leg from underneath Adrian.

The devil from both my dreams and nightmares levels Ryan with a harsh glare. A shiver zips down my spine, even though it's not directed at me.

He could kill with that look alone.

"This is your first and final strike." Adrian digs the sole of his shoe into Ryan's calf, making him cry out. "Touch her again and I'll make sure you're paralyzed for life."

Ryan nods rapidly, frantically. I'm sure he can see the black halo surrounding Adrian like a second skin. Or maybe I'm the only one who can see his unmodified nature.

"Fuck off." Adrian removes his foot and kicks the back of his thigh. Something for which Ryan sobs out loud as he struggles to his feet.

He faces us while heading to the stairs as if expecting Adrian to come at him from behind again, knowing this time, he'll make good on his promise.

I steal a look at the ballerina couple who were making out when I first got here, but there's not one soul in sight. I inhale, not realizing I stopped breathing. While I usually don't care, the last thing I want or need is to be associated with a mobster.

"Don't defend another scum like him in front of me again."

My attention flits back to Adrian. My fingers are still digging in his shirt, and my heart continues to beat in and out of sync as if I'm still watching the scene with Ryan play out in front of me.

"Do you understand?"

I shake my head, taking a deep breath to gather my thoughts before releasing him. "You don't get to treat people as if they're disposable garbage."

"That's exactly what he was." He takes my hand in his and

I shudder when he raises it to his mouth and nibbles on my pinkie the slightest bit. The gesture is possessive and shoots straight between my legs. "You're trembling."

"I'm okay."

"Don't say that again."

"That I'm okay?"

"That word doesn't suit you. It's juvenile, when you're anything but." He watches me, his eyes running over my body in a full sweep as if he's checking to see if I've grown something since the last time he saw me. "Are you all right?"

I nod, completely baffled by his caring nature. Witnessing him kill once and almost repeating it again tonight has allowed me a front row seat of this brutal personality that terrifies me to the core, so to see him act concerned is giving me whiplash.

"How is your foot? Try moving it."

I rotate it slowly and release a breath when I realize most of the pain is gone. "It's fine."

"Are you sure or are you trying to stop me from catching up to that fucker and paralyzing him?"

"It's really fine." I scowl. "And stop that."

"Stop what?"

"Threatening other people's lives and dreams. You're like a true villain."

His lips twitch in rare amusement. "You thought I was a fake villain?"

"If I did, you've completely proved me wrong."

"I'm happy to do so." He's still gripping my fingers near his mouth, sending tiny sparks down my spine with each word against them. "If anyone touches you again, I'll make sure it's their last time to touch anyone."

I shudder, and I'm not sure if it's because of his words or his hold on my hand—or both.

All I'm sure about is that this man is a lot more dangerous than I thought.

"How will you know?"

"Know what?"

"That someone has touched me. Are you going to stalk me?"

He raises a brow.

"Right. You're doing it already or you wouldn't have found me here." I pull my hand from his with more force than needed.

Adrian grabs it again, his hold not brutal but firm enough to crush my fingers against each other.

"That's the second and final time you pull away from me."

"People don't like to touch their stalkers."

"Is that what you believe, Lenochka? That I'm your stalker?"

"Aren't you?"

"No. Stalkers are cowards who are afraid to get close. Do you see me watching from the shadows?"

"You were. If Ryan hadn't done what he did, would you have come out or would you have disappeared into thin air like that day?"

"Do I hear hurt, Lia? Were you disappointed that I left?"

"I never said that."

"You didn't have to. I can see it in the depths of those beautiful eyes. I can sense it in every shiver of your body. And you know what else your reaction tells me?"

I shake my head, not wanting to listen to him psychoanalyze me. I hate that he's so observant of my every move and that nothing escapes him. Not even the little things that I'm not aware of.

His voice lowers with a dark, seductive undertone. "It tells me that you were disappointed I left that day. You wanted more, didn't you? You wanted me to tear into that tight cunt of yours and fuck you into the mattress until my cum covered your every pore while you screamed my name."

My thighs clench and the familiar sensation of falling into

a deep hole grips me. I can feel myself disintegrating, being caught in his web all over again.

Lifting my chin, I gather whatever's left of my dignity. "I would never let you touch me if it were up to me."

"That's why it's not up to you."

"I hate you."

He nods as if he's suspected that all along. "Understandable. I'd hate me, too, if I were you."

"Don't you feel even a sliver of remorse?"

"You desperately want that to be a yes, don't you? But you already answered your own question when you labeled me a villain. Tell me, Lenochka. Do villains feel remorse?"

I purse my lips. I know what he's playing at. He wants to make this about me. Since I already picked a name for him, I shouldn't be surprised by his actions. If anything, I need to expect them and act accordingly. But if he thought he'd get a lamb, that's far from reality.

Adrian grips my chin and lifts it up with two fingers, forcing me to gaze into his merciless eyes. "Answer my question. Do they?"

"No."

"Correct."

"But that doesn't give you free access into someone else's life to wreak havoc as you please. To come in as you see fit and get out when it suits you."

"That's exactly what the lack of remorse gives me, Lenochka. The freedom to do what I want without feeling that little thing called guilt."

He really is a monster. There's no other word to describe the man within. When you're dealing with someone without any moral compass, it's impossible to beat him.

But I'm already caught in his trap and I'm more than certain that he won't let me go. If I fight, he'll subdue me, and considering his sadistic nature, he'll probably enjoy it, too.

If I flee, he'll follow.

To have any chance of winning, I need to start speaking his language. To take as much as I can from him as insurance for myself.

Sucking in a breath, I resist the urge to pull my hand from his and put distance between us, because the more he touches me, the deeper I'm caught in his web and the harder those marionette strings dig into my neck.

"If you get bored of me, will you let me go?" I ask with a calm I don't feel.

"Probably."

Okay. I can work with that. His type usually gets bored easily.

They're thrilled by the chase, the hunt, and the ability to track someone. Catching their prey is only a reward, and once they do, all the fun is over.

I'm not going to play hard to get. I'm not going to let him follow me around, heightening his need to chase. If I want to get rid of him, I need to pretend I'm playing into his hands.

I need to become so boring, that he'll leave and never return.

But instead of being obvious about it, I whisper, "Tell me something."

"Something?"

"Anything about you that the world doesn't know."

He seems to consider that for a second as he drops his hand from my chin. "Why?"

"Because I want to know you as you wanted to know me." And I need as much information on him as possible to figure out how to deal with him.

"What makes you think I want you to know me?"

"Isn't that how these things work?"

"These things?" he repeats with an edge of mockery.

"You know."

"I don't know."

"Just you and me."

"Just you and me. I like that."

My head lifts at the satisfaction in his tone. He really does sound like he likes it, but why?

A rare gleam passes over his ashen gaze as he nibbles on my pinkie again. "If I tell you, do I get something in return?"

A shudder goes through me and I hesitate.

"I don't tell things about myself without getting something in return, Lia."

"Okay."

"What did I say about that word?"

"I can't just get rid of it."

"You will learn to. In time. Or there will be consequences."

I stare up at him, my mouth agape. "What type of consequences?"

"You'll see."

"Ok—I mean, fine. So?"

"So what?"

"You said you want something. What is it?"

"I'll let you know later."

I don't like the sound of that. "Why don't you tell me now?"

"Because I don't want to."

Ugh. This asshole.

Before I can allow my tongue to curse him and possibly ruin any chance of getting what I want, he says, "I was born outside of marriage. My mother was my father's mistress before she killed my stepmother and married him."

My lips part, not only at the load of information, but also at the apathetic way he says it. As if it's normal, everyday life.

Is he really a sociopath?

"But how…?" I sound as bemused as I feel.

"You asked for one thing, Lia." He pulls me to his side. "Now, it's my turn."

Tendrils of both anticipation and fear coil inside me as I murmur, "Your turn…for what?"

"You'll find out once we're in your apartment."

TWELVE

Lia

ADRIAN DOESN'T SPEAK AS WE WALK DOWN THE hall to my apartment. He doesn't speak when I put in the code, trying to hide it from him after I changed it a few days ago.

He also didn't speak on the ride here, and neither did his guards, who were the same solemn-faced ones from the last time.

To say I'm nervous would be an understatement.

I'm the one who came up with this plan to lure him in so he'd leave me sooner rather than later, but I never thought that the actual moment would be this nerve-wracking.

It doesn't help that he looks as lethal and as handsome as ever. His physique is really impressive, whether it's his straight nose or his chiseled cheekbones or the black clothes that add a dangerous edge to his muscular frame.

He's the type of beauty one should only admire from afar. Whenever anyone gets close, he'll snuff them out like a deadly exotic animal.

I step into my apartment and don't turn around to make

sure he followed since hushed footsteps fall behind me. I stop in front of the long, narrow table that I usually use for my keys if I haven't left my car at the theater.

Releasing a shaky breath, I shrug off my coat and hang it above the table. It takes me a few seconds of inhaling deeply before I gather my courage. "We're inside my apartment. You said you'd let me know when—Ohhh."

My words end in a gasp mixed with a moan when he grabs a fistful of my hair and bends me over the table. My cheek meets the cold surface and my heart clenches in my chest as my eyes widen. I have no freaking clue why the sound I just released was a moan. It should've been a squeal, a scream, a call for help.

Anything but a moan.

His nose touches my hair from where his fingers are imprisoning me in place, then trails down to the soft flesh of my throat. Shudders and goosebumps break out on my skin, covering each other and allowing new ones to form.

His hot lips meet the shell of my ear and he nibbles down before he whispers in tight words, "You think I haven't figured out what you're doing, Lia?"

My eyes must double in size as I try to look at him, but his unyielding grip prohibits me the slightest movement. "W-what?"

"You've been waiting for this moment all night. Or…let's say for part of the night. Did that busy brain of yours think you could get rid of me by being an obedient slut?"

My molars grind together as I snap, "I'm not a slut."

"Then don't fucking act like one." His words are as scathing as his rare cursing.

"I'm not."

"Yes, you are. Do you want to be treated like a slut, Lia? Is that it?"

My words catch at the back of my throat when he lifts my

dress to my waist. Cold air covers my backside despite the heat that's on in my apartment.

Adrian cups me through my plain cotton panties and I gasp. Him touching me isn't a novelty but more like meeting an old lover. And not just any lover, the only skilled lover who's ever known how to twist my body in all the right ways possible.

But I've never had such a lover before. I've never been caught in an erotic maze by a mere touch as I am with Adrian.

Why did it have to be him, of all people?

"Mmm. You're soaking wet. Is it because of being called a slut or being forced into this position?"

Either. Both. I don't know.

I honestly have no clue what's going on right now.

I should feel shame at being held down with my half-naked body in his full view. I should fight and get away from his strong killer hands and all the havoc they wreak.

But I can't.

I tell myself it's so he'll leave me alone afterward. I tell myself it's some fling like all the others, but those words fade into the background when he puts his hands on me.

Adrian bunches the underwear in his hand so it's snapped in a tight line and rubs it against my clit in harsh, merciless strokes. My thighs clench in a fruitless attempt to stop the madness, but Adrian ups his rhythm until I'm trembling against the table.

The pleasure he wrenches out of me hooks against my bones and pulls me under. It's not even about the pleasure, it's about the monster who's inflicting it. The unapologetic, savage monster who will stop at nothing to get what he wants. As I fall apart, biting my lip to stop from screaming, I realize that's the reason I've been caught up in him since the first time he kissed me.

I've always secretly liked the type of man who takes whatever he wants while flipping the world the middle finger. No clue what that says about me as a human being, and in my defense, I've been doing just fine hiding that guilty pleasure all these years.

But before now, I didn't have this mountain of a man in my life. I didn't expect I'd meet someone who would put that fantasy into a literal application.

I'm still riding my orgasm when a slap reverberates in the air and the burning sting registers on my ass cheek. I freeze, my heart nearly stopping from the sudden onslaught of pain over pleasure.

Adrian just…spanked me.

"What…what was that for?" I ask in a breathy tone, still fighting the remnants of my orgasm.

"That was for hiding your voice from me. Don't do that again." He slaps me a second time and I jolt against the table, both of my hands gripping the edge tightly.

"Okay, I w-won't."

Slap.

My body jerks at the assault and foreign tingling erupts between my thighs.

Holy shit.

"I said I won't…" My voice breaks with the need to contain my moans.

"But you used that juvenile word." He spanks me again, leaving a pulsating burn on my skin and a clenching in my core.

I gasp, heat rising to my ears. "What was that for?"

"Because I wanted to. Mmm. You're surprisingly responsive." He teases a finger at my entrance and I flinch at the hot contact, or maybe it's me who's hot. "You like being spanked into obedience, Lenochka."

"No…" I moan the word, unable to stay still.

"Oh, but you do. Look at how your cunt is inviting me in."

"Stop it."

"Stop what?"

"Torturing me."

"Why do I think you like it? You hate how much you want it, but you don't hate the sensations it creates inside you."

I dig my nails into the wood, waiting, holding my breath for him to do something. He teases my entrance, coating it with my own juices and pushes his finger inside, but before I can really feel him, he pulls out.

It takes everything in me not to groan in frustration. It's been a long time since I was this turned on, this attuned to my body's needs as if it was the only path to my survival. Hell, I've never been this turned on in my life, except for the last time he brought me to orgasm.

"You want my fingers, Lia?" he asks in a seductive tone, one I've never heard before, one that's heightening the state of my arousal.

"Mmmm…" I release an unintelligible sound.

"What was that? I didn't quite catch it."

"Yes…" Shame rings in my ears as I breathe in and out, unable to gather my bearings.

"That's a good slut."

"I'm not…a slut," I manage to mutter.

"Then are you a good girl?"

My heart thuds faster at those words.

"Whether you're a good slut or a good girl depends on how you obey orders, Lia."

My stomach clenches and the malevolent butterflies from the last time slash through it, wrecking any semblance of control I thought I was wielding. It was cartoonish all along, meaningless, and with no actual impact. Because the one who has been holding the power in his brutal hands from the get-go is the man who's standing behind me, confiscating my air and my sanity.

"You won't get my fingers, though."

"W-what…?"

"It's time I claim you." While he's still gripping me by the hair, I hear the unmistakable unbuckling of a belt and the unzipping of pants.

The rhythm of my heart turns scary. Worse than when I have intense workout sessions. Worse than any frightening moment I've experienced in my life.

And I realize with terror that it's because the fear is now mixed with something entirely different. It starts with my sticky inner thighs and ends in my overstimulated core.

He leans over my back and I'm acutely aware of the massive erection nudging against my ass.

Oh, God.

I don't need to see him to know he's huge. It's been a long time for me, so there's no way in hell I'll be able to take him.

I close my eyes when his hot breath meets my ears and he murmurs, "I'm going to fuck you so hard, you won't be able to move, Lia, and when you do, you'll only feel me inside you."

I don't get to analyze his words as he tugs on my underwear and rips them off me. I gasp, both at the barbaric action and the friction that follows at my clit.

Adrian palms my hip and parts my legs with one of his knees, and then he's rubbing the head of his cock at my entrance.

I suck in a sharp breath when he drags it all the way over my folds and against my clit before going back again. He does it a few times.

Up.

Down.

Rub.

Down.

Up.

My head swims in a dizzy mixture of sensations, unable to take the torture anymore.

"Adrian…" I moan.

"Impatient, Lenochka?"

"Please."

"Please what?" His voice hardens with arousal and authority.

"Please..."

"I asked, please what?"

"Don't make me say it." I'm breathing out the words now, sounding wanton to my own ears.

"I want to hear you say it."

"Adrian..."

"What?"

"Do it."

"Do what?"

"Fuck me," I murmur, my ears exploding in flames.

"I didn't hear that."

"Fuck me...ahhh." I moan, then gasp when he sheathes himself inside me in one savage go, his groin slapping against my ass with the force of it.

I choke on the air as it's knocked out of my lungs. My fingers are white and clammy around the table's edge as I catch my breath and get used to the sheer size of him.

Did I think he was big? He's so fucking massive, I can feel him everywhere inside me, all around me, and especially behind me.

I want to turn my head and look at him, see if his expression is as bewildered as mine must look right now. See if the mere penetration is affecting him like it is me. He's not even moving, but the feel of him inside me pushes me to that edge all over again.

Adrian's firm hold forbids me from staring at him as he starts moving, thrusting slowly at first, but it's so deep, I feel the stretching of my walls around him.

"You're so tight, Lia." He strains, as if moving inside me is a chore. "So fucking perfect."

My heartbeat roars in my ears as he ups his speed, hitting a secret part inside me that I didn't know existed.

"Ahhh…Adrian…"

"You feel that, Lenochka?"

"Yes…yes… I never…never…ahhh…" I trail off as he hits it again, then pulls my legs farther apart to reach it fully.

"You never what?"

"Never…felt like this…" And it's not just because of the sharp pangs of pleasure that come with each of his thrusts against it or how he's taken complete hold of me. It's about how a monster like him is able to wrench such strong emotions from me, how he hasn't only entered my body, but is also forcing entry into my soul.

"And you never will at the hands of anyone else. From now on, you'll forget about any bastard who touched you in the past." His rhythm becomes uncontrollable, unforgiving, as he rams inside me with a force that rattles the table and my insides.

When he hits that spot again, I'm screaming in a voice I never knew I possessed. It's so long and raw, like standing at the peak of a mountain and shouting at the top of my lungs to my heart's content.

And just like that, I'm free. Like that day in my bedroom, I'm having an out-of-body experience where everything is trapped in a halo.

Adrian powers inside me over and over again, never slowing down. As he promised, he fucks me so hard, my front slides back and forth on the table, straining my hard nipples on the harsh surface.

That added burst of pleasure triggers another submerging wave that transports me to an alternate space. I couldn't fight it if I wanted to. And I don't want to, because at this moment, I feel wild and free like I never have in my life.

"Adrian…"

He wraps my hair around his fist and pulls me by it so that I'm suspended in mid-air while he drives into me. The position isn't exactly comfortable, but it gives him more depth and my orgasm more force.

"Say it again. My name."

"Adrian…" I manage on a whimper as my eyes clash with his. They're ashen, but sparking with lust that mirrors mine. It's so strong that I can taste it in the small space between us.

"You'll never say anyone else's name in that tone again." The raw possessiveness registers for a second before he rubs my clit and I'm falling again.

This time, he uses my hair to drag me closer and crashes his mouth to my aching lips, plunging his tongue inside. He twirls it against mine with the same rhythm he's fucking me. I'm delirious, the triple stimulation my undoing. I don't even know if I'll get back from this one, but I fall anyway.

That's how I've felt about everything to do with Adrian since I first met him. He has a way of making me abandon my inhibitions and just…fall.

It's liberating as much as it is dangerous.

Delicious as much as it is terrifying.

My eyes are drooping when I find myself in his arms again, his tongue at the back of my throat and his cock ramming into me with the harshness of a warrior.

He goes rigid at my back and grunts in my mouth as warmth fills my insides and then trickles down my thighs when he pulls out of me.

I'm yanked out of my haze when I realize that he just fucked me without a condom. Holy shit. How could I not think about it until now?

I've been on the pill for years to regulate my period, so that will protect me from pregnancy, but there's something worse than that nowadays.

Adrian releases my hair, and before I can say anything, he

picks me up. I squeal, arms looping around his neck to stop myself from falling.

He walks with absolute nonchalance toward my bedroom. His pants are hanging open, but other than that, everything else is in perfect order. His face is hard and unwelcome, and one would never think he'd reached his peak of pleasure just now. However, he feels more relaxed than when we first arrived. His muscles aren't filled with tension and his hold feels a bit tender.

"You didn't use a condom," I murmur.

His gaze slides to mine and I feel cornered in it. "So?"

"STDs. Ever heard of them?"

"I haven't been sexually active for months and I've always used condoms, so I'm clean."

I trap my lip beneath my bottom teeth, my mind strangely going to the part where he hasn't been sexually active for months. Who was his last victim? Someone like me?

That makes my skin crawl and I quickly shoo it away.

"Why didn't you use a condom just now?"

He pauses. "I forgot."

"You forgot?"

"Yes, am I not allowed to?"

"No, it just seems that you're the type who would never forget."

His eyes ease. "Correct."

"So why did you?"

"I wish I knew."

The quiet in his tone gives me pause as I ask, "What if I weren't on birth control?"

"You obviously are, so why fuss about it?"

The nonchalant way he speaks bothers me. It's like he really wouldn't care even if I wasn't on birth control. Does he truly lack any sort of remorse? Would he throw me out and regard the baby as collateral damage if I were to get pregnant?

"Would you like to have a shower first?" He pulls me out of my chaotic thoughts.

"First? Why? What's going to happen after?"

"I'm taking you again." He stops in the middle of my room, nuzzling his nose against my hair and inhaling me in. "Fucking roses."

Goosebumps cover my skin and my thighs clench, because even though I haven't come down from the first high, the need for another one hits me with a slamming force.

Still, I go the logical route. "I…I thought it was a one-time thing."

"You thought wrong, Lenochka." His voice is as calm as the devil, and just as lethal.

And I know, I just know that my life will never be the same again.

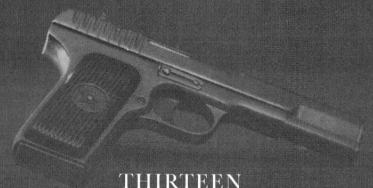

THIRTEEN

Adrian

I PULL MYSELF FROM BESIDE LIA.

She's been sound asleep for the past hour. At first, her body was relaxed, slightly pushing into mine, almost snuggling, but then she slipped back into her rigid posture.

The death posture.

It seems like the norm for her, some sort of a habit she developed over the years and eventually fell into subconsciously. People usually find their comfort zone, their self-made box, and stuff themselves in it.

But that's the thing about Lia. Although a part of her is confined, tucked away from the world, another completely different part climbs over the stage and flies as if attempting to touch the skies.

She's a contradiction through and through. One I'll attempt to dissect inch by fucking inch.

I watch her for a beat, taking in her soft features, her full lower lip tipped by a tiny teardrop in the middle, and her flushed cheeks.

They've had the same color since I fucked her against the

table. It wasn't supposed to happen that way, in the entrance, as if I had no control over myself.

But that's the thing. I lacked my steel-like control. I didn't have the will to stop, not after what happened in the club.

I was still fuming with pent-up frustration for not strangling that fucker who put his hands on her, who didn't only touch her, but also did it intimately and then threatened her.

In that moment, I never wanted to see life leave someone's eyes as much as I craved to strangle it out of him.

Despite my background, I don't really have a strong blood-lust like Damien, or even Kirill and Vladimir. Killing someone is merely a means to an end for me. I don't take pleasure in the act; however, I'm not repulsed by it either.

It's just a necessity.

But that blond fucker? Yeah, I would've enjoyed every second of the air leaving his lungs.

If someone were to ask me what came over me back then, I wouldn't know either. One moment, I was watching from the shadows—like a stalker, as Lia likes to point out—and the next, I was seeing red as I never have in my life.

I'm not the type to see red. I've always believed anger was beneath me—it's an emotion that will just cloud my vision and deter me from making the right decision. In fact, aside from when Aunt Annika died, I don't think I've ever felt strong emotions. After that, all the anger and the irrationality that came with it seemed to vanish out of my system to be replaced by a cool head.

Until that scene at the club.

Until all I could see was fucking red.

This woman hasn't only been messing with my patterns, but she's also provoking a part of me that I bid farewell when I was a child. A part that I will smother to death before it invades me again.

I had to prove to myself and her that I'm in control and always will be.

That's why I took her against the table as soon as we were inside. She thought she could get rid of me and I thought that, too. For a moment before I flipped her down, I had this idea that I'd fuck the anger out of her and erase the chaos that's related to her.

I didn't.

If anything, it's become bleaker, harsher, and darker. With every thrust into her tight cunt and every moan from her pink lips, I felt an invisible thread form between us. I'm not the type who forms a bond with my sexual partners. They're simply there for me to use and give pleasure back to if I see fit. They know me to be rough, callous, and demanding, but they keep coming back for more.

They know me to be cold and easily bored, and that's why I pull out after release.

That was not the case with Lia.

For the first time in my nearly thirty-one years, I took a woman again right after I was finished with her. A dark obsession grabbed hold of me, and I needed to hear her moans and watch her petite frame shake as she unraveled around me. I had to engrave in my brain the way her face contorted with pleasure as she cried out my name and dug her nails into my shoulders when it got to be too much.

In fact, all I want right now is to wake her and pick up where we left off. I want to touch every inch of her body, study it, and tease it to heights even she wouldn't have thought possible.

Then…I'd eventually destroy it.

What a fucking waste.

Taking a strand of her hair between my fingers, I inhale it, letting the scent of roses barge into my lungs and carve a place there. Everything about her is soft, even her personality.

But being soft doesn't mean she's naive. Lia knows when to stand up for herself if need be, but she carefully picks her battles.

Like a survivor would.

Considering her background, the tactic makes perfect sense.

Not that I gave her any choice. It was either my way or death. And while that's how I usually deal with everything in my life, I find myself taking a different approach with her.

One I don't fully understand myself.

I get up from the bed and note the pills on the nightstand. They've changed position from last time, so that means she's been taking them these past couple of days.

Not bothering to pull on my boxer briefs, I head to the kitchen and take out a bottle of water from the fridge. I pause with it halfway to my mouth as I study the notes attached to the door.

Buy groceries.

You didn't actually slip and break your ankle. That was a nightmare.

Try to reach L again.

I remove the last two, studying her neat cursive handwriting.

She's reminding herself about her nightmares. Hmm. Does this mean her case is getting worse since the last time she saw her therapist?

My finger taps over the last note and my body turns stone cold, even with the heat in the apartment.

Try calling L again.

Who the fuck is L and why is she writing their name as an initial as if she's keeping it as a dirty little secret?

Is he an ex-lover of hers? Friend with benefits? The more I think about it, the faster the red from the club threatens to return.

I slam the note back on the fridge before I can crumple it and give my snooping session away.

While I don't give a fuck, I know she does, and then she'd

start one of her psychoanalyzing sessions that only end up hurting her more than necessary.

She'll soon see my uncensored side. How soon, is the question. My gaze flits over the living room, noting the places where I'll have Kolya and Yan install cameras when she's out.

There's also a nook in her bedroom, right over her vanity, where it would be the perfect spot to insert a surveillance camera.

She's right. I am a stalker.

But it's either that or torture her for answers. What am I if not the perfect villain? I prefer to do things smoothly, not harshly.

It'd be a pity to draw blood from that porcelain skin; however, marking it is a different story altogether.

Seeing my red handprints on her ass brought out the beast inside me, the one who craves more marking, more claiming.

Just *more*.

After drinking the small bottle of water, I throw it in the trash and go back to the bedroom.

Lia is still sleeping in her death-like position, but the sheet has slipped, revealing a perfect pink nipple.

And just like that, I'm getting hard again.

Fuck.

I lie beside her, propping my head on my elbow to watch her intently. Unable to resist, I lean in and take the naked nipple into my mouth, lapping my tongue against it like a teenager with a tit obsession.

At first, Lia remains still, but then her dead position breaks and her lips part. "Mmmm…"

The sound goes straight to my dick, hardening it to the point of torture. I bite down on her nipple enough to cause slight discomfort, hoping she'll open her eyes, but she moans again, her hand moving under the sheet.

I pull it down to watch her touching her cunt, rubbing her clit in that soft but erotic way that's meant to get herself off.

Not again.

I might have watched the last time, but there will be no touching herself when I'm around anymore.

Wrapping my hand around hers, I still it, my fingertips brushing against her wet folds.

"Mmmm," she mumbles, trying to pull her hand free and continue her task.

I nibble on her nipple once more, and this time, she gasps awake, her deep blue eyes staring at nowhere at first before she slowly focuses on me.

"What…?" she trails off when she sees my mouth around her nipple and my hand over hers on her cunt.

A red hue spreads over her fair skin, covering her neck and face and even her ears. Her self-implicated feelings of shame are interesting, and I find myself wanting to engrave them deeper into my mind.

Or perhaps, what I really want is to see her flushed and at my mercy.

I speak against her nipple, making her squirm with each of my breaths against the wet, sensitive tip, "You were touching yourself again, Lenochka, but these soft fingers don't satisfy you anymore, do they? I can give this cunt what it truly craves."

She places her other hand on my shoulder. It's to resist me, to stop me as that smart brain of hers dictates, but she and I know that can't go on for long.

"Are you going to be a good slut or a good girl, Lia?"

She sucks in a sharp breath, attempting to withdraw her hand that's on her clit from underneath mine. But I keep it imprisoned and she gasps as I push it in a little.

I straddle her in a swift move, my knees on either side of her parted legs. Lia lets her arm fall to her side and whispers, "When are you going to be done?"

"Don't act like this is a chore, Lia. That's another form of lying and you know I don't appreciate it."

She glares at me, her tiny features scrunching with the movement. "You're a sadist."

"Then that makes you a masochist, Lenochka."

"I-I'm not."

"Yes, you are. Can you feel your arousal coating both of our hands?"

She tries to stare at the opposite wall, but I pull her back with a firm hold on her chin. "Don't do that again. Keep your attention on me when I'm touching you."

"So now, I'm only allowed to look at you?"

I like that. In fact, I like it so much, it's fucking disturbing, and I don't usually consider anything disturbing.

"If you can help it, yes," I say in a nonchalant tone that doesn't betray the thought I was having.

"You're a disaster…ahh," she whimpers as I align my dick with her entrance.

"Then you shouldn't get in my way, Lenochka. I will ruin you, break you and mess you the fuck up."

"Aren't you doing that already?"

"Not truly, no. You'd be smart not to provoke that side of me." I release her chin and place a hand behind her back, lifting her to a sitting position, then fling her legs so that they are positioned beside my knees as I slam inside her at the same time.

Fuck. She feels like the first time. No, it's even better, her walls more inviting and her body more used to mine.

Lia cries out, the sound turning into a soft moan as I power into her tight heat so deep, our groins slap against one another with our hands in between.

Lia stares down at where we're joined, her face turning a deep crimson, and she starts to glance away.

"No. Look at us."

"Don't make me," she begs between moans.

"You called me a disaster, but this is the true disaster, Lia. You and me."

She complies, her lips parting, and a sparkle shines in the depths of her eyes, making them lighter, almost as if she's on a high.

Using her fingers, I make her tease her clit, my thumb adding pressure. Her hand is tiny compared to mine, small and sophisticated like everything about her. It shakes with my ministrations, but she doesn't attempt to pull it away as we rub on her clit in the way she likes while I thrust inside her at the same time.

She throws her head back, which causes strands of her rose-scented hair to brush against my face. I breathe her in and memorize the complete abandon on her features as I fuck her in a rhythm that leaves her whimpering for a release.

She came more times than either of us can count tonight, but Lia still wants more. She still comes apart around me when I pull back, then drive back in.

Her fingers halt underneath mine and she moans the only name that she's allowed to from now on, "Adrian...yes...yes... Adrian..."

The sound of her throaty whisper sends me crashing into my own release. My back and balls tighten as I empty myself inside her in one go.

Fuck condoms.

She falls against me, her head nestling into my chest. A sheen of sweat covers both of our bodies as we breathe each other in.

Soon, she'll try to pull away from me as she did earlier, but right now, her body is completely slack against mine. Now, she looks docile and content and even releases a small sigh.

I choose this moment of peace to offer her another bit of truth. The lone truth that rattles me to my bones.

"You asked when I'd be done. The answer is never. I'll never be done with you, Lenochka."

FOURTEEN

Lia

I DON'T EVEN KNOW HOW I MAKE IT THROUGH rehearsal today.

Due to the thorough fucking like I've never experienced in my entire life, I woke up sore and groggy and…in a haze of pleasure.

I thought I wouldn't be able to move, let alone rehearse.

But sometime in the early morning, I felt Adrian wipe between my legs with a warm cloth. The sensation alone was enough to make me moan in absolute bliss.

After I woke up, I was rolled in a clean duvet, and the one stained with the evidence of our sexual activities was in the washing machine.

I found breakfast on my nightstand. Coffee without sugar, my salt-free toast with bio cheese, and an apple. There were also painkillers with a bottle of water.

I should wonder how he knows what I eat for breakfast, but it wouldn't be too hard to figure out since that's all I have in my kitchen.

Despite wanting to question him, I was oddly touched by

the fact that he brought me breakfast in bed. No one has ever done that for me before, and in my own house, no less.

But the fact remains, he disappeared.

There was no trace of him or his clothes. If it weren't for the tender ache between my legs and his red handprints on my ass, I would've suspected he was never here in the first place. That everything which had happened last night was another cruel punishment created in my head.

But he was here. I can still feel his merciless thrusts and savage touch that oddly turned caring afterward. My nipples still ache from how he bit and fondled and twisted them. My ass still burns from how he spanked me while fucking me as if knowing how much it drives me mad.

But after he exhausted my body till I was spent, he left.

Again.

We didn't even get to talk or anything like normal people after he announced he'd never be done with me.

He just used me and left.

However, is it considered using if I enjoyed every second of it? If I touched myself to thoughts of him while I was sleeping?

God. Maybe I'm broken beyond repair for liking it, for reveling in his rough handling and unapologetic fucking when I hate the man. I should be glad that he disappeared, not disappointed.

I went through the motions during today's rehearsal, trying to distract my head from any thoughts about Adrian Volkov.

Philippe and Stephanie gave me an earful about how I left without notice last night. I apologized, but it's not like I could tell them what actually happened, or that I possibly had the best sex of my life just to wake up to an empty apartment.

And no, I'm not still salty about that.

One thing changed, though—or one person. Ryan.

Starting this morning, he didn't try to touch me outside of rehearsal. He hasn't looked into my eyes too long either, as if he's afraid of what I—or someone else—will do to him.

At least he learned his lesson and will keep the distance he was supposed to a long time ago.

"Lia."

I turn around at Stephanie's voice. She catches up to me so that we're standing in front of my car, my keys dangling from my fingers.

She takes out a cigarette and lights it, inhaling, then exhaling a large cloud.

"What is it, Steph? Please don't tell me it's another night out."

"No, but that was a dick move yesterday." She puts her hand on her hip.

"I'm sorry. I wasn't feeling well." And I really wasn't until Adrian fucked me like a savage before he disappeared.

Is he going to make this a habit and keep leaving after taking care of his sexual needs like I'm some sort of slut?

Damn him.

Why the hell am I so hung up on that part, anyway? After all, I allowed for everything to happen just so he *would* leave.

He's a killer, Lia. A fucking killer.

I wait for the disgust to invade me at that reminder. I wait to feel nausea at allowing a murderer to touch me so intimately.

Yet nothing comes.

Am I *that* broken?

"Whatever." Stephanie stares me down as if she doesn't believe me. "Anyway, I learned something I thought you'd be interested to know."

"What?"

"That Russian mafia guy you were asking about yesterday. Matt's associate?"

My grip tightens on my keys as I try to hold on to my cool. "What did you learn?"

Stephanie gets closer, searches her surroundings, then half-cups her mouth before she whispers, "Apparently, he's a higher-up in the Bratva. Like *very* higher-up."

I swallow. Even though this information shouldn't be a surprise, it hits differently than I'd expect when I learn about it.

"How do you know?" I murmur back, dread getting the better of me.

"I heard Matt mention it to one of his minions."

Stephanie is a true eavesdropper and loves gossip to a fault.

She steps back and takes another drag of her cigarette. "Now, girl, tell me why you're interested in knowing about him?"

"I-I'm not."

"Uh-huh. Lie to someone else. I can see that gleam in your eyes whenever he's mentioned."

Shit. Am I that obvious? "It's really nothing. I just…find him scary."

"That's because he is." She rubs my arm. "There's a crowd we should never mingle with. He belongs to that crowd."

Too late, Steph.

I offer her a reassuring smile and get to my car. By the time I arrive home, I'm hungry, exhausted, and my mind is fried from the number of theories I've been conjuring about Adrian.

He told me he's a strategist, so according to what Stephanie said, he plots the Bratva's movements.

God. He's part of the freaking Russian mafia.

A shiver runs down my spine at the thought. I don't know anything about the mafia except for *The Godfather* trilogy, and those films are a far cry from reality.

The real thing must be more dangerous.

Wiping my clammy fingers on my skirt, I tap in my code and get inside.

I throw my bag and keys on the entrance table, trying not to think about what happened on that same table last night. How he owned every inch of me and gave me a dark type of pleasure I'll never be able to forget.

Shaking my head, I hang my coat and freeze.

Between my two other coats, there's a different one. Gray. Male.

His.

I kick my shoes away and step inside, the sinking weight that's been settled over my stomach since this morning lifting with each step I take. My feet come to a halt on the heated flooring at the scene in front of me.

Adrian is placing a few plates on the small dining table situated between the kitchen and the living room.

He's dressed in his usual black pants and shirt, the first few buttons undone, revealing his hard, muscular chest that I buried my face into last night. His sleeves are rolled to his elbows, revealing the intricate design of his tattoos. Both extend in sleeves from his shoulders to above his wrists. Surprisingly, there are none on his chest or back like I'd expect from a gangster.

"You're back," he says without lifting his head from his task. There's a frittata and a big bowl of salad as well as a few cut apples.

"What are you doing?" I murmur, unable to make sense of the situation.

"What does it look like I'm doing? Preparing you dinner." He still hasn't met my gaze. "Go wash your hands."

My feet carry me toward him as if I'm floating on air and I grab his bicep. "I said, what are you doing in my apartment, Adrian? How did you get in?"

He continues setting the plates in a meticulous kind of way—geometric, even. "I saw you put in the code yesterday. Not that it would've been a problem if I hadn't."

"This is called breaking and entering."

"Do you always feel the need to label everything, Lenochka?" This time, his gray eyes that are the color of harsh winters collide with mine. "Does it make you feel better?"

"I'm naming things by what they're called."

"By all means, do what makes you feel comfortable. Now, go wash your hands so we can eat."

"And if I don't want to?"

He releases a breath. "This is one of the situations where you pick your battles. If you don't, I'll be happy to sit you on my lap and shove food down your throat."

I glare at him, then storm to the bathroom to wash my hands. By the time I get back, he's already seated with a plate of what looks like ham frittata.

With a sigh, I settle opposite him and stab a fork in my salad that's placed in front of me, while the frittata is for him. I hate that he knows what I eat and doesn't act like other people who are constantly telling me, "Hey, some comfort food won't hurt." I didn't get this far by allowing myself luxuries.

To be at the top, there's always a dire price to pay. I don't even smoke like many of the other ballerinas, so I have no way to kill my appetite except for sheer determination.

For a moment, we eat in silence. We both take our time. Me, because it makes me full faster. Adrian, because he seems like the type who savors his food, deliberately taking every bite. I try not to watch how his masculine fingers wrap around the fork and knife. He's so sophisticated, like someone who's upper class, not a mobster.

"Is the salad to your liking?" he asks.

I lift a shoulder. "It's fine."

"Would you like a glass of wine?"

"So I'll get drunk like last time? No, thanks."

His lips twitch in what resembles a smile but isn't quite there. "Your drunk version is more honest."

"Or more stupid."

"I'll go with honest."

I lift my head, my fork playing between the tomatoes and lettuce. "You want honesty, Adrian?"

He places his utensils beside his plate and takes a sip of his water. "Sure, let's hear it."

"I think you're sick and twisted. You're the type who gets off on subduing someone weaker than you, closing all doors in their face so they're forced to have dinner with you. Are you *that* lonely?"

Although I think my words will trigger anger, he merely taps his finger on the table twice. "If sick and twisted is what you like to label me, we'll go with it. But you're wrong. If there's anyone who's lonely between us, it's you, Lia."

"I'm not lonely."

"We'll have to agree to disagree."

"What gave you the idea that I'm lonely?"

"Aside from your obvious lack of friends and your uneventful life, you also chose ballet when you knew full well it would make you hated when you climbed to the top. You didn't fight the process of being envied and gossiped about. If anything, you used it to bury yourself deeper in your lonely bubble where no one can reach you."

My lips part at his careful and horrifyingly precise analysis of my life. This man will swallow me under if I'm not careful.

"You did," I counter with more venom than needed.

"I did what?"

"You reached inside my bubble."

He picks up his utensils and cuts into his food. "That's because you didn't have a choice in the matter."

"What if I want to have a choice?"

"Too late." He stares at me with those unnerving eyes. "I already claimed you as mine and there's no going back."

My fingers tremble at that word. *Mine.* But it's not out of fear, it's something else that I can't quite pinpoint, so I blurt, "That's called coercion."

"Always with the labels, Lia. It's getting tedious."

"I told you. I'm giving things their name."

"It changes nothing except offering you some sense of fragile justice."

"Justice is not fragile."

"Oh, but it is. Those who believe in it fail or are slapped in the face by harsh truths."

"Then what do you believe in?"

"Patterns."

I'm taken aback by that. After I take a bite of my salad and swallow, I speak, "How does someone believe in patterns?"

"Patterns are a powerful tool that allow me to see the outcome before it happens."

I scoff. Of course someone like Adrian would like that type of power.

"You don't agree, Lia?"

"Not particularly. I'm just not surprised you'd be attracted to that sort of thing."

"You're starting to get to know me. That's progress."

"I don't know you, Adrian, and I prefer it stays that way."

"Why? Because you can bury your head in the sand and pretend like none of this is happening? You do realize that's useless, right? The more you resist, the more pain you bring upon yourself."

"Let me worry about that. Whatever I feel or don't feel is none of your business."

"Watch that tone, Lia." His voice lowers with an unveiled threat.

"Or what?"

"Or I will take my belt to your ass."

"You…"

"Go on." His eyes spark with pure sadism. "By all means, give me a reason to punish you."

Fire explodes in my chest and I try to swallow it down, to no avail.

Jesus. This man is a true devil.

I stuff my face with the salad to keep from spouting whatever is trying to come out.

"Slower," he reprimands. "Or you'll get indigestion."

"As if you'd care."

"Of course I would. I'm not that heartless."

"Yeah, right."

"I truly am not—under the right circumstances."

"You mean the ones you lay out?"

"Correct."

"So it's your way or the highway?"

"More or less."

I bite my lower lip, then quickly release it when I find him watching it with undivided attention and a frightening sheen of lust.

"What's going to happen when you're done with me?" I ask the question that's been niggling at the back of my mind.

"I said I won't be."

"Surely you'll get bored. Everyone does."

"I'm not everyone, and it'd be wise not to compare me to anyone you know."

As if I would ever find someone like him.

Luca is a bit elusive, like Adrian, but he's not as intense, and I've always considered him a friend, so he doesn't really count.

I clear my throat. "Point is, this phase will end. Like everything about life."

"I'll think about that when it comes to it."

"Is that what you did to the others? You thought about their fate when the time came."

"The others?"

"The ones who came before me."

"I've never done this with anyone before you, Lenochka."

Bolts of both thrill and fear spark through me. For some

perverse reason, I like that this is also a first for him, that we're at least equal in that regard. But knowing I'm his first, that he broke a pattern for me when he appreciates them so much, is also enough to make me imagine the worst.

Shooing that thought away, I ask. "What does that mean?"

"What does what mean?"

"Lenochka?"

"Bright light."

My lips part, not believing he just called me that. Surely, it must be a play of my imagination. "You think I'm a bright light?"

"That's what I said."

"But you think I'm lonely."

"That doesn't make you gloomy. A rose shines brighter alone than when it's in a field."

"Is that why you plucked me?" My voice lowers as I stare at the bowl of salad.

"Possibly."

"Just so you know, the prettiest roses have the deadliest thorns."

He stands up. The motion isn't abrupt, but I sink in my chair, partially regretting what I said and partially proud of it.

The proud part wins, because I lift my chin. Fuck him. If he thinks I'll just cower away because he tells me to, he'll be disappointed.

He stands beside me, his sheer size towering over me like doom. "You think that scares me?"

"I didn't say it to scare you. I'm just relaying facts."

"Here's a fact for you, Lia. Deadly thorns thrill me."

I swallow. "But they injure you."

"It's worth it." He motions at my forgotten plate of food. "Are you finished?"

"Yeah, why?"

"Because I'm going to fuck you until you scream, my deadly thorn." And with that, he picks me up and carries me in his arms toward the bedroom.

FIFTEEN

Lia

FOR TWO WEEKS, WE FALL INTO A SORT OF ROUTINE. I go to rehearsal, and when I get home, I find Adrian waiting with either takeout or home-cooked food he brings over. I know he doesn't cook here, because he said he brings them from his house.

Then he carries me to the bedroom and fucks me until I fall asleep. Sometimes, he does it on the table, making me straddle his lap as he owns every inch of me. Other times, he grabs me as soon as I step inside, lifts my skirts and fucks me in the entrance.

But it doesn't end there.

It never ends there.

After that, he takes me in the bedroom or in the shower. Sometimes back to back as if he can't stop touching me, as if he craves me again as soon as he's finished.

When I can't take it anymore, which basically means I'm sobbing through my orgasms, he cleans me up or carries me to the shower. He makes sure I'm fully comfortable and sometimes dresses me, though just in a nightgown or a long shirt so he can touch me as he pleases during the night.

I try keeping my distance from him by scooting to my side of the bed or sleeping with my back facing him. But the moment he stimulates me, I'm right there with him writhing and begging for a release that I'd had not long before.

It's crazy how I've become addicted to the pleasure only he can conjure. How I crave his rough manhandling and savage fucking.

Maybe he's right. Maybe I am a masochist. Because all I can think about is what he'll do each night. How he'll take me, spank me, and set my world ablaze.

In the mornings, however, he leaves. Every fucking morning, he goes out like a thief. Like I'm his slut and he doesn't want to be seen with me.

Ever since the first time we had dinner at the diner, he's never taken me out again. I haven't asked for it either, because that would mean I want some sort of a relationship with him.

I don't.

The only thing I'm waiting for is for him to get bored and leave me alone.

He doesn't seem to be getting bored, though. If anything, his appetite for my body seems to be growing over the days to the point where he takes me again almost immediately after he comes. I don't know if he's easily stimulated or has a strong stamina, but I do know that I've been slowly but surely emulating his rhythm.

He's made me get used to him—addicted, even—so that all of my lines have blurred.

I tell myself that it's wrong, that I shouldn't want a man like Adrian this carnally or with this much abandon. And yet, I also know I can't stop it. To my doom, it's not just because of his threats and invisible hold on me.

Ever since he came into my life, my rehearsals have become smoother and easier. I've never grasped a character as much as I do Giselle. In a way, I'm projecting my situation onto her. The fact that I had no choice in falling into the hands of a much more powerful man who can hurt me.

The only difference is that I know what I'm in for.

Something that's only physical.

Adrian's sole connection with me is stimulating my body so he can satisfy his crazy sex drive. But I've been using what we have to grasp Giselle's character.

Even Stephanie and Philippe have noticed it. The director has been telling me it's his favorite performance by me yet, and for the first time, I agree. For the first time, I don't think that I could do better.

Stephanie and Philippe keep chastising me about how I don't join their night fun anymore. Little do they know that I have my own fun. And honestly? I would rather spend quiet nights at home rather than at a club.

Well, as quiet as they can get with all the sex.

Other than that, nights with Adrian are calm. He keeps his words to a bare minimum, even when he's the one who strikes up the conversation.

We talk about my rehearsal, or he asks me how I'm doing, and I end up talking more than needed. Ballet and classical music are my only subjects of obsession, the only things I can talk about forever to soothe my nerves. Ever since Adrian figured that out, he asks me how my day went like we're some old couple.

When I once countered and asked how his day went, he raised a brow and said, "Are you sure you want to know?"

No. I didn't. I really didn't want the reminder of what he is and what he does. It makes it easier to have him inside me every night when I pretend he's just a stranger with whom I have a mind-boggling type of chemistry.

Only a stranger.

On my way home from rehearsal, I stop by a boutique to buy new panties. Adrian has ripped most of mine, even when I told him I'd remove them myself.

I falter in front of a row of red lingerie, reaching out to inspect their low cut and the invisible lace. I pull my hand back before I touch them. God, what am I doing? Am I really thinking about wearing lingerie for Adrian?

I'm about to turn around and head to the comfy underwear section when someone appears by my side.

At first, I think it's just one of those strangers who get too close, but then I recognize his leather jacket and the black hat he wears too low, while holding a phone to his ear. Then, my nostrils fill with a familiar scent: bleach.

"Luca?" I whisper.

"Don't look at me and keep inspecting the clothes, Duchess. You're being followed."

I stare ahead, running my fingers over the red lingerie. Am I really being followed? I knew Adrian was a damn stalker. I've seen a black car and a shadow of his guard, Yan, a couple of times, but I thought those were one-offs. I should've known better.

"Bring out your phone and pretend you're talking on it," Luca says in his nonchalant voice.

I do as he says, one hand on the underwear and the other holding the phone to my ear. Luca is always careful not to be caught out in public. That's why we've only been talking over the phone lately. Or before Adrian came into the picture, at least.

"Why haven't you called me back?" I don't hide the hurt from my voice. I've really needed a friend these past couple of weeks and he's the only one I have.

"I was out of the country. Besides, you're full of fucking traps, Duchess. You're as hard to get close to as the president."

"What?"

"Adrian has you all bugged. Your phone, your house. Even your car."

The information strikes me deep. Even though Adrian is a stalker, why would he go to the trouble of bugging everything?

He has me, doesn't he? Why would he need to log my every movement? Then another realization hits me.

"Wait…how do you know about Adrian?"

"I know everything about you, Duchess. We promised to have each other's backs, remember?"

I do. Since the time we escaped our old lives, we said that we would have a new beginning that's not defined by who we were. Luca chose a completely different road from mine.

"He's…" I swallow. "He's dangerous, Luca."

"I'm dangerous, too."

"No. He's *really* dangerous."

"I thought you'd need my help to get rid of him. Are you defending him?"

I pause. I do want to get rid of Adrian, but resorting to Luca's methods isn't the way to go. That's not any different from acting like Adrian.

Although Luca has been keeping me out of his world, I know that he's involved in shady business with shady people. He's a lot like Adrian, but I've known him since we were children. I know he won't hurt me.

"I'm not defending him," I murmur.

"So do you want to get rid of him?"

"I don't like to harm people, Luca."

"Sometimes you have to or they'll harm you."

I remain silent, mulling over his favorite words. Luca has always had that philosophy about life and people.

"I'll get rid of Adrian."

His words cause a strange clenching in my chest. "I said I don't want to hurt anyone."

"It's not only because of you, Duchess. Remember the people I work for? They want him gone."

"But why?"

"Because he knows too much about things, and if he's gone, the brotherhood will be weakened."

He really is a higher-up if people like Luca's random employers want him gone. Just what type of business is Adrian involved in? I've made it my mission to not get mixed up in that part of his life, but is that the wisest decision?

"Before I get rid of him, I need you to keep an eye on him, Duchess."

"What?" I hiss.

"You heard me. I want to know if anything suspicious arises. You're currently the closest person to him and the only one who can figure out his system."

"His system?"

"He has a system where he watches everyone and everything, predicting things before they happen."

Patterns. I recall Adrian said he believes in them. That's why he's a strategist.

I shake my head the slightest bit, bunching my hand on the lingerie. "I'm not going to be your spy, Luca."

"Why not?"

"It's Adrian. He'll know."

"He won't."

"How can you be so sure?"

"He's blinded by you."

My lips part. "Blinded by me? You must be kidding."

"I'm not. For the first time in his life, the meticulous Adrian Volkov is letting a woman close. If that's not a weakness, I don't know what is."

I don't like that, the idea of me being Adrian's weakness. The more Luca talks, the more I want to shut him up.

"All you have to do is act as you've been doing all along. Don't try to find his bugs and don't get out from under his thumb."

"No."

"Lia..." his voice softens. "Have you forgotten what we promised?"

"I haven't, but I also didn't sign up to be a part of this game."

"You were signed up a long time ago."

"What?"

"Do you want me to tell you who was behind your parents' deaths?"

A rapid thump takes over my chest as if a wild animal has been awakened. My limbs tremble and the black box seems to close in on me like when I was a kid. "You know?"

"I told you I'd find out and I kept my word."

"Who is it?" My voice quivers as the noises from that day filter back in, the silence, the screams, the hushed footsteps. My ears ring with the harshness of them and it takes everything in me to remain standing.

"That's not how it goes, Lia. Give me what I want and I'll give you what you need."

With that, he turns and leaves. The meaning behind his words remains with me.

I'll give you what you need.

Luca worded it perfectly. He, of all people, knows that uncovering the truth behind my parents' deaths is what's been haunting me since I was a small girl.

It's why I have those visceral nightmares and take those pills. It's why I'm too scared to live and too scared to die.

And to free myself, to choose a final destination, I need to spy on the devil himself.

SIXTEEN

Adrian

I'M RUNNING OUT OF TIME.

In fact, I've been running out of time since the first encounter with Lia in the parking lot. If it were any other person, I would've ended it as soon as it started.

But it's not.

During the past four weeks, I've been bargaining with myself to get on with it, to extort what I want from her and go. To throw her to the wolves, as per the original plan.

But every time I see her, sink inside her, and own her, I'm left hungry for more. I thought I would have fucked her out of my system by now, but it's proving to have the opposite effect. Every time I touch her, I'm starved for more, and a part of me keeps wanting to take this to the next step and offer her another one of my truths. One that will either make her more suspicious or give herself to me fully.

Now, I'm seriously contemplating other options about how to go about her. The evening meeting with Sergei and Igor goes longer than I'd like. They both need progress reports about the Italians, something I haven't brought to the table yet because of a certain ballerina who shouldn't be involved in this life.

But I already dragged her in. It might have started the day she saw me kill or the day I went to watch her shine on the stage, or her fate might have been sealed the first time I kissed her—or fucked her.

At any rate, Lia Morelli is in.

She might not have a single clue about what's happening, but her life and mine are intertwined closer than she'll ever know.

I still hang on to the fact that she's far enough away from the brotherhood and everything in it. She's doing her thing with the ballet and I'm doing mine behind the scenes.

Dealing with Sergei and Igor isn't hard. They know I don't fail. *So far.* If they want something about the Lucianos, they'll get it. Only the method might have changed.

Yan releases a bored sigh as soon as we get in the car. Kolya, however, meets my gaze through the rear-view mirror with a furrowed brow. "They're getting more insistent."

"I will keep them busy." I stare at my watch. It's past ten, so Lia is probably fast asleep.

Fuck long meetings.

I dial Boris, the one who's been watching Lia, and he picks up after one ring, speaking in gruff Russian, "Boss."

"Anything out of the ordinary today?" I ask in the same language.

"It was the usual." He pauses. "She stopped by a lingerie shop before going home."

I can't help the brow that raises or the erection that presses against my pants at the thought of her in lingerie. My Lenochka was buying lingerie.

That's...interesting.

She's always worn plain underwear and has never gone out of her way to be presentable for me. Not that I care, but the fact that she's putting an effort into it now is intriguing me more than it should.

"Anything else, Boris?"

"Nothing out of the ordinary, Boss."

I hang up, tapping my finger against my thigh. Lia bought lingerie and I wasn't there to unwrap it—and her. Sergei and Igor have the worst timing ever.

"Sir."

I lift my head at Kolya's voice. Yan is smoking and I didn't even notice when he lit the cigarette. I sigh. "Put it out, Yan."

"It's almost finished." He pauses, then adds as an after-thought, "*Sir.*"

"Yan." Kolya elbows him.

"Fine. Whatever." Yan takes one last drag and throws it out the window, grumbling. "What do you want to talk about, Kolya? By all means, we're all ears."

My senior guard ignores him, focusing on me. "Sergei and Igor's patience can only go on for so long."

"I know." I stare at the city lights through the window.

"If you know, why don't you act on it?"

"Kolya, you bastard! Are you suggesting he hurt Lia?" Yan sounds disapproving. "She did nothing."

"Whether I hurt her or not is neither of your concern. And since when are you her advocate, Yan?" My tone is more biting than usual.

"She's…innocent, Boss. She did nothing to deserve…" he trails off.

"Me?" I finish for him.

"I didn't say that."

"You didn't have to."

And in a way, he's right, but being innocent doesn't exempt her of her fate. However, people like Yan will still try to allevi-ate their conscience. I never had that—a conscience, that is—so I don't worry about it.

The car stops in Lia's parking lot, but I don't step out right away. Instead, I fixate on both of my guards. "I need more men on Lazlo Luciano, as many as possible."

"We're already watching him," Kolya says.

"It's not enough. I need a full report of his daily habits, of the places he frequents, and even his waking and bedtime. I want to know his meals and his lifestyle and have the hackers dig into his and his wife's phones and laptops. Don't let his underboss get suspicious, because he's more paranoid than Lazlo and would react at the smallest trigger. I want no mistakes."

"But why?" Yan cranes his head back toward me. "What would that information give us?"

"I'm forming another plan." And with that, I'm out of the car.

It doesn't take me long to reach Lia's apartment. I'm fully prepared for the darkness and finding her asleep. I didn't ask Boris if she had dinner and I didn't have the time to check the surveillance cameras during the meeting with Sergei and Igor.

The automatic light goes off in the entrance as soon as I'm inside. There's low symphonic music playing in the background. I'm surprised to find her small figure lying on the sofa. Lia is sleeping on the side, her hand under her ear, and she's covered with a fuzzy woolen blanket.

Her lips are slightly parted and her legs are tucked behind her. She looks so soft, so breakable, my Lenochka. She can be marked just as easily, too, and that part of me, the part that I shouldn't be giving weight to, is demanding that.

I turn off the music using the remote and plan to carry her to the bedroom, but as soon as the sound dies, her eyes flutter open.

She sits upright, and when her gaze meet mine, panic and something else whirls in the depths of the mesmerizing blue.

I hate that look. I want to erase it so that it's not her first reaction to me.

It's been more than a month and she still considers me the villain she painted me as that first time. While I didn't give a fuck about her labels at the beginning, I now want her to let her guard down when around me, without me having to touch her sexually.

Lia might revel in my touch and even crave the depravity, but she's still surrounding herself with barbed wire and the deadly thorns she mentioned the other day.

Wires and thorns I plan to eradicate.

"Adrian," she says softly, tucking her hair behind her ears. "I thought you weren't coming."

"I'm here, aren't I?"

Her demeanor stiffens, all softness purging from her delicate features. "For how long? Until the morning?"

"For as long as I please."

"You can't come and go as you please. I'm not your whore."

"Then what are you?"

I can tell my apathetic tone pisses her off since her cheeks turn a deep red. "I don't want to be your anything."

"Are you sure it's not the opposite?"

"Stop putting words in my mouth, you crazy, sick bastard."

"One strike."

"For calling you what you are?"

"For being angry at yourself for illogical reasons and taking it out on me. Now, come here."

"No."

"Two. If you don't do as you're told in the next second, the count will keep going up."

She glares up at me, crossing her arms over her chest.

"Three. I see that spanking has no effect on you anymore. Have you gotten used to your punishments, Lenochka?"

"You need help, okay?"

"Four. And you do, too, because I can see that anticipation in your pretty eyes."

"It's called hatred."

"Five." I pause for a second. "Six." Another. "Seven."

Her face reddens even further and I can tell she's fighting her pride to save herself. That she knows I won't back down and it'll only end badly for her if she keeps up the attitude.

Finally, she scrambles to her feet, eyes flashing with fire. "Fine. Do your spankings and leave me alone."

"Oh, no." I unbuckle my belt and pull it out. "I'm upping my methods."

SEVENTEEN

Lia

A RUSH OF ADRENALINE STIFFENS MY LIMBS AND AN urgent need pulses through my veins.

Run.

Hide.

Run and hide.

But I'm frozen in place.

Not one muscle moves as I stare at the belt in Adrian's hand. He loops it around his masculine fingers twice, making a show of what he has in store for me.

My legs lock in place and his handprints on my ass from last night start throbbing, tingling, *burning.*

I realize now that I shouldn't have provoked him, shouldn't have felt confident enough to think I'd win this and come out of it unscathed. We're on different sides of the chessboard, he and I, and there's no room for us to play the same game.

After what Luca told me, I should've been on my best be-havior, should've flown under the radar to watch Adrian, but my frustrations got the better of me.

Because even though he's owned me every night and has

taken care of my every need, come morning, I've been nothing short of a slut he's spent his nights with.

That's why I defied him, and that's why I will now pay.

It's then that I realize I'm slowly shaking my head, still focused on his belt.

He looks larger than life, dressed in a white shirt and dark gray pants that match the color of his unforgiving eyes. Adrian has always been a force to be reckoned with, a beautiful master of manipulation. It's like he was born with a handsome face to help him lower people's guards before he attacks.

I'm currently one of those people.

Because I have no doubt that he's coming after me and that I'm completely trapped with no way out.

"Get on your knees facing the sofa, Lia." The firm tenor of his voice sends a rippling shock down my rigid spine.

I continue shaking my head, a tinge of terror sparking through my chest. If his hand brought immeasurable agony by only spanking me, his belt is going to be pure torture.

"You can take your punishment now or..." he trails off, his gaze roaming down my naked thighs. I'm wearing a cotton shirt that stops below my ass, barely hiding my panties. The top buttons are undone, and the material of the neckline matches the fluffy socks covering my feet.

"Or what?" I murmur, squirming under his intense scrutiny.

His gaze slides back to my face. "Or you can take it later, after the count goes up."

"You really think that's a choice?"

"It is since you have two options. It's up to you to pick the less painful one."

"They're both painful."

"Correct, but one is definitely more merciful than the other."

"You're anything but merciful, Adrian. You're sick."

"And your labels are getting boring and repetitive, Lenochka." He grabs a fistful of my hair and I yelp when he turns me around and shoves me down on my knees. They sink into the carpet as he yanks the shirt over my head in one go.

I gasp as goosebumps break out on my skin. My nipples peak into sensitive buds, throbbing and pulsing in a rhythm that matches the one in my core.

Adrian throws the shirt aside and pushes me down against the sofa so my aching nipples meet the surface. I stifle a moan at the torturous sensation. It doesn't matter how much I fight myself or him, the moment he touches me like he owns me, sick pleasure courses through my veins.

He reaches a hand between me and the sofa, then pinches a painfully hard nipple, twisting it between his thumb and forefinger until I release a broken moan.

"Always sensitive and responsive, my Lenochka. Do you like it when I torture your pink nipples until you're soaking wet?"

"Mmmm..."

"Do you like the preparation for what's to come and the anticipation it creates in your little cunt?" He twists my nipple again and the motion, coupled with his crude words, nearly sends me over the edge.

"Oh...God...Adrian..."

"Yes, me. Only me." His voice lowers as he grabs a fistful of my hair and yanks me back by it. I'm suspended in mid-air, both of my hands gripping the sofa while he peers down on me, still pinching my nipple. "Say it."

"Say...w-what?"

"That I'm the only one you get wet for. The only one you allow to torture your nipples and fuck your tight cunt until you're spent."

My thighs clench together at the effect of his words, but I couldn't speak even if I tried.

His fingers dig into my scalp and his hold becomes merciless, non-negotiable, as his darkened eyes hold mine in an intimate cage. "Say, it's only you, Adrian."

"It's…only…you…Adrian…"

"I'm the only one who gets to touch you, aren't I, Lenochka?"

"Yes…"

"The only one you completely let go with?"

"Yes."

"The only one who punishes you?"

"Yes…" I briefly close my eyes, horrified with how true my words are.

How…liberating.

Adrian pushes me down by the hair so my cheek meets the sofa's warm surface, then releases me. But he doesn't disappear, standing behind me like both a threat and a promise.

He wraps a hand around my panties, and I yelp when he rips them away in one savage tug that coats my inner thighs with arousal.

"Would you stop ruining my underwear?" I breathe out.

"I'll ruin anything that gets in my way." His calmly spoken words send a sharp sting down my back, the unspoken intent tying me in knots.

I'm well aware of the fact that Adrian is dangerous, a killer, and a ruthless one at that. So I have no doubt he'll ruin even me if I get in his way.

That thought wraps ghostly fingers around my neck. If Adrian finds out I'm spying on him, he won't hesitate to strangle me, tear me apart.

Kill me.

His fist tightens on my hair again, pulling my attention to the present. "What are you thinking about?"

"I have very few panties left," I blurt.

"You can buy new ones." His voice lowers as he whispers near my ear, "Now, count."

A swish echoes in the air before the first strike comes down on my ass. I cry out, my scream bouncing off the walls.

Holy shit.

That hurts like nothing I've ever felt. It's like my skin is breaking, but it's not. The pain is trapped between the air and his belt.

"We'll start over, Lia."

"B-but why?"

"I told you to count."

His belt comes down on my ass again and it's even worse than the first one, burning my skin and carving himself a place beneath it.

"Should I start over again?" His voice is nonchalant, but it couldn't be any crueler.

"One…" I whimper.

Swish. Slap.

"Two!" I scream, tears gathering in the corners of my eyes and my ragged breath bouncing off the sofa.

Slap.

"Ahhh…three…" My voice breaks as my legs shake and my stomach flips.

That's when I feel it.

The deep contraction in my belly and a harsh finger forcing its way through my folds.

"Mmm. I knew you needed pain with your pleasure, Lia."

"No…no…" I want to erase the evidence he's gliding his fingers through, the arousal, the deep tingling I've felt only a few times before this started when he shoved me facedown on the table and took me without holding back.

Only, now, it seems to have intensified, reaching a new height I never thought existed.

Oh, God.

Is there really something wrong with me? Is that why I'm reacting to his perverse punishment and sadistic dominance this way?

"Deny it all you like, Lia, but your cunt knows what it wants."

Swish. Slap.

Swish. Slap.

My ass throbs and my arousal keeps coating his fingers. Shamelessly. Relentlessly.

"Four…five…" My voice finishes on a throaty cry when he whips me again. "Six!"

I'm a sobbing mess right now. My tears wet the sofa and seep into my mouth, making me taste salt. A sheen of sweat covers my skin and my burning ass.

I wish that was all there was to it.

I wish I was sobbing only because of the pain, but my pussy pulses with a need as violent as the flames exploding on my ass. The need for release claws to be set free.

The sound of the belt in the air adds more torment and anticipation to the upcoming hit. When it meets my flesh, I sob, "Seven…"

I want to sigh in relief that it's over, but the ache in my pussy forbids me to. If the whipping managed anything, it definitely got me hot, tingly, and damn fidgety.

The belt hits the ground and Adrian releases my hair. I think he's finally done, but I feel him sinking to his knees on the carpet behind me.

Before I can watch what he's doing, his hands grab my aching ass cheeks and he parts them. I moan because of the pain, relief, and something else.

"Adrian…" I sob. "I…please."

"Please what, Lia?"

"I…don't know."

"Of course you do. You just don't want to admit it."

"*Please…*"

"Please make you come?"

I purse my lips, tasting my tears.

"Say it, Lia."

I shake my head slightly.

"The more you defy me, the harder I deny you."

"I can't say it."

"Yes, you can. You need to own up to your pleasure with me or you won't get any of it."

I peek at him behind me. He's so broad compared to my tiny body, it's both frightening and a turn-on.

That man will take from me as if he were always meant to, he'll own me just because he wants to, but he's also willing to give back just as hard.

However, he has a steep price for that—my complete submission.

"Should I make you come or leave you hot and bothered?"

I swallow.

"I'll tie you up so you won't touch yourself all night long, Lia."

My lips tremble. "Don't…"

"Say the fucking words."

I suck in a shaky intake of air. "Please…"

"Please what?"

"M-make me come," I whisper.

"I didn't hear that."

"I want to come."

His face creases with a beautifully cruel smile that slams straight into my throbbing chest. "There. Good girl, Lenochka."

And with that, he dives between my legs, his hot tongue sliding from my folds to my swollen clit.

Holy…

"Adrian…ohhh…" My voice is robbed from me when he thrusts his tongue in and out of my opening. His big hands knead my ass, adding a sharp tang of pain to the pleasure he's eliciting from my core.

He tongue-fucks me like it's an extension of his

punishment, but at the same time, it's the most erotic thing I've ever experienced.

The assault of his tongue in and out of me, licking, biting, sucking, coupled with the burn in my ass is too raw, too hot.

Just too much.

When he nibbles down on my clit, I scream out my orgasm, coming all over Adrian's tongue. It's the strongest I've had. The most damning, too. I feel like I'm never coming down, that everything is whirring and buzzing and my poor heart will stop, unable to take it all in.

I want to collapse here and now, but I'm more tempted to look at him, to cement this moment by getting a read on his expression.

Still gripping my ass, Adrian unzips his pants and releases his raging hard-on. I swallow at the size of him. His cock is just like the rest of him, beautiful and scary.

He gives it a single violent stroke that leaves me breathless. I love it when he touches himself with that sure masculinity. A drip of precum travels down his length and I find myself wanting to lick my lips and him.

Still gripping his cock with one hand, he cups my jaw, gliding his thumb over my tear-streaked face. "I love it when you cry because your tiny body can't contain the pleasure I give you. It makes me rock fucking hard to see your arousal tears. Did you cry during sex for other bastards?"

"No," I whisper, strangely turned on by his words. Am I sick that I'm happy he likes my pleasure tears?

His gray eyes darken with raw possessiveness as he presses down on my cheeks. "These tears are only mine, aren't they, Lenochka?"

"Yes…"

"And they always will be."

"Yes…"

He leans over so the warmth of his chest is an inch away

from my back and his hot breaths tickle the side of my face. "I'm going to fuck you and you're going to cry for me."

My spine tingles, and the orgasm that still didn't release me yet rushes back in with wrecking force.

Adrian slams inside me in one ruthless go that knocks the breath out of my lungs and the thoughts out of my head.

"Fuck," he groans when he's sheathed deep inside me, and I meet it with a moan, because no matter how many times he does it, being this tangled with him always feels new. Like this is our first time, or worse, like we both get more addicted with each touch, each fuck, each joining of our bodies.

Adrian grabs a fistful of my hair and my assaulted ass as he thrusts deep inside me, hitting that sensitive spot over and over.

I'm so close to the edge that I'm sobbing again. Tears stream down my cheeks and my moans echo in the air.

He releases my hair and glides his strong, lean fingers across my cheek, taking the tears away before pressing his middle and index fingers against my lips. I open, letting him slide them inside.

"These tears and moans are fucking mine, Lenochka."

I suck on his fingers as a reply while he slides them in and out of my mouth, matching the rhythm of his cock inside me.

The moment he slaps my burning ass, I'm coming again, clenching around him with a wordless cry.

Adrian joins me soon after, his body going rigid before the familiar warmth of his seed fills me.

Then, in the midst of the carnal pleasure, everything turns black.

EIGHTEEN

Lia

I'M FAINTLY AWARE OF STRONG ARMS CARRYING ME IN their cocoon. Ones I recognize even with my eyes closed.

I'm placed on a soft mattress and a warm cloth wipes between the valley of my breasts, brushing against my nipples before sliding to my sticky core.

"Mmmm." I sigh in my half-asleep state as I bask in the soothing sensation.

I probably would never admit this out loud, but Adrian's aftercare is addictive. It's so tender in contrast to his brutal touch. So patient, too. He takes his sweet time cleaning my every pore like he finds pleasure in touching me this way.

I'm about to fall back asleep as usual when his strong voice filters in the silence, "Who were you talking to in the lingerie shop, Lia?"

My eyes snap open, my breath hitching when I find him standing over my lying position, the contours of his face shadowed by the dark. "W-what?"

"The man you were touching that red lingerie in front of. Who the fuck is he?"

Shit!

"A-Adrian…"

His hand wraps around my jaw. "It's better that you freely divulge information or I'll find him and rip his heart out while you watch."

"No, Adrian…please."

"Who is *he*?" His tone is frightening, harsh.

I shake my head frantically.

"It was me."

Our attention snaps to the figure sliding inside my room from the balcony. I gasp as Luca comes into view, holding a gun.

"Looks like you have to die sooner rather than later, Volkov." And then he shoots, the bullet lodging straight in Adrian's chest, and he falls face-first against my lap, blood exploding on his white shirt.

"Noooo!" I shriek, bolting up.

My eyes open, and I quickly take note of my surroundings. I'm in my room, the morning light filtering through the balcony's muslin curtains.

Luca isn't in view.

There's no blood either.

Please tell me that was a nightmare. Please.

I retrieve my phone with trembling fingers, going straight to Adrian's number. He entered it the first time he was here in case I need him, but he's always the one who texts to ask what I want for dinner.

This is my first time to contact him.

My unsteady thumb swipes over his name and I place the phone to my ear. I'm shaking, my limbs sweaty as I listen to it ring.

Please tell me he's busy working or doing whatever he does when he leaves my apartment.

Heavy footsteps come from outside the bedroom before Adrian appears in the doorway, wearing only his boxer briefs. A sheen of sweat covers his sun-kissed skin, causing the full tattoo sleeves to shine in the morning glow. His glorious abdomen and chest muscles ripple with every movement.

His long legs cross over each other as he motions at his phone in his hand. "You called me?"

At first, I don't believe what I'm seeing. I think it's another sick play of my imagination. That this is the nightmare and the one from earlier is reality.

I dig my nails in my wrist and release a sigh of relief when pain rushes to the surface.

Without thinking, I scramble out of bed. Then I cry out, stumbling over the sheets when burning pain explodes in my ass.

Holy shit. That hurts.

Adrian is beside me in a second, grabbing me by the arm to stop me from falling.

I hold on to his forearm as I regain my footing and study his chest and side, making sure that it was indeed a nightmare.

"Take it easy, Lenochka. We don't want you to hurt those talented legs." His voice holds mild amusement.

My lips part at the fact that for the first time, I didn't think about my obsession with keeping my legs safe in my haste to make sure he was okay.

That's when the current situation dawns on me. "You're… here."

"Isn't that obvious?"

"But you always leave in the mornings."

"I don't have work early today."

"Oh." Is that why he was leaving early all along? Or is this only another excuse?

"*Oh* isn't a word. Use actual ones."

I blush at the obvious way he's openly checking my nakedness. I find myself watching him, too, the way his muscles are taut to perfection or how the fine hairs travel to the waist of his boxer briefs.

"What…" I swallow. "What were you doing?"

"Push-ups."

The sweat makes sense, but I still can't force my gaze from him. Adrian has physical perfection that's so different from what I've witnessed before. I'm used to seeing models and dancers who don't shy away from removing their clothes and changing in semi-public places. But that type of beauty is pretty—aesthetic, even. Adrian's rugged, harsh, and comes with an edge that's complemented by his calm yet ruthless personality.

"Why did you call me?"

I force my gaze to slide up to his face. "Huh?"

His lips twitch in what resembles a smile. "The phone call, Lia."

"Uh…nothing."

"People don't make phone calls for nothing."

I rack my brain for something because I really don't want to tell him I was on the verge of hyperventilating due to a visceral nightmare I had about him.

"Lia…" It's a single word, but the warning is clear. Adrian is a damn dictator sometimes, I swear. He doesn't tolerate having his questions ignored and will keep demanding an answer until I finally give it.

"I was going ask what you're bringing tonight for dinner," I blurt.

"I can send you whatever you like, but I probably won't be able to make it."

I fight the tug of disappointment that sinks to the bottom of my stomach.

Adrian raises a brow. "Aren't you going to ask me why?"

"I don't care," I say with so much stubbornness, it leaves even me stunned.

"As you wish." He wraps his arms around my waist, pulling me against his chest. My tender nipples harden against his skin and I suck in a fractured breath through my parted lips.

Will this pull between us ever end? Will there ever be a day where I'll be in Adrian's vicinity and not wish to be closer?

"You didn't have a nightmare last night," he murmurs.

That's because I had it this morning.

I frown. "How do you know I have nightmares? Wait...you watch me when I sleep?"

"I do."

My mouth opens, and when it finds no words to say, it closes again. It shouldn't be a surprise since he cleans me up every night, but I dislike that he studies me in my ugliest form.

"You know, for someone who claims not to be a stalker, you have obvious stalkerish behavior, Adrian."

"A stalker would never openly admit to watching you sleep. If anything, they'd keep it a secret for as long as possible."

I narrow my eyes on him. "You're still a stalker."

"If you say so."

"You really don't care, do you?"

"No, and neither should you, Lenochka. The world means nothing if you decide it doesn't."

"I'm not you, Adrian. I care."

"Why would you when it'd only hurt you?" His hand glides in circles on the small of my back, eliciting shudders from my skin. "You're better than that."

"No, I'm not."

"Yes, you are."

"How do you know?"

"I just do." A strange look passes in his eyes. It's brief and quickly disappears as he says, "Since when did you start to have nightmares?"

"No particular date. Everyone has them."

"Not like you. They seem more...raw."

"It's because they are. Sometimes, it takes me long minutes to differentiate between reality and a nightmare. Sometimes, what I have a nightmare about comes true." My lips tremble at that, recalling how he was shot by Luca. Is that also something that will happen in the future?

"I presume this started a long time ago?"

I shake myself out of those thoughts. "Since I was a child. How did you know?"

"They seem deep-seated, and childhood events could produce that type of wild subconscious."

"Are you my shrink now?"

"Not your shrink, no. I'm merely trying to understand that part of you better."

I don't know why that warms my heart, why everything in me becomes even more tender at those words. He shouldn't care, he really shouldn't, so why does he?

"There's nothing to understand, not when I don't understand it myself."

"Hmm. We'll see."

I pause, watching the easy expression on his face. "How about you?"

"Me?"

"Do you know about trauma from childhood events because you went through something yourself?"

"Perhaps."

"Is that a yes or no?"

"Neither."

"It's not fair if you're the only one who knows things about me, Adrian."

"I told you. Fairness doesn't exist. Besides, weren't you the one who made it clear that you don't want anything to do with me?"

"I changed my mind."

"Why?"

"Well, you're obviously not leaving me alone, so I can at least get to know you better."

"So you can escape me?"

"N-no."

"You're lying, and that's one strike for the day." He narrows his eyes. "But it doesn't matter, because you won't be able to."

The promise of his words hits me in the bones and it takes a few inhales of oxygen to get my bearings. "Then tell me."

"What do you want to know?"

"Your childhood. Did something happen in it?"

"The real question would be what didn't happen."

"Was your stepmom evil?"

A distant nostalgic look fills his eyes. "It was the other way around. My mother was the villain and my stepmom was the real-life Disney princess who didn't get saved."

That's the first time he's talked so openly about his family. "Why was your mother the villain?"

"Villains don't need reasons."

"Yes, they do. You said it yourself that they're heroes in their own stories and, therefore, they want something."

"Do you remember everything I said, Lenochka?"

"I have a strong memory." My cheeks burn. "So?"

"So what?"

"Why was she the villain?"

"Power. It was her first and last goal, and Aunt Annika got in the way, and though it wasn't by choice, she still paid the price."

"What price?" My voice is low, haunted like the look in his eyes.

"Her life. She died when I was seven."

It dawns on me then. Judging by the way he appears nostalgic talking about his stepmother and even calls her *Aunt*, he must've loved her. He must've had some sort of a bond with her. I can almost imagine a younger Adrian holding on to his stepmother's light because his mother and his mobster father didn't emanate any.

After her death, I assume a part of him died, too. His

human side. That's why he's now an unfeeling monster who cares about no one's demands but his own.

"Do you miss her?" I whisper.

"She's dead."

"You can still miss her."

"I don't."

"Why not?"

"Because I have no clue what that word means."

"You don't?"

"Not in the practical sense, no."

"I can explain. It's when—"

"I don't want you to explain," he cuts me off.

"But—"

"Drop it, Lia." The bite in his tone suggests that he's done entertaining my questions.

I glare up at him. "You're insufferable."

"If you say so."

His hand lowers until he cups my ass cheek. I wince, gripping his muscled bicep for balance. "You're sore. Let me take care of that."

He sits down on the bed and pulls me over his lap. The position is so vulnerable and causes heat to rise to my cheeks and I squirm. "I can lie on the bed."

I whimper when Adrian cups my assaulted ass cheek. "Or you can stay still."

He reaches for the ointment he keeps on my nightstand. My attention is robbed by the intricate tattoos on his arms, the way they swirl around his skin, adding another mysterious layer to his personality.

"What do the tattoos mean?" I ask before I can stop myself. I've always wanted to know, but I figured he wouldn't answer. This morning, he feels closer somehow. It could be because he didn't leave before I woke up or because he told me about himself as normal couples do.

Wait. We're not a couple.

Right?

Adrian retrieves the ointment and slathers the cool cream on my backside. I wince but soon moan when he rubs it in gently.

"In the Bratva, each tattoo has meaning." His voice is as cool as his repeated strokes.

"Like?"

"The red rose means I've killed before."

I gulp at the reminder.

"What is it, Lenochka? I thought you wanted to know."

"I do," I blurt. "Is the map of Russia?"

"Correct."

"Do you love it, Russia?"

"What type of question is that? Who doesn't love their country?"

"I mean, do you love it enough to tattoo it on yourself?"

"No. It's for another reason."

"What is it?"

"The vacation I never got to take as a kid."

"Is that why you have a compass on top of it?"

"That's to remind me of how far I've come."

"What about the skull."

"That's because I'm a thief."

"A thief?"

"Hmm. How to explain this. The Bratva is also called the Vory, which is to say we're thieves."

"So it's a brotherhood of thieves?"

He dips his finger against my folds. "Something like that."

I suppress a moan. "Do you like it? Being a thief."

"I like the surge of adrenaline it brings."

"So you like the lifestyle?"

"Yes, I do."

A pang of disappointment hits me at his assertive words. I

don't know why a part of me hoped that he didn't have a choice in being who he is, that he can quit if he chooses to. But I was only fooling myself. Adrian willingly chose this life because he likes it, and there's nothing that will deter him from it.

Letting the subject go, I fall into the sensations he's eliciting in me, how he's stroking my ass and gliding his fingers through my folds and to my opening.

My eyes flutter closed as I rest my cheek against his naked thigh.

Hot breaths tickle my ear as he whispers, "Don't fall asleep, Lenochka."

"Mmm. I'm not."

"Good. Because I'm going to fuck you so hard, you'll feel me inside you until tomorrow."

NINETEEN

Lia

ADRIAN MADE GOOD ON HIS PROMISE.

Getting through rehearsal is torture. I can feel him with every move, every jump, and every damn step. I had to wear boy shorts to cover the welts on my upper thighs. Every time I touch them, I recall last night and the amount of pleasure I got out of it.

The dark type.

The type that's hushed in corners and kept secret.

Then I recall how I felt when I thought he'd been shot. I shouldn't have had that reaction. I shouldn't have been worried, pained, and damn confused.

He's a mobster, a killer.

But those facts seem to fade day by day whether I like it or not.

After this morning, I feel closer to him more than ever. As if a bridge is building between us slowly but surely. It might be fragile, but it's there.

Something's changed.

I could feel it when he fucked me against the shower wall

and when we prepared breakfast together like it was a normal occurrence. I felt it when he sat me down on the counter just so he could kiss me. And I sure as hell felt it when he kissed me again before he stepped out.

Those aren't things a man would do with his whore.

My long day is finally over when Philippe announces it's a wrap. This is one of our last rehearsals before the opening next week.

I've never been this excited about a performance. About taking on a character as complex as Giselle.

Ryan releases me, turns around, and heads to the dressing room without a glance back. I love the type of relationship we have formed since the night at the club—professional. That's how it was supposed to be from the beginning.

Hannah gets in my face as soon as he's out of view. "What the fuck did you do to him, bitch?"

I allow myself a taunting smile. "Why don't you ask him what *he* did?"

"He won't talk to me!"

"Doesn't seem like my problem. He got what was coming to him." I lean in to whisper, "You deserve each other."

And with that, I leave her and head to Stephanie.

She smiles, interlacing her arm with mine. "Come with us to this great company opening Matt invited us to."

"I don't know, Steph."

"Don't leave me alone with Philippe and how he randomly switches to French when he's drunk, as if the world is fluent in the language."

"Then curses you when you speak in English?"

"Exactly, girl. Come on, it'll be just the three of us."

"Fine." I don't have anything to do, anyway, and I need to stop thinking about Adrian for one night.

Or try to.

After this morning, I want to see him again more than I ever have before.

"Yes! I love you forever." Stephanie walks with me.

I grin back as a response.

She stops in front of my dressing room and pinches my cheek. "You're glowing more lately."

"I'm not."

"Yes, you are. Is your lover the reason why your Giselle is so haunting?"

"I-I don't have a lover."

"Of course you do. He's the reason why you hurry home every night and refuse my and Philippe's invitations."

"That's…how did you know?"

"It's clear if anyone focuses hard enough. Lately, you seem to be firmly on the ground instead of floating somewhere no one sees you. You need to introduce me to Mr. Hot Stuff."

"It's not serious," I murmur. Adrian is not my lover and never will be. What are we, anyway? We can't be friends with benefits because we're not friends.

Sex partners? Probably, but do sex partners go to the lengths Adrian does to make sure I'm fully comfortable?

"How about you invite him to our opening?"

"Huh?"

"Yes!" She claps her hands. "It would be the perfect opportunity for him to see your Giselle and for us to spy on the man who got your heart."

"He doesn't have my heart," I say defensively, then pause at the thought Stephanie just planted in my head.

Should I invite Adrian?

Since he's part of the reason for how I shaped my Giselle, I'm sure I'll perform even better knowing he's there.

Or worse.

I shouldn't take that risk, but at the same time, a part of me wants him there. In the midst of the thousand strangers, I want to step onto the stage, knowing Adrian's among them.

"I guess I can ask him," I tell Stephanie, who squeals.

"I'm getting you a VIP ticket." She winks at me and hurries down the hall.

I laugh at her enthusiasm and go in to change.

Half an hour later, I'm wearing a blue dress with a double V-neck, complementing the look with a dainty sterling silver necklace—the only memory I have of Mom.

My heart tugs at the reminder of her and I tuck those black memories to the back of my brain. I wear low heels and let my hair fall in loose waves down my shoulders before I put on my coat and meet Stephanie and Philippe.

She shoves a VIP ticket in my hand, grinning like an idiot.

"*Chérie.*" Philippe kisses my cheek as we walk to his car. "I'm glad you could join us."

"I won't make it a habit."

"I'm happy with what I can get. Don't spoil my fun."

We leave the theater together in the midst of glares from other dancers. I learned to tune out their envy a long time ago. Adrian was right, in a way. If I care too much, I'll be the only one who suffers.

Matt, who's tall and obese, meets us at the venue where the event is being held. Apparently, it's the opening for some subsidiary of a large corporation named V Corp. Our producer has associates here and owns some shares. While leading us inside, he keeps reminding us to be on our best behavior like we're children.

The hall is enormous and majestic as is expected of a large corporation. Gold glitters everywhere as if they want to shove the fact that they have money down everyone's throats.

Men in tuxedos and women in gowns are scattered all around, chatting happily.

I'm glad Philippe and Stephanie ignore the commotion, choosing to attack the long lines of the buffet and the open bar.

I climb onto a stool and wait for them to stop arguing over which food is fattening and join me.

"What can I get you, miss?" the bartender asks.

"Nothing." The voice coming from my right gives me pause.

The young bartender pales before he retreats to the corner, going to serve the customer farthest away from me.

I stare up to find Yan, Adrian's younger guard with the long hair, standing by my side, his face as stoic as usual. "You need to leave, miss."

That's the first time he's ever addressed me in the month I've known Adrian. He has a subtle Russian accent that resembles Adrian's, but it's less sophisticated.

Wait. If Yan is here, does that mean his boss is here, too?

I hate the fluttering in my belly as I stare around Yan, searching for the most threatening and dangerous man in the room.

"Miss." Yan repeats, impatiently this time.

"Why do I need to leave?"

"You have to."

"Says who?"

"Boss."

"Well, your boss doesn't get to tell me what to do. And if he has something to say, why doesn't he do it himself?"

Yan's gaze shifts sideways as if he's nervous or lost about what to do. "You can follow me willingly or I'll have to carry you out by force."

My lips part. "What the hell?"

"Orders are orders."

"Are you a robot?"

He pauses at that as if he's offended. "By force, then."

Yan grabs my hand and pulls me down from the stool. I'm about to scream the whole place down when I catch a scene over Yan's shoulder.

Adrian.

He's wearing a black tux that flatters his tall, muscular body. It's the first time I've see him in such formal clothes and it suits him to perfection, making him appear like the latest hot model on a men's magazine. His hair is styled back and his lips are tilted in a smile.

One he doesn't give me.

One that's now directed at a slender blonde with stunning features and a bombshell body to go with it. She doesn't need to be naked to showcase it either. Her red dress is long-sleeved and stops right above her knees. It's modest and beautiful, giving her a classy look I could never pull off.

She touches Adrian's arm as she speaks, and he continues smiling, obviously enjoying the gesture.

Yan follows my field of vision, then mutters, "Fuck."

"Who is she?" I murmur, my tongue heavy in my throat.

"You don't need to know."

"Is that the reason your boss wants me away from here?"

Yan's lack of words is the only answer I need. I don't know what I'm thinking when I shove away from him and march toward them. If anything, it's like I'm not thinking at all.

Yan calls after me, but I'm faster, barging through people and getting cursed a thousand times.

There's been a burn in my chest ever since I saw Adrian with that woman. I don't know if it's because he never takes me out, yet he accompanied her to a grand opening, or because he's smiling at her and never does at me.

Or because he stood me up tonight for her.

It's probably all of the above.

I stop right in front of them. Adrian stares down at me like I'm a stranger he's meeting for the first time.

Worse. It's like I'm a rock in his shoe.

"Excuse me?" the blonde asks, and her voice is as soft and classy as she is.

I glare up at him. "Explain this."

"Who the fuck do you think you are?" Adrian's cold, harsh words stab me deeper than anything ever has.

An elderly man joins our circle. His features are solemn and he speaks with a Russian accent, "Is something wrong?"

"I don't know, Papa." The blonde stares between me and Adrian. "This woman came out of nowhere."

The elderly man, her father, watches me with a critical eye, all while I stare speechless at Adrian, trying to figure out what the hell he just said.

It must've been a figment of my imagination. Adrian didn't just imply that I'm a stranger in front of his date.

"Do you know her, Volkov?" the man asks.

"No." Adrian doesn't look at me, his voice casual.

If I thought his earlier words hurt, these ones cut so deep, I feel the knife digging inside. The bridge I felt forming between us this morning dissolves into thin air.

Yan finally catches up to me and tries to pull me back by my wrist. I snap out of my daze, attempting to wiggle away. "That's not—"

"Throw her out," Adrian says to Yan, jabbing the knife deeper.

The old man looks at me again. "Do you know my daughter's fiancé, young lady?"

I freeze.

Did he just say his daughter's fiancé?

My gaze shifts from him to his daughter's questioning eyes and then back to Adrian's cold gray ones, and the only answer I can give under the circumstances tumbles from my throat, "No."

And with that, I let Yan drag me out.

I'm too stunned, too shocked, to move on my own, so I follow his steps mindlessly.

"You should've come with me the first time," Yan mutters under his breath.

Maybe so, but if I had, I wouldn't have been shaken by this wake-up call.

Adrian has a fiancée. All blonde and beautiful and Russian.

I was only a game to him all this time.

TWENTY

Adrian

IT TAKES ALL OF MY SELF-RESTRAINT NOT TO WATCH AS Yan drags a half-dazed Lia out of the venue.

If I do, if I look at her, I'll be tempted to go after her, and that's the most foolish thing I could do under the circumstances.

By the time Boris informed me she was here, thanks to that fucker Matt, who's a close associate of the brotherhood, I barely had time to tell Yan to get her out.

That plan was obviously a clusterfuck since she came to me as if she had every right to be by my side.

She doesn't.

Even though I don't stare at her, Igor and his daughter, *my fiancée*, Kristina, do, both measuring her up until she disappears with Yan.

Igor's attention finally comes back to me, his face hard. "Do I need an explanation, Volkov?"

"No," I speak with an ease I don't feel.

"Good. Because I won't allow you to disrespect my daughter."

I nod in a show of respect, but he doesn't nod back as he turns around and leaves.

Kristina continues to stare at me, then at the door through which Lia left, her face remaining as emotionless as her father's. As a mafia princess, she was born ready to be married within the brotherhood. Pretty and flawless, Kristina's role in life is to bring honor to her father and become the obedient wife.

When Sergei suggested this alliance a year ago, I didn't see why not, especially since Igor and his brigade are surrounded by a high wall no one can penetrate. I thought this would bring me closer to his methodical reign.

If I had to marry one day, Kristina seemed like the safest and most logical choice.

I can see the doubts on her face, but she doesn't voice them. She wasn't raised to. For Kristina, being the obedient wife is everything that matters.

Unlike my Lenochka, whose feelings are usually written all over her face, Kristina's are locked under a makeshift façade.

"If you're keeping her as a mistress, let me know." She fakes a smile. "Have a lovely night."

And with that, she turns and leaves as if nothing happened.

It takes everything I have to continue with the dull event. While I loathe the empty socializing these parties are all about, I need the networking and information they provide.

However, it's hard—almost impossible—to concentrate when I recall the shock and hurt in those blue eyes. Conjuring those emotions in her was everything that I initially strived for, but now it feels like a rusty knife in my gut.

After some thirty minutes of mindless talking to influential men whose only worth is their networks, my phone vibrates in my pocket. I excuse myself and check it.

Yan: She's in the apartment.

I should take it out on him for not escorting her out soon enough, but it's pointless. I couldn't have kept her in the dark for too long.

Adrian: Stand guard.

Yan: Got it.

The night feels like a thousand years. Lia's ballet producer comes to talk to me, introducing the French director. He says his prima ballerina is here somewhere, but he can't find her.

And he never will.

After the night is finally over, I ignore the small gathering Sergei is having with the other leaders and leave. Kolya drives at high speed until I reach Lia's apartment.

Yan blows smoke from his cigarette and nods from his position in front of the door. I motion at him to join Kolya downstairs, but he hesitates.

"What?" I don't bother hiding my impatience.

"You said you'd talk about a new plan for Lazlo."

"This isn't the time to discuss that, Yan."

"I'm just saying, we need to do something about this situation." He tips his head toward the apartment door. "She didn't seem to be doing so well."

He leaves before I can say anything.

I put in the code and go inside.

The light flicks on as the door closes behind me.

"Is she really your fiancée?" Lia's apathetic tone greets me. She's standing at the entrance to the living room, crossing her arms over her chest and still wearing the blue dress that gives her a softer edge. Her face is flushed, but her eyes are ablaze with a mixture of volatile emotions.

I start removing my coat.

"I wouldn't do that if I were you," she bites out.

"Why not?"

"Whether you're leaving or staying is up to the answer to my question."

I throw the coat on the entrance table, not bothering to hang it, and charge toward her. She startles when I grab her by the chin, my hold harsh and firm, prohibiting her from moving.

"You seem to have some misconceptions, so understand this, Lia. Whether I leave or stay is only up to me. You don't get a say in it, never have and never will."

Her eyes are wide, lips pale, and chin trembling. She's obviously scared, but she meets my gaze as she repeats, "Is she your fiancée?"

"Whether she is or isn't doesn't concern you."

"Of course it concerns me! I will not be the other woman!" she strains, trying to squirm free from my hold.

I wrap a hand around her waist and slam her front against me, knocking the breath out of her lungs. "You are whatever the fuck I say you are."

She shakes her head. "No…no, Adrian. Don't…"

"Don't what?"

"Don't put me there."

"Put you where?"

"In this damn position." She hits my chest with closed fists. "I'm *not* your whore."

"I own your cunt, Lia. I own *you*. Titles don't matter."

"It matters to me!"

"Why? You think if you're my whore, you'll want me any less? You'll open your legs for me any less? You're a slut for me, Lia."

She raises her hand and slaps me across the face. Hard. The sound reverberates through the silent apartment as the sting etches across my skin.

My vision reddens, but it's not with the need to hurt her for hitting me. It's for the reminder of what being hit means. My fucking mother.

I close my eyes for a brief second, tightening my jaw.

When I open them again, Lia's eyes have widened further and tears cling to her lids as if she's realizing exactly how fucked she is.

Literally and figuratively.

She opens her mouth to say something, but my lips crash to hers. She thins them in a line, her small hands pushing against my chest. It's her rebellion against me, one that doesn't last when I bite down on her bottom lip. She tries to fight me, to hold on to her anger, but I tilt her head back to plunge my tongue inside and feast on her. She whimpers as her fists go limp against my chest and a tear slides down her cheek, clinging to my lips until I taste salt.

But that's not the only thing I taste. There's also her desperation, betrayal, and lust. I take all of those as I kiss her, sucking her soul from her lungs.

Using my hold on her chin, I push her small body backward. Her lips part with a gasp as her ass flattens against the wall. I pull her dress up and bunch her panties in a fist, tugging until they rip into shreds.

It takes me a second I don't have to unbuckle my pants as I lift her leg and loop it around my waist. Then I'm ramming inside her with an urgency I haven't felt before. My back snaps in a line as I thrust into her tight heat with a rhythm that leaves her gasping for air against my lips.

Her leg squeezes me as more tears slide down her cheeks, soaking us both. I'll take her emotions and everything she has to offer.

My fingers dig into her thigh as I power into her, feeding off her moans mixed with sniffles. Off the way she holds on to me, even when she hates me.

I hit her sensitive spot over and over until she's sobbing out her orgasm. She tightens around my dick like a vise and I empty inside her with a deep growl, my harsh breathing echoing in the air.

It takes me a second to come back to the world of the living. Lia turns her face away from me while still crying, her body shuddering as she whispers, "I'll never forgive you for putting me in this position."

"You are mine. Get used to it." I pull out of her and watch my cum streaking down her thighs to her ankles.

That view will always be my fucking favorite.

I grab her by the elbow to test her balance, but she pulls away from me, using the wall as an anchor.

Gritting my teeth, I tuck myself in, then I turn around and step out of the apartment before I lose the cool that I'm barely holding on to.

Before I confiscate her from the world and keep her for myself.

Maybe that's what I should do, anyway.

Because tonight, I made irrevocable decisions.

Lia isn't the other woman. She's *the* woman.

And I'm not my fucking father.

TWENTY-ONE

Lia

I'M NUMB ON THE LAST DAY OF *GISELLE* REHEARSALS.

In fact, I've been numb since the moment Adrian fucked me against the wall, then left me crying on the floor. Right after he made me the other woman.

His *whore*.

That was three days ago.

Three days since I found out he has a fiancée. A blonde, beautiful one. A Russian, just like him.

One he shouldn't have looked away from. I don't have a low opinion of myself, but even I can tell her type—classy, blonde, and with legs that go for miles—is the one that suits him.

I've been going through the motions since that day, but I haven't been living. All I keep thinking about is a way to stop being *that* woman. That despicable bitch who's stealing away an engaged man.

I hate him so much for putting me in this position. Even more than when he lured me under his thumb and made me crave him.

Despite the murkiness of that situation, I was able to let

go, to let him invade my world. But this situation is completely different and against every principle I have.

And because of that, I need to break away from him. Knowing Adrian's domineering character, he won't end it with me just because I demand it. If I fight, he'll subdue me and even punish me for it. I have to be smart about this and do something that will make him disgusted enough with me that he'll leave my life in peace.

But no matter how much I've racked my brain these past few days, I haven't found a way.

I'm glad Adrian left me alone during this period, but knowing he'll eventually come back makes me restless.

Whenever I walk into my apartment and don't find him there, a mixture of relief and annoying disappointment hits me.

I wish he'd get bored of me, already, but he implied he'd never leave me that day.

If he'd said those words that morning, I would've felt different. Slightly scared but probably excited. However, now, all I feel is bitterness, because even the moments we shared that morning weren't real.

He has a fucking fiancée.

In my parking garage, I spot Yan in his Mercedes right across from my car. He's been openly watching me. Sometimes alone, other times with another buff, scowly guard who isn't Kolya.

I usually ignore him, but today, my nerves are shot. I'm anxious about *Giselle*'s opening, and the whole thing with Adrian is making me lose sleep, startling awake at any sound, expecting him to show up.

I march to Yan and he gets out of the car before I reach him, standing in an erect position. "Do you need anything, miss?"

"Yes, leave me alone."

His expression doesn't change. "I can't."

"Why the hell not?"

"Boss's orders."

"Tell your boss to go fuck himself."

"I'm afraid I can't, but you tell him yourself if you like."

My hold tightens on my bag as I glare at him. A look that he returns with a neutral one.

"Why is he doing this to me, Yan?"

"Honestly?" He lifts a shoulder. "No one but him knows."

"You're his guard."

"Believe it or not, that doesn't give me access to his complicated brain."

I pause at the sarcasm. I always thought Adrian's guards were as stoic as him, but Yan seems to be different. Despite being calm in my presence, he's not as solemn-faced as Kolya. Besides, he's pretty to look at.

"Do you know what he plans to do?" I ask.

"Not really."

"Is he ever going to let me go?"

He winces. "I don't know."

"But he has a fiancée." My lips tremble around the word. Is it supposed to hurt this much whenever I think of it or say it aloud?

"It's tradition, miss. He's supposed to marry into the brotherhood. Kristina Petrov is the daughter of one of the leaders and was handpicked to be Boss's wife, to bear his heirs, and so on."

Yan's tone is nonchalant, meant to make me feel better, but it just manages to dig the knife in deeper. Kristina Petrov is not only the most suitable woman for Adrian, but apparently, she's the perfect candidate, too.

"Then why is he betraying her with me?"

"He's not."

"He obviously is."

He pauses. "It's somewhat normal to have…"

"Mistresses?" I bite out, finishing for him.

He gives a hesitant nod.

"I'm nobody's mistress," I mutter from between gritted teeth. "If I have to fight Adrian tooth and nail to not be one, I will."

"Please don't." He retrieves a pack of cigarettes. "May I?"

"Sure, I'm used to the smell." I pause. "What did you mean by what you just said?"

He lights a cigarette and takes a long drag, then releases it through his nostrils. "If you use violence against him, you'll be met with violence. I don't have to tell you who will win in that case."

"Do you suggest I stay silent?"

"I never said that. Just…be smart about it, miss. That's the only way you can get anything from him. Boss is a practical man, and while he might seem robotic at times, he weighs everything and will always choose logic above anything else."

I mull his words over in my head, finding them true. Going at Adrian full force would just blow up in my face.

"Thank you," I say. At least Yan isn't as desensitized as his boss.

He raises both hands in the air. "I said nothing. Don't get me in trouble."

I smile a little before getting in my car, and when I head out, Yan follows close behind me in his Mercedes. After the talk we just had, I don't feel as stifled. He's just doing what he was ordered to do.

At rehearsal, I go through the final motions and preparations. Costume designers and makeup artists are all gathered to make sure there are no loose ends.

Philippe tells me to do one last demonstration with Ryan because he wants to see his grasp of the emotions.

We do a few routines in which Philippe criticizes his laziness. Ryan says he had a cramp and will take care of it with the company's physician.

The staff buzz around the empty theater and the other dancers stand behind the curtains, watching us. Stephanie, Philippe, and a few of their assistants are on stage as we're about to perform the routine one final time.

I wipe the sweat off my brow with the back of my hand. I overworked my ankles today and I will pay a visit to Dr. Kim later.

The scene is a solo between me and Albrecht, played by Ryan. It's when I choose to save his life even after he doomed me to death. He didn't do it on purpose, but my life ended as soon as I knew he had a fucking fiancée. A princess.

It's where love proves what it truly is, a masochistic feeling where you want the best for the one you love despite what they've done to you.

Bullshit.

I twirl on pointe for a few seconds, then jump into Ryan's arms a fraction of a second early. He extends his hands, but he misses by a breath.

It's a single breath.

Just one.

Time freezes for a moment and everything turns into white noise.

Both of our eyes widen as I land in an unnatural position. Shock ripples through my leg and then a haunting, ugly sound echoes in the air.

Pop.

TWENTY-TWO

Lia

I T'S A NIGHTMARE.

I wait for it to end.

For reality to kick back in.

I've had a thousand nightmares about breaking my ankle, my hip, my leg.

But no matter how gory or frightening they are, I wake up.

I write notes about them to remind myself they aren't real.

Not this time.

Now, the searing pain is a constant reminder that this is far from a nightmare.

This is reality.

I lie on the hospital bed, my leg in a cast and propped up high on a wedge.

I broke my tibia and the bone punctured the skin. I'll never forget the sight of the bloody white rod protruding through my torn flesh. A surgery was needed to set the bone back in place, one I entered in a state of shock and exited numb.

I held on to the hope that the whole ordeal would be over

with the surgery. That Dr. Kim would tell me it was just fatigue, that I should take my pills and everything would be fine.

He didn't.

Instead, he said the words that almost always end a dancer's or an athlete's career, "We were able to set the bone back in place and suture the wound so that the scarring will be minimal. Fortunately, the fibula wasn't broken, but there will be a permanent deformation near your knee. With rehabilitation, you'll be able to walk normally again and run sometimes, but not for long. A full recovery is, unfortunately, virtually impossible."

In other words, I'll never be able to be a ballerina again.

I'm still not grasping it fully, and it's not only because of the doctor's words. I think I heard the end of my career with that *pop* and the silence and gasps that followed from everyone present.

But at that point, I was still praying for the nightmares that have scared me my whole life. I want the nightmare.

Someone give me the nightmare.

Dr. Kim asks me if he should call someone close, but I don't have anyone. People have friends and family, I have ballet. I sacrificed my youth and my life for it. I survived my parents' deaths and relocating from one country to another with it.

When people went clubbing, I went to rehearsals. When they slept, I timed my stretches and the care of my ankles. When others ate real food, I settled for apples or a salad.

I never considered it a sacrifice or a chore, because I was doing something I loved. Something I was damn good at. I was living my dream and getting rid of my excess energy through flying where no one could catch me.

Now, my wings are broken.

Now, the dream is over.

And I can't bring myself to force those feelings to the surface. Not a single tear leaves my lids as I stare at the hospital room's white ceiling.

There's a soft knock on the door before it opens. Philippe and a teary-eyed Stephanie walk inside.

I stare at them as if they're in a snow globe and I'm looking through blurry glass.

"Oh, Lia!" Stephanie rushes to my side, holding my limp hands in her trembling ones, the tears now running freely down her cheeks. "I'm so sorry, so terribly sorry."

"*Chérie...*" Philippe sounds pained, on the verge of breaking as well.

Their compassion and emotions bounce off my chest and disappear. They're not able to penetrate my numb state or provoke the grief that needs to be let out.

"We can get a second opinion..." Stephanie trails off when Philippe shakes his head at her.

"Can I please be alone?" I whisper in an apathetic tone that I don't recognize.

"Are you going to be okay?" Stephanie asks.

I give a perfunctory nod.

"Call us if you need anything," Philippe says in a voice filled with sympathy.

I can't bring myself to move any of my limbs, so I stare at them until they go out and close the door behind them.

My gaze flits to my cast leg supported in the air. My useless broken leg that ended everything.

I never got to show the world my Giselle. She was killed before she was even born.

And with her death, all of my dreams and my coping mechanisms perished.

I tug on the leg until it falls from the wedge onto the bed. Pain explodes from it, but it's like I'm caught in an alternate reality.

My movements are robotic—mechanical, even—as I sit up and yank the IV tube from my wrist. Droplets of blood trickle down my arm, but I can barely feel the sting.

I swing my good leg to the floor and stand on it, letting my broken one drop with a painful thud.

Dragging it behind me, I gingerly limp to the window and open it. Cold winter air flips my hair back as I pull a chair over and use it to climb onto the ledge, bringing my cast with me. Bursts of pain pulsate harder with every move, but I ignore them.

It'll all end soon.

The freezing air filters through my flimsy hospital gown as I stare down at the moving cars. They look like ants from this height. At least ten stories up.

It'd be easy enough to finish everything, for me not to feel numb and desensitized.

One step.

One breath.

And it'll be all over.

I'll be free.

"Lia."

The sound of my name with that voice scatters my thoughts for a fraction of a second. I stare over my shoulder to find Adrian standing a short distance away from me.

At first, I think he's an illusion. That all of this is my brain's way of seeing him one final time before everything ends.

But the pain in my cast proves this is real. The fact that he's here, looking larger than life, as usual, with his calm expression and his black clothes and brown coat.

"Come down, Lia." His voice is tender, gentle, in complete contradiction with the shadow casting over his face.

I shake my head once. "For nearly twenty years, I've only lived for ballet. Now that it's gone, I have nothing to live for. You said it yourself, I'm lonely and have no friends or family. I only had ballet."

"You can find other things to live for."

I scoff. "No, I can't."

"You can. Circumstances shape you, but they don't dictate your fate." His voice lowers with a soothing undertone. "You do."

I shake my head again as a single hot tear slides down my cheek. "It's over."

"Not if you have a say in it. Whether it's ballet or anything else, you can always rewrite your own story." He reaches a hand out, the corners of his eyes softening for the first time since I've met him. "I'll help you."

"Why would you?" I'm crying now, and even the freezing air is unable to make the tears less hot and stinging.

"Because I want to."

"I will not be your mistress, Adrian. Never."

"You won't be."

"But you have a fiancée."

"Not anymore."

My lips part. "W-what?"

"I got rid of her." He takes a step forward. "Now, come down."

I stare at his hand, at the promise he's offering and what he did. I said I didn't want to be his mistress and he listened.

He got rid of her.

Adrian, of all people, has managed to pull me out of my numb state and provoke my tears.

My full-blown grief.

My hand trembles as I place it in his. As soon as our skin touches, he pulls me down, wrapping both arms around my waist and holding me up so I'm not putting any weight on my legs.

I burrow my face against his shirt through the small opening in his coat. A wracking sob mounts, catching in my throat before it bleeds out of my insides.

For a moment, we stand like that as I cry into his chest, my voice turning hoarse and my head pounding. Through it all,

Adrian holds me in his strong arms, stroking soothing circles on my back and being the silent anchor I didn't realize I needed.

"It hurts…" My voice breaks.

"I'll call the doctor."

"Not that pain." I slam a closed fist against my chest. "Here. It hurts so much, I feel like I'm being cut open by a thousand knives."

Adrian wraps a hand around the back of my head, caressing my hair. "It might feel like you can't take it, like it would be better to die, but that's not true. It'll heal, maybe not right away or in the near future, and it might not heal completely, but the wound will close and you will look back on this day as the moment you changed."

"But I'll be scarred for life," I sob, hitting my chest again. "Right here."

"Scars mean you are alive and strong enough to survive." He kisses the top of my head. "I'll worship each of your scars until you're able to face them, Lenochka."

I lift my eyes to stare at him through my blurry vision. "Why would you?"

There's a softness in his gaze, the closest thing I've seen to affection in them. "I told you. Because I want to."

"What if you stop wanting to?"

"That won't happen. You have my word."

I don't know if it's because of my desperation or the rare tenderness on his face, but in this moment, I believe Adrian.

I believe that this man, this killer, is my only hope to repair my life.

Or what remains of it.

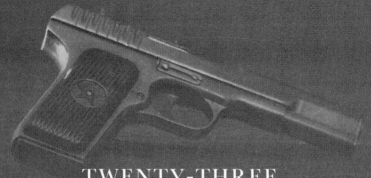

TWENTY-THREE

Adrian

LIA IS FAST ASLEEP AFTER THE NURSE INJECTED HER with tranquilizers.

Her frail hand is weightless in mine, almost like it barely exists.

Tears still cling to her long lashes that are fluttering against her pale cheeks. Even though she's sleeping, her lips remain twisted and her brow is furrowed in discomfort.

I reach out and smooth the crumpled space on her forehead with my thumb. Here's to hoping she doesn't have nightmares tonight, though that's completely wishful thinking.

Since my youth, I've learned to stop wishing for things, because they won't come true. I grew up and made things happen on my own. So knowing that, how come I find myself wishing for a different outcome for Lia's career?

Yan called me as soon as she broke her leg and was transported to the hospital. But I was in a meeting with Igor and Sergei and couldn't answer. My *Pakhan* and my former potential father-in-law are displeased with me for ending my engagement with Kristina so abruptly and without a convincing reason.

Everyone in the brotherhood knows I don't make a move unless I've studied its impact on generations to come. Ending the engagement wasn't a 'me thing' to do, considering that Kristina is the most logical choice for my wife.

However, it seems I'm sacrificing that part of me—the methodical, logical one—more often than not since Lia came into the picture. I do have a plan, though. One that will give Sergei and Igor the reason they need, and, at the same time, give me Lia.

That plan also includes Lazlo Luciano. After the close surveillance I put on him, I have a good handle on his life and his goals. He regards most of the New York Italian families as his enemies, especially the Rozettis since he has a lifelong grudge against them. They feel the same for him because he's made it his mission to wipe them off the face of the earth.

The grudge can be used to my advantage. It's my perfect opportunity to get in Lazlo's good graces without raising his suspicions.

Due to the sensitive nature of my plan, where every detail needs to be in its rightful place, I had to listen to Sergei's and Igor's grumbling all afternoon. That's why I couldn't answer Yan's calls.

As soon as I finished, I found out about Lia's accident and came here. If I'd gotten here even a second later, I would've come to collect her corpse.

I slowly close my eyes, my grip tightening on her hand before I release it and let it rest on the bed. The thought of losing her brings an ache I thought I'd never feel again after Aunt Annika's death.

I will make sure Lia's fate is different from my stepmother's.

Her career is probably finished for good, though. I spoke to her attending physician and he mentioned that the nature of her fracture is impossible to recover from in the professional sense.

Which brings me to the reason behind her *accident*.

I stand up and brush a kiss on Lia's forehead before I turn for the door. After her suicide attempt, I'd rather not leave her side. However, my next course of action needs to happen, if not for anything else, then for her beloved justice.

I meant it when I said that I don't believe in justice, but I do believe in an eye for an eye.

Blood for fucking blood.

Besides, the sooner I'm done with this, the faster I can get back here and take care of her.

The moment I step out of her room, Yan, Kolya, and Boris stand erect, their expressions more closed off than usual. Kolya and Boris were with me all day, but Yan hasn't left Lia's side.

"Did you see it with your own eyes?" I ask Yan, not that I need a reason to get on with my plan.

"Yes, sir," he snarls. "That motherfucker did it on purpose."

I stare at Kolya. "Have you managed to get me footage?"

He nods, then shows me his phone. My three guards and I watch as the scene unfolds in front of our eyes. It's not that I doubt Yan's words, but I want to see it for myself—the exact moment when the fucker signed his death certificate.

The shocked expression on Lia's features guts me. She must've known it was going to be the end as she was falling, and that pain, that desperation, makes me clench my fists on either side of me.

"Have you located him?" I ask Kolya with a calm I don't feel.

"He's at a club. One of our men, Fedor, is keeping an eye on him."

"At a fucking club," Yan snarls. "I'm going to torture the bastard to death."

I shake my head once. "You stay here, Yan."

"But, Boss—"

"Stay here and protect her until I get back."

"Why can't Boris do it? I want to kill the fucker."

"Yan. It's an order."

He opens his mouth to say something, but Kolya shakes his head at him before he and Boris follow me out.

My knuckles hurt from the amount of clenching I do during the ride to confront Ryan. My guard, Fedor, calls us and says he left the club alone and he's following him home, and since I've had my men watching him, we know the route he'll take.

Kolya strategizes with him so we can intercept Ryan in the alley he always drives through. Fedor hits his car from behind and we're already waiting for Ryan in the shadows.

Ryan gets out, cursing and checking his car. He doesn't sway on his feet, so he must've not drunk a lot.

I step out of the vehicle at the same time as Fedor, who nods at me. Boris and Kolya stand on either side of Ryan so that the four of us are surrounding him.

The fucker turns around, his expression ashen as he meets my gaze. I see the exact moment when he knows he's fucked.

People know when death is coming. Sometimes, they can feel it and hope leaves their greedy eyes. Some fight, some know it's useless. Others fight even when they know it's useless.

Like Ryan.

"What…what do you want from me?" He stares at me, then at my men, looking like he's ready to piss his pants. "I didn't do anything."

I step in front of him, retrieving my gun with the silencer attached to it. "Yes, you did, Ryan. I should've killed you that night at the club. A mistake I will not repeat again."

"No, please… I…I kept my distance…"

"Then you decided not to catch her at the last second."

His eyes widen.

"Did you think I wouldn't know? I saw the sadism in your eyes when you decided you wouldn't catch her."

"No… Everyone witnessed it… She jumped a second too early."

"You could've caught her. You just chose not to." I point the gun at him. "That's your final fucking strike."

"No, please, please…"

"We'll start with the legs, then I'll make you beg to be killed. Only after you've paid for every tear she's shed will you be allowed the mercy of death."

I shoot him in the tibia, right where her leg broke.

Ryan shrieks like a toddler as blood explodes from his wound. As he falls to his knees, I shoot his thigh.

He wails, his ugly voice bouncing off the buildings and fueling my need to inflict more pain. Pain greater than what Lia will be going through.

This is going to be a long night.

When I'm done with this scum, he'll disappear as if he never existed.

Just like her career.

This is my form of fucking justice.

TWENTY-FOUR

Lia

I SPEND THE NEXT TWO WEEKS AT HOME, RECOVERING.

Or more accurately, trying to survive my mind.

Every day, I wake from a nightmare replaying the moment I fell, the exact moment the haunting sound of my leg breaking echoing in the air.

And every time, soothing hands wrap around me, pulling me close to a strong chest. A chest that I've grown so used to along with the compassion that comes with it.

A compassion I never believed Adrian to be capable of.

He didn't leave my side during the first couple of days, but then he had to go back to his work. I don't want to think about the fact that he's going back to torture and kill people, that after caring for me, he went back to destruction.

But it's not like I could stop him. Adrian made it clear that he enjoys what he does, and there's nothing I can do or say that will change his mind.

Not having him around is hard. It's even harder than I would like to admit.

Since I took Adrian's hand and cried into his chest,

something between us changed. The bridge I thought was ruined has been slowly building since that day. It might have something to do with his attentiveness or silent support, but he's become a pillar in my life. He distracts me from my head and every vile emotion that comes with it.

But when he's gone, all those emotions barge back in.

The walls close in on me as if intending to trap me in the confines of the dark box from my childhood. I keep stealing peeks at my ballet clothes, at the shoes and the leotards, and try not to break down all over again.

I deleted my Instagram account and all of my socials to get a reprieve from the outside world and the press.

Stephanie and Philippe have been calling and tried to visit, but I avoided their advances and changed my number. They're associated with the world I can't go back to. Seeing them and talking to them would only bring that fact to the forefront of my head.

Besides, after my injury, the entire crew had to start anew and delay the opening. I bet Hannah is ecstatic to play Giselle instead of me.

I lean against my crutch, facing the closet, looking at all of my leotards, tutus, tights, and ballet shoes. I don't know how long I stand here, staring at the evidence of my ended career, but it's long enough that my injury under the cast tingles.

Then I charge inside and bring every last piece of clothing down, tossing the hangers and the shoes. I try ripping the leotards with my hands and lose my balance, falling to the floor. I crawl to a drawer, yank it open, and grab the scissors. Then I cut through every piece of ballet clothing, destroying the muslin and tulle and everything I once considered beautiful.

I kill the remainder of the dream that was murdered for me.

Maybe this will help me get free. Maybe the walls of my

apartment will stop closing in on me as if they're monsters. Every corner of this place reminds me of ballet, of dancing, of rehearsing on my own until I exhausted myself.

When I first got this place with my extravagant salary, I felt proud to have a place of my own, to have accomplished this with my skills. But now, it feels like my custom-made hell. One I can't escape.

I need to kill all the memories associated with ballet so I can live. So I can find another path for myself.

Even if the idea brings burning tears to my eyes.

Due to my injury, my contract was terminated with the New York City Ballet, and although I got a generous compensation wired to my bank account, I couldn't care less about it.

I have a small fortune that's able to sustain me for a long time, but it was never about the money for me.

Ballet was my defense mechanism against my screwed-up head. Now that I don't have it anymore, how am I going to stay sane?

The front door clicks open, but I don't stop ripping through the clothes. It isn't until a shadow falls over me that I finally look up. I figure it's Adrian, but it's daytime and he never shows up before nightfall.

Yan stares down at me with a softened expression. It's not exactly pity, but it's something more subtle. I don't ask why he has the code to my apartment since Adrian must've given it to him in case of an emergency.

"Don't even try to stop me." My voice is brittle. "I need to do this to get it out of my system."

"Want me to help?"

My lips part. "Would you?"

"If you'd like."

"Can you bring them all down?"

He gives a curt nod and methodically knocks down every hanger, skirt, leotard, tutu, and shoe. He even pulls out the drawers with my glitter makeup and jewelry, surrounding me with them.

As he does that, I cut through everything in sight, slicing it all to shreds. Yan stands there watching me with his eternal cool.

By the time I've cut through most everything, I grow lethargic, my anger and grief slowly subsiding. Yan is still in his usual position, hands crossed in front of him.

"Do you think I'm insane?" I murmur.

"I think you're just in pain."

I sniffle, even though there are no tears. I cried enough for a lifetime the day Adrian saved me from my own mind and hugged me. He held me like he wanted to protect me, like protecting me is his mission in life.

"Can you get rid of these?" I ask Yan.

"Will do."

"The awards, too. I want them gone."

"If you want."

I pause, staring at the scissors in my hand. "Where does Adrian go during the day?"

I hate to admit that I miss him and his words, no matter how few they are. Since the day at the hospital, he's been the one person who can get me out of my head.

It's a strange change of dynamics. Before, the only time Adrian and I could get along was when he was fucking me or sexually punishing me. But during these past couple of weeks, his touch has never gone in that direction. He's only held me, made sure I ate, and helped me shower and change clothes. He sat with me underneath my wool blanket as I watched a mindless movie and then maneuvered my head on his lap so that I was more comfortable. His fingers stroked my hair back in a way that made me nearly purr like a kitten.

I've been feeding off that care like a starved animal who's never had affection.

"He works," Yan says.

"I know that, genius. Where? With whom?"

"He mostly works at home with Kolya."

I pause at that information. Aside from the first restaurant date, Adrian and I only ever meet here, so I never considered the notion that he has a separate home.

"He doesn't go to do mafia things?"

Yan smiles at that. "He does those mafia things at home. He doesn't go out unless absolutely necessary."

For some reason, that makes me feel more at ease. At least he's not in danger of being shot in the streets like all those mob bosses I read about.

And yes, I might have searched about the mafia's history in New York. But the articles are filled with stuff about the Italian mafia and their hits. There's little to no information about the Bratva. I'm not surprised, though. Taking Adrian's secretive nature into account, I assume the rest of his organization is similar to him.

But I still haven't been able to get those images of assassinated mob people out of my head, and I recently started having nightmares about Adrian suffering from something similar.

Wait. Does that mean I'm worried about him?

"Miss."

I stare up at Yan. "Yeah?"

"Let me help you up."

"I can get up on my own." I get on my good knee, pull my crutch over, and lean all my weight on it to stand. Yan's body is turned toward me, ready to catch me if I fall, but I manage to stay upright, keeping my cast off the ground.

"What about...*her?*" I whisper.

He raises a brow. "Her?"

"Kristina Petrov." I haven't talked to Adrian about his engagement since that night in the hospital, and part of the reason is because I wanted to live in this peace for a while. To not think about the fact that I took another woman's fiancé.

"I believe he ended it."

"You *believe*? As in, you're not sure?"

"It's better if you ask him about it."

"Tell me, Yan. What's going on?"

He runs a hand through his long hair. "You didn't hear it from me."

"Cross my heart."

He smiles again, and I'm struck by how pretty he really is. If he hadn't chosen the mafia life, he would've been a perfect model.

"So?" I urge.

"Remember when I told you Boss is expected to marry Kristina?"

I nod.

"Just because he wants out of it doesn't mean he can. Not only is Igor, Kristina's father, a powerful member of the Bratva who will take no disrespect, but the *Pakhan* himself is also against ending the engagement."

My heart shrinks and any semblance of peace I managed to feel the past couple of weeks crumbles. "So, what? He will *marry* her?"

"I don't know. He's thinking of solutions to get out of it, but if he doesn't come up with a reason that will satisfy both Igor and the *Pakhan*, he'll be put in a bad position and might lose his power within the Bratva."

My stomach churns and its contents nearly spill to the ground.

Either Adrian marries Kristina or he'll lose his power.

I know exactly which option he will choose. He lives for power, control, and patterns. He'll never sacrifice his work for someone like me.

Besides, I shouldn't want him to. It's not like I love him or anything.

My chest squeezes as I softly thank Yan and hobble back to

the bedroom. He brings in large bags from the kitchen and gets rid of the torn clothes and everything in the closet.

As I sit on the bed, the only thing I can think of is how Adrian will marry Kristina.

The beautiful Russian Kristina, who was basically made to be his wife.

A dark emotion simmers underneath my skin, one even I don't recognize, but there's one thing I do recognize.

I need to stop him from marrying her.

꙳

Another week goes by and I fall into a loathsome routine. My lack of purpose is eating away at my soul. I'm so used to conditioning or rehearsing, and now that all of it is gone, I feel a hole eating away at my soul.

I try going out to the park and Yan accompanies me, sometimes with another guard named Boris. I hate it when Boris joins us, because Yan doesn't act as carefree as when it's just me and him.

Then I go back home and start dabbling in cooking to occupy my time. Adrian doesn't like that, however, because my leg is still in the cast and he says I stand for too long.

But I need to do something; otherwise, I'll go out of my mind waiting for him to come back.

I've become attuned to his footsteps. They're heavier and more powerful than Yan's, but still silent enough considering his build. Like right now.

His scent sometimes precedes him, or maybe I've gotten so used to him that I can smell him, even from a long distance away. I can get lost in that wood and leather scent, like it's the only one I've ever smelled.

I scramble to my feet from my position in front of the TV and go to meet him. Adrian is removing his coat and hanging it by the entrance, revealing his white shirt and black pants. Not a day has passed where he hasn't looked breathtakingly beautiful in a rugged sort of way.

Dangerous, too.

But I guess some part of me yearns for that danger, or I wouldn't have fallen for him so easily. And I need that danger to make me forget about the black hole eating away at my soul.

Nowadays, I don't get to see him for long or touch him enough. Well, I don't touch him, anyway, since he's the only one who does that. Even though he doesn't leave until after I wake up, he usually spends the entire night on his phone, typing away. Sometimes, he steps out to talk to Yan and Kolya. He barely sleeps by my side and he's stopped initiating sex.

From the day he barged into my life until the evening of my accident, he never once spent a night without fucking me. And now that the sexual touch is gone, I feel an emptiness like nothing before. I went years without sex with other people, but it never had the impact these past twenty-one days have. Actually, it's been twenty-five since that day he fucked me against the wall.

And no, I'm not counting.

It doesn't help that he's getting more attractive, too much for his own good. Or maybe I'm just getting sexually frustrated.

Adrian releases a breath when he sees me in the entrance leaning my useless leg against my other one. "You shouldn't put pressure on your injury, Lia."

"It's okay."

He narrows his eyes.

"It's *fine*. Jesus. Are you the vocabulary police?"

"Only when it comes to that word." He reaches me in two strides and picks me up, carrying me and the crutch in his arms. It's the closest I'm able to get to him lately, and that's probably why I make it a habit to greet him at the door every day.

I wrap my arms around his neck and search his harsh but

ethereal gray eyes and the light in them. There are exhaustion lines on his face, and it takes everything in me not to smooth the crease between his brows.

Yan refuses to divulge much about Adrian's business, but I can tell he's been overworking himself lately. If anything, coming here is taking more time and effort than he probably should give.

I want to ask about Kristina, but fear of his answer always stops me. What if I've been a mistress all along and I just don't know it yet?

Adrian sets me on the sofa and places the crutch by my side. "Wait here. I'll get dinner."

"I ordered takeout. It's on the counter."

He raises a brow. "Are you finally listening to me, Lenochka?"

I lift a shoulder. "I didn't like the scent of food when I was cooking."

Adrian observes me for a second, and it's intrusive, as if he's peeling away the exterior and trying to peer at what's inside. I don't think I'll ever get used to being the subject of his interest. It always feels odd, yet strangely endearing, for a cold man like him to care about me.

He's cold to the world, but not to me.

Then he strides into the kitchen. The TV is on, broadcasting some cooking show, but my entire attention is on his agile movements, on the easy and purposeful way he moves around the room, setting out the food with plates and utensils.

Soon after, I hobble to the table and he sits beside me with the containers between us. I ordered Lebanese because I had it in my teens, and it's remained on my mind ever since. Since I can eat anything—and that's not just limited to salad anymore—I've been stuffing myself like a pig. I don't even know where I got the sudden appetite from.

Adrian doesn't comment on my choice of cuisine, digging in

without any fuss. Now that I think about it, he's never mentioned disliking anything.

"Is there any food you don't eat?" I ask.

"Not really." He stares at his phone that's lying on his lap.

"Not a fussy eater?"

"I didn't have that luxury when I was growing up."

I recall what he said about his mother being a mistress who killed his stepmother. That she was a villain.

"Were you poor?"

He chews slowly and swallows. I think he uses that time to consider his reply before speaking it aloud. "Not really. My mother was a doctor, but she didn't like cooking, so I had to fix my own food."

"I'm sorry."

"I'm not. It's better that way." His gaze slides from the phone to me. "Are you a fussy eater?"

"I hate seafood."

"Really?"

"I can't stand it. I feel like I'm eating the sea's cockroaches."

That makes a small smile crack on his beautiful face. I love it when I'm the reason behind his smile. Could be because they're as rare as hell or that he looks lethally attractive.

"No cockroaches. Noted."

We fall into easy conversation about food and different cultures and I'm impressed by how much Adrian knows. He's definitely more well-traveled than me.

After we finish eating, he takes the empty containers to the kitchen, disposing of them while still watching his phone. It finally rings and he picks up after a few seconds, his tone firm. "Volkov."

He listens for a beat and his face relaxes as he answers with a thick Russian accent, "Name a time and place, Don."

Don?

As in, the Italian mafia?

"I'll see you then," he says, hanging up.

When he returns to the living room, he appears less tense than he did earlier.

"You have to go somewhere?" I ask.

"Not today." He pauses. "But starting tomorrow, I might not come over for a few days."

"Why?" My voice is spooked.

"Business."

"Are you sure it's not because of your fiancée?"

He frowns. "I told you she's no longer my fiancée."

"Is it as easy as you make it seem?"

"Why wouldn't it be?"

"Tell me, Adrian. Am I your mistress?"

"Why? What are you going to do about it?"

"I begged you not to put me in that position."

His eyes darken, and I can see him wanting to put me in my place using his domineering power like the other times. I brace myself for it, but he just releases a long sigh. "You're not."

"How can I be sure?"

"You'll have to trust me."

"Yeah, right." I stand up abruptly and the world spins. A strong sense of nausea hits me and I clutch my stomach from the force of it.

Adrian is by my side in a second, grabbing me by the arm. "Lia? What is it...?"

"I think I'm going to throw up," I manage between gritted teeth.

Adrian lifts me in his arms and hurries to the bathroom, then carefully helps me lower myself in front of the toilet. I grab it and empty my dinner in violent heaves.

Strong hands stroke my back in soothing circles as my stomach releases ugly sounds.

By the time I finish, Adrian is crouching by my side and says with utter calm, "Let's get you to the doctor."

"Why?"

"I think you're pregnant."

TWENTY-FIVE

Lia

I STARE AT THE SMALL GRAY DOT ON THE ULTRASOUND monitor, my lips parting.

Adrian was right. I am pregnant. Five weeks.

First, the OB-GYN confirmed it through a blood test, and she's now showing us the baby.

I've been shocked, numb, like the day I got out of surgery to learn I could no longer be a ballerina.

But the moment I see that life? Something inside me shifts.

At first, I wanted to demand an abortion because of ballet. But I don't have ballet anymore, and whether I have children or not will have no effect on my ended career.

But now, as I watch the tiny figure on the screen, strong feelings like I haven't had since the day my career ended invade me all at once.

That baby is mine. Something I conceived.

A tenacious life which survived all the stress I've been through up until now.

I stare up at Adrian, who's standing next to my hospital bed, also observing what will soon grow into a fetus, in his utter calm. He's been like a rock during this entire night—carrying me, taking care of procedures, and being the anchor anyone would hope for.

However, he hasn't shown a single reaction since the doctor confirmed his suspicion. Although it wasn't really a suspicion since he announced it before the doctor did.

My eyes widen. Did he…do this on purpose?

The thought thunders through the rest of me like wildfire. When I told the doctor that I'm on birth control pills, she mentioned that the pill isn't one hundred percent effective, especially if I didn't take it at the same time every day.

But pregnancy would've been so much more probable if he actually switched my pills out.

The feelings I was basking in only a few seconds ago slowly evaporate as I focus on the man standing beside me. And not just any man, a killer and a mobster. I can't let someone like him father my children. How the hell did I allow myself to be even the slightest bit happy about the idea?

The doctor offers me the sonogram picture, but I don't take it, afraid to look at that life one more time. Adrian thanks her, pulling it from her hand. I go through the motions as I cover myself and grab my crutch to stand up.

Adrian tries to help me, but I squirm free. He gives me a look and grabs me by the elbow, forbidding me from getting away from him until he helps me into a chair in front of the doctor's desk.

Instead of taking his own seat, he remains standing by my side. "Is her injury going to cause a problem with the pregnancy?"

The doctor, a middle-aged lady with soft features and her white hair done in a pixie cut, says in a melodious voice, "Not at all. Thankfully, the injury didn't happen during one of her late trimesters. When do you get the cast off, Ms. Morelli?"

"In three weeks," I murmur.

"It should be fine, but until then, please pay extra attention to your stress levels. The first pregnancies are usually the most fragile."

Adrian gives a curt nod, schedules an upcoming appointment, and leads me out of the office.

I pull away from him as soon as we're down the hall, hobbling as fast as my crutch allows me to do so.

He catches up to me, grabs me by the waist, and glues me to his side. Then he speaks in a low, threatening tone, "That's the second and final time you flinch away from me. And walk slowly so you don't put too much pressure on your leg."

"Stop it," I hiss, twisting against him.

"Stop what?"

"Stop acting like the most caring person alive when you planned this all along."

"This?"

I halt near a fire escape staircase and point a finger at the envelope in his hand. "You switched my pills to make *that* happen."

His expression remains the same, as if I didn't say anything. "You were pregnant before I had to do that."

My lips part. "You…you planned it?"

"Yes."

"You really switched my pills?"

"I said I didn't have to. As the doctor said, birth control pills aren't a hundred percent effective."

His methodical, apathetic tone, coupled with his words, nearly send me into a state of hysteria and pure black rage. It takes everything in me not to shout as if I've lost my mind. "Are you even hearing yourself? How could you do this to me?"

"I didn't."

"You were planning to."

"For the *third* time, I didn't have to."

"But you wanted to. Why the hell would you even want to impregnate me?"

"Because it's the only way to keep you close." He checks his watch. "Speaking of which. I think we can make it."

"Make it where?"

He places his phone to his ear as he slowly but firmly guides me to the elevator. "I need a priest. Wake him up if you have to… We're heading to the church…make sure Emily has everything she needs before we get there."

The door of the elevator shuts and we head to the parking lot as he makes two more calls, speaking in Russian.

By the time he's finished, I'm breathing so harshly, I can barely focus on what's going on around me. "What are you doing, Adrian?"

"We're getting married."

The words leave him with utter ease, as if they're the most normal occurrence, as if he didn't just suggest that we take vows when we barely know each other.

"Please tell me you're joking."

He stares down on me. "I told you I don't do that."

I'm about to wiggle free, but he pins me in place, his eyes darkening with a warning. "Stay still and stop aggravating your injury."

"I won't marry you! That's for devoted couples, not for… for…*us*!"

"You're pregnant with my child. There doesn't need to be any other reason."

"Of course there does."

"Not for me."

"I *need* more, Adrian."

"Too bad you don't get to decide, Lenochka."

Frustrated tears well in my eyes and I suck in a deep breath. "We didn't even discuss the child, and now you're talking about a wedding?"

"Why?" He tilts his head to the side. "Were you considering not keeping it?"

Was I? No, not really. But I didn't even get to think properly about how I will go about this. Ideally, I want Adrian away from me and the child until I clear my head. Marriage is the last thing I want right now.

"People have kids outside of marriage," I try to bargain.

His eyes flash with menace more terrifying than I've ever witnessed before. His jaw clenches when he speaks in a low tone, "My child will *not* be born outside of marriage. Is that fucking clear?"

My spine snaps upright at the change in his demeanor. This is the first time the calm façade has cracked and I've actually seen him this angry, this callous, and without any semblance of light in his gray eyes.

That's when I recall what he said. Adrian was a mistress's son. *Shit*. No wonder he doesn't want to put his offspring in the same position.

But that doesn't give him the right to force me into this marriage.

"At least give me time to think about it." I sigh with resolution.

"And then what? You think you get to say no?"

Of course he won't allow me such an option. So I try to appeal to any sliver of humanity inside him. "I'm barely surviving the end of my career, Adrian."

If I expected any sympathy, I find nothing in his closed off face. "You'll survive it better when you have something to occupy your time."

"Wow, great. Thanks for thinking of me."

"Drop the sarcasm, Lia. It doesn't suit you."

"So now you know everything about me?"

"Not everything, no, but I know this is happening tonight."

I try to free myself from him, but that only manages to tighten his hold around me. "Just give me time. Let me process this."

"You'll have all the time you need to process it afterward."

The elevator door opens before I can utter a word and Adrian carries me to the awaiting car.

Kolya and Yan are in the front, and the latter gives me a sympathetic look as his colleague drives away.

The news of the pregnancy has become the least of my problems now that he's using it to make me marry him.

"Adrian…"

He faces me with an exasperated look. "What, Lia? What is it?"

"Don't make me do this."

"Would you rather I go back to Kristina and marry her?"

"W-what? What does she have to do with anything?"

"It's either you or her, and if you play stubborn and say I should go to her, I'm going to make you watch me marry her, then fuck her to put an heir inside her."

I gasp, the image forming in my head as if it's indeed a reality. I can clearly imagine Adrian's glorious naked body powering into the beautiful tall blonde, and bile rises to my throat, threatening to empty my stomach again.

He…wouldn't be so cruel as to do that, right?

The question must be written all over my face, because Adrian grabs my hand and leans over to whisper in harsh words, "Go ahead, Lia. Make the foolish choice if you're ready to bear the consequences. But understand this, I'm never letting you go. I'll make you watch me with Kristina every night before I fuck you. She'll have to adopt your child as hers, too, because I will not allow my offspring to be treated as a bastard. So what's it going to be? A wife or a mistress?"

A tear rolls down my cheeks, clinging to my lips as I taste salt. I have no doubt that he'll make true of his word, that he'd torment me in such a way so I'd regret going against him.

"You're a monster," I breathe out.

"And you're marrying this monster." He releases me with a

shove and I glue myself to the back seat, my heart nearly hammering out of my chest.

He's really left me no choice. He knows I would never be the mistress, no matter what. That I would rather go through any craziness he's planning instead of being his side piece while another woman is his wife.

And not only that, but the jerk would take my child away, too.

When we arrive at a large old building, nausea fills my stomach.

We're at a church.

He'll really make me marry him tonight.

Adrian carries me out of the car and leads me to a back door. A blonde in a sharp skirt suit greets us with a smile.

"Mr. Volkov." She nods at me. "Miss."

"Do you have everything ready, Emily?" he asks with his non-negotiable Russian accent.

"Yes, sir. Everything's as instructed."

"Make it quick." He places me to my feet.

I'm thinking of ways to somehow escape when hot breaths tickle my ear and he whispers, "If you resist, let alone attempt to run, I'll catch you and we'll do it my way. I assure you that's the last thing you'd want, Lia."

And with that, he turns around and leaves, utterly sure that I won't do it.

And to be even more certain, a few black cars line the perimeter of the church, all of them filled with men dressed in black, like Yan and Kolya.

He brought his guards to the ceremony. Isn't that romantic?

Emily leads me inside and introduces me to two of her helpers. I'm back to the numb state as I let them treat me like Adrian's doll.

The asshole.

The fucking asshole.

Every time I think we're falling into some sort of an understanding, he does something to prove his monstrous nature. I sometimes get the idea that he might care for me, but it'll always be his way or the highway.

Emily and her helpers don't waste any time. They wash my hair and pull it up in an elegant twist before carefully attaching a long veil to it.

After that, they apply a natural touch of makeup, painting my lips a soft pink.

Soon enough, I'm dressed in a white silk wedding dress with a large skirt that covers my cast. Its train is long and circular, matching the length of the veil.

The dress has a jewel neckline with a lace V-back that shows my skin. It's elegant and fits me to perfection, as if it's been specially made for me—which I wouldn't put past Adrian.

"Is this tailored?" I ask Emily, who's fussing with the veil.

"Yes, miss." She beams. "We're so glad we had it made in such a short time."

"How long?"

"About a month."

Since before I found out about the engagement. Adrian ordered for this dress to be made while he was engaged to Kristina. He's intended to marry me since then.

I don't know what to think about that. Should I be flattered? Angry? Both?

Emily says I should stay in my flat shoe since it'll keep me comfortable. Besides, it's covered by the dress, anyway. After finalizing the look, she retrieves a camera and grins. "Smile."

I don't know if I do as she takes the picture. I stare at my reflection in the long mirror and it's like I don't recognize myself. I look beautiful with slightly red cheeks, like a blushing bride.

But it's the exact opposite.

That red is for anger, for the way Adrian is taking everything away and not giving me a choice.

Though he did give me one—being his wife or his mistress—but that's merely another way of manipulating me. He never intended to go with my decision, not after he spent nearly a month preparing me a wedding dress.

Or maybe he would've thrown it away and had another one made for Kristina.

One thing's for certain, I now know he'll never let me go.

"You're good to go, miss." Emily smiles. "Want me to help you?"

"No, thanks."

I lean on my crutch, head held high as I step out of the room. If I'm going to sacrifice myself, I'm not doing it with tears in my eyes or like a damsel in distress.

Because there are no knights in shining armor. What waits for me at the end of the aisle is a monster.

One I willingly let into my body and nearly allowed to destroy my soul.

Not anymore.

Adrian has added a black jacket to his outfit and stands in front of a sleepy-looking priest, with Kolya and Yan by his side. Other than that, the church is empty.

I hobble toward him and refuse to stare at the slight awe in his eyes, at how his expression lights for a bit before it completely closes off like the rest of him.

The moment I'm within reach, he squeezes my waist, and in spite of my crutch, he carefully pulls me close so his chest nearly crashes against mine.

The stormy winter skies in his eyes bore into mine as he orders the priest, "Start."

I don't want to look at his eyes or get caught in the lack of empathy there. Sometimes, they're too apathetic, too black. Like now.

However, there's something else in there, something akin to carnal possession.

I rip my gaze from his to focus on the priest, an old man with a half-bald head who speaks with a thick Russian accent.

"Skip that," Adrian orders again when he starts to talk about marriage and its values.

"Do you, Adrian Volkov, take Lia Morelli as your wedded wife, to be with you always, in wealth and in poverty, in disease and in health, in happiness and in grief, from this day until death do you part?"

"I do," Adrian says with so much conviction, I want to stab him for taking such vows so recklessly.

The priest turns toward me. "Do you, Lia Morelli, take Adrian Volkov as your wedded husband, to be with you always, in wealth and in poverty, in disease and in health, in happiness and in grief, from this day until death do you part?"

I stare at Adrian, at the promise of retaliation in his closed off features if I don't say the words he wants me to.

He really shouldn't have threatened me, because now, I'll be completely on board with Luca's plan. If not for anything else, then to get rid of him and the negative influence he has on my life.

Ever since he walked into it, I've lost complete control and I need to get it back.

During the past few weeks, I was planning to tell Luca I wouldn't spy on the man who's taking care of me, but Adrian showed me his true colors tonight.

"I do," I say meekly, with no emotions at all.

"Are you sure, miss?" the priest asks, and Adrian stares at him as if contemplating whether or not he should chop his head off.

"I am," I say. Because I'm going to make Adrian regret everything he's made me live through since the day I first saw him in my parking garage. While I was ready to overlook that with the connection I thought we'd formed, nothing can forgive what he's done to me tonight.

I'm still not over my ended career, but now, I find myself pregnant and also forced to marry him.

Adrian takes two small boxes from Kolya and slides a diamond ring onto my finger. It's big, perfectly cut, and elegant. Simple and a flawless fit. However, I find no joy looking at it. If anything, it feels like an imaginary weight on my hand.

He places the other ring, a simple white gold band, in my palm and I turn off my emotions as I glide it onto his finger.

"I now pronounce you husband and wife," the priest says with a regretful tone. Maybe he knows exactly what type of man Adrian actually is and he's pitying me. "You may kiss the bride."

Adrian pulls me against his chest as he grabs me by my nape. "You're now mine, Mrs. Volkov."

I hate having his last name attached to mine. For some reason, it feels like I've sold my soul to the devil.

Worse, I actually married him.

But while Adrian considers this a win, for me, it's only the beginning.

He forced me to be his wife? Fine.

But it's by his wife's hands that his life will end.

I don't close my eyes as he presses his lips to mine. His kiss is all-consuming and meant to dominate me, to tear all my walls down.

But I've already lost everything.

Now, all I can do is win.

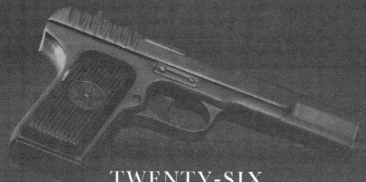

TWENTY-SIX

Adrian

I T'S DONE.

Lia is now my wife, bound to me for life, whether she likes it or not.

If I wasn't so pressed for time, I would've done this under different circumstances, after her leg was healed. It would've happened anyway, but my methods could've been gentler.

However, not only did she fall pregnant sooner than I expected, but I also finally have an alliance with Lazlo Luciano without having to get her involved.

I planned it for weeks on end, creating the perfect circumstances so I'd somehow end up in the same club as Lazlo during a meeting with one of the other Italian families, the Rozettis.

I had to make Yan into an assassin, have him kill one of the other Italians to save Lazlo, who's always been at the crux of territorial wars. Even though the Lucianos have been ruling with an iron fist, they have a bloody history with the Rozettis, so it wasn't a first that one of them would try to kill him.

By killing one of their capos and saving Lazlo's life, I

assured myself a direct line to the Don of the Lucianos. One he confirmed when he invited me to his house over a phone call.

Today has been productive.

My gaze flits to Lia, who's sitting beside me in the car. She stopped pleading and trying to escape her fate, the desperation replaced by quietness. Maybe tying the knot has made her realize that there's no way out for her.

Though I doubt she'll accept it that so easily. She's never really gotten used to having me in her life, and now, I've taken it a step further. But as I said, she'll have all the time in the world to process it. After she's safe from everyone—aside from me.

I take my time observing her as the lights outside reflect off her soft features. Her hands lie limply on her lap. They're as delicate as the rest of her—breakable, even.

Just like her leg.

When her dream shattered in front of her, I felt a twisting in my gut. One I haven't experienced since Aunt Annika's death. I wanted to shield her from the world and everyone in it, and I knew that the only way to do that would be to bring her under my protection—officially.

She'd become a target, too, but as long as she's in my sights at all times, I'll be able to take care of her. Because there's no way in fuck anyone is taking her away from me.

I may not be able to fully grasp the extent of my obsession with her, but the need to protect her and own every inch of her is a raging, insatiable beast.

Lia is still that delicate flower. However, there's always been a simmering strength behind her apparent fragility. An inner energy humming under the surface, waiting for a chance to burst free. I've felt it when she's underneath me while I'm fucking her, and also during her nightmares.

She bottles things up until they eventually explode, whether in the form of passion or bad dreams, no one knows.

The dress is a perfect fit, hugging her soft curves and enhancing her elegance. This look is probably my favorite of hers, not only because of the wedding dress, but also because of what it signifies.

She's my bride.

My wife.

Fucking *mine*.

A dark sense of obsession takes hold of me, urging me to rip off that dress and sink inside her tight heat.

It takes everything in me to stop such thoughts and focus on what's left to do tonight.

"This isn't the way to my apartment," she says meekly, her voice quiet.

"We're not going back to your apartment. Ever."

"What?"

"The lease is ending in a month, anyway. Besides, as my wife, you'll live in my house."

Her hands ball into fists. "When were you going to inform me of such facts?"

"I just did."

Her sharp glare cuts to me like a double-edged sword. "What if I said I don't want to leave my apartment?"

"Then you'd be lying, and I told you not to do that. You've been suffocating in there for the past couple of weeks, getting more depressed by the day because it reminds you of ballet."

"And your house will be the magical solution?"

"Probably. It's also better secured." And I can leave her without obsessively watching the cameras and splitting up my guards all over the place to keep her safe.

Her lips purse as if she wants to argue more but thinks better of it. "I want my things from my apartment."

"They will be in my house tomorrow."

"Why can't we go now?"

"Because we have somewhere else to be."

A delicate frown creases her features. "We're not going to your house?"

"Not yet."

"Why not?"

"You need to pay respects to my *Pakhan* first."

Her face pales and her throat bobs with a gentle swallow as her voice lowers. "Do I have to?"

"Yes. We already got married without his presence and we can't forgo this step. You don't have to talk. Just kiss his hand when he offers it—that's all."

"Does this mean I'll be part of your organization now?" She sounds spooked—terrified, even—but what she doesn't understand is that her taking this step was merely a matter of time. It would've happened anyway, and the sooner she accepts it, the better.

"You're part of me, Lia. That's all you need to worry about."

Her lips part as if to say something, but she purses them again and stares out the window until we reach Sergei's house.

I help her out, then lift her in my arms when she struggles with her long dress and the crutch. I expect her to fight, but she doesn't, her tiny body remains inert against mine as I carry her inside.

Only Kolya follows us in as Sergei's guards nod at my entering. Lia watches her surroundings like a cornered animal searching for an escape, her brow creasing deeper the farther I stride up the stairs and down the hall.

While her arms are around my neck, her attention is elsewhere. I will have to deal with her attempts to pull away from me whether in body or in mind later.

I put her to her feet a few steps away from Sergei's office, and Kolya hands her the crutch. Before I can say anything, the door opens and Vladimir steps outside.

He pauses at the sight of us and runs his gaze over Lia in

a mechanical observation. Even though there's no other intent behind it, I'm tempted to poke his eyes out.

Lia steps into my side and I relish in the fact that she's chosen me as protection. In her eyes, Vladimir is a bulky bearded man with a permanent scowl, who appears as if he's ready to murder everyone in his path.

Since I've known him for many years, I don't see him as a threat. However, this is Lia's first encounter with him, and the initial impression people usually have of Vladimir is that he's deadly, probably the most dangerous-looking among the elite.

"Is this why you asked for a meeting with Sergei?" he asks in Russian.

"Yes, but I don't see why you should be here," I answer in the same language.

"I came for other matters." He stares at Lia one last time, then shakes his head and leaves.

I take Lia's frigid hand in mine and lead her to the door. "Not a word," I remind her before I knock.

"Come in," Sergei says in Russian.

I push the door open and she hobbles on her crutch, following me.

We stop in the middle of Sergei's grandiose study which was originally his brother's, the late *Pakhan*, Nikolai. He hasn't changed a thing about it, as if he's keeping Nikolai's memory alive through the grim decor and the countless book editions in Russian.

Sergei is sitting in the lounge area with Igor across from him. I called him over, too, because he needs to see this for himself.

After I broke off the engagement with his daughter, Igor demanded my punishment from the *Pakhan*, but since I'm Sergei's 'golden boy,' as Kirill likes to call me, he gave me a chance to explain myself.

I prefer action over words.

Igor's features contort with obvious displeasure as he studies Lia in her wedding dress and the bands around each of our fingers.

She remains in place, but her features pale when she recognizes him.

"I thought you didn't know her?" Igor doesn't hide his accusatory tone as he speaks in accented English.

Lia's fingers stiffen in mine.

"I didn't," I lie. "We had a one-night stand."

I can sense Lia peeking at me, but thankfully, she keeps her words to herself. Any misstep in front of these men and everything will be over. It doesn't matter that I put a baby in her or married her. Any show of disrespect, and they will take that baby and kill Lia.

"How dare you?" Igor slams his glass of vodka on the coffee table.

"Kristina said it was fine if I had any mistresses at the time," I say. "You can confirm that with her if you like."

"So what, Volkov?" Sergei's critical gaze slides to Lia, measuring her up like she's a maid he doesn't approve of. "You chose to marry your one-night stand instead of Igor's daughter. Is this your explanation?"

I can tell when Sergei gets angry. He turns eerily calm, like right now. That's the difference between him and Nikolai. The late *Pakhan* would go on a killing rampage, but his younger brother will kill you with silence.

His point is logical. Sergei is taking offense on behalf of Igor, whom he hasn't only known for the past forty years, but is also the closest of friends with in the brotherhood.

"No," I speak in my signature composed, even tone. "I married her because she's expecting my heir."

Both of their gazes flit to her stomach, as if they can see a child there and question him about his origins. The attention causes Lia to squirm, so I retrieve the envelope from my jacket and hand it to Sergei. The sooner we're done with this, the faster I can get her out of here.

The *Pakhan* places his drink on the table and studies the sonogram and the doctor's report, then sighs. "Is this truly yours?"

"Why would I even give her the time of day if it wasn't?" Lia flinches as if I've slapped her across the face.

I struggle to keep my cool. I don't want her to think she's nothing to me, but if she believes it, so will they.

And I fucking need to get her off their radar. It won't be easy, considering the position I hold in the brotherhood, but if they think she's only here because of the child, they won't have any expectations of her and I can keep her safe from this life. Even if it's only partially.

"I didn't want to disrespect Kristina by forcing her to raise a child that isn't hers, Igor," I tell him. "She deserves better than that."

He takes a swig of his drink, refusing to answer me, but both he and Sergei know my views on raising a bastard child. I lived it and would never, under no fucking circumstances, put my son or daughter through that fate.

"At least Kristina is Russian." Sergei doesn't hide the disregard from his voice. "This one looks American."

"Don't worry, *Pakhan*. My child will be brought up the Russian way."

"That goes without saying." He studies her crutch. "What's wrong with her?"

"I broke my leg," she says with a clear voice.

I tighten my hold on her hand so she'll stop talking. She really doesn't want to attract their attention—at all.

Sergei raises a brow. "So you do have a voice. We went out of our way to speak English for you, and you're only now delighting us with your words."

"Adrian said it's better not to speak, but I dislike being talked about as if I'm not in the room."

Fuck me.

The strength that's always lurking inside her bursts out, and even though her fingers are trembling in mine, betraying her fear of the two Bratva leaders, she still holds her spine upright and stares at them head-on.

I really need to keep her contact with the brotherhood to a minimum. I've seen that look before, the determination and stubbornness in a world filled with men.

My mother had it as soon as she got rid of Aunt Annika and married my father.

There was greed, too.

But her ambition was snuffed out before she could do anything. Anyone who challenges the *Pakhan* is sentenced to death, no matter who they are.

"I see Adrian has a lot to teach you," Sergei says in a grim tone. "She's better when mute."

Lia opens her mouth, probably throw a retort, but I squeeze her fingers until she winces.

"Will do, *Pakhan.*"

He nods me away, and I nudge her so she hobbles in front of me as we leave the office.

Time to teach my bride her first lesson.

TWENTY-SEVEN

Lia

MURDEROUS DOESN'T EVEN BEGIN TO EXPLAIN the atmosphere as soon as we leave the *Pakhan*'s office.

Adrian doesn't say a word during the entire ride, but he doesn't have to. Not that it's surprising. He's the type who lets his anger build, the type who'd hand out pain to prove a point.

The type who makes you fall into his proximity and forces you into marriage, then tells his bosses that you mean nothing.

I don't know which part sliced me open the most. His coercion or how he talked about me in front of his higher-ups.

The silence in the car is suffocating, feeding off my boiling rage and Adrian's simmering ire.

Kolya and Yan are also quiet, not daring to look behind them.

It feels like forever until Adrian's second-in-command slows to a halt outside of a large metal gate that opens with a loud creak. Soon after, we're going down a long, endless drive-way and then stop in front of a mansion.

It's grandiose, larger than life, dark and cold. Just like its owner.

So this is my new gilded cage.

I used to at least have some semblance of control in my apartment, but now, Adrian has stopped pretending or making an effort for my sake. His caring attitude and the soft ways he treated me were only a façade, a preparation phase so he could get me here.

In his monster cave.

Adrian steps out before the car properly stops. I flinch at the sound of the door slamming from his side, despite arming myself with anger all the way here, despite my new resolve to ruin his life as he destroyed mine.

When he opens my door and I attempt to grab my crutch, he pulls me out in one firm yank. I try resisting him, but he throws me over his shoulder like some Neanderthal and barges inside the house. My large veil falls down his back and skims the ground. Blood rushes to my head from the position and the humiliation of being seen this way by all of his damn guards who followed us from the church.

I don't even get to focus on my surroundings as he eats the distance in large steps as if he's on a mission.

Twisting, I bang on his back. "Let me go!"

He doesn't respond, not when I dig my nails into his jacket, and not even when I bite and squirm. It's like he doesn't feel my hits, as if they're the rebellion of a toddler.

"Let me down!" I scream.

His hand comes down hard on my ass and I yelp as the slap echoes in the air. But my muscles don't lock up until his sharp words pierce through my chest. "You screwed yourself over tonight, Lia, so it'll be wise to shut the fuck up. You don't want to test me right now."

I go limp in his hold, and it's not only due to his threat.

If I want to come out of this marriage unscathed—or as

unscathed as possible—I need to be smart when dealing with him and pick my battles.

Adrian's anger doesn't seem to lessen, even after I stop struggling. If anything, his strides widen as he carries me down the hall and kicks the door of a room open, then slams it.

He places me down on the bed, and if I'm not imagining things, I'd say he was gentle so as not to hurt my leg. But of course I'm imagining things. Adrian's caring side is merely a damn illusion that he uses for his own favor as he pleases.

What's the use of thinking about it, when he stained my entire life with today's wedding and everything that followed?

The pregnancy is the only thing that I don't mourn, because I felt—and continue to feel—an instant connection with my baby. However, Adrian is far from being the model father or husband. He's just using the child and the marriage to crush me under his thumb.

He yanks his jacket free and throws it behind him, then unbuttons his shirt, revealing his taut, muscular chest and his rippling, cut abdomen.

I look away from him because I refuse to get caught up in his physical beauty, in how attracted I actually am to him.

All of those feelings are hormonal and physical reactions. They mean nothing.

I lean on my hands on the bed, carefully maneuvering my dress and my cast on the mattress so that I'm sitting with both legs stretched out in front of me. He can show me his worst tonight, but I'll separate my body from my mind and my heart. It's time I wake up and see Adrian for what he truly is—an unfeeling monster.

He removes his belt and loops it around his strong hand, and when he speaks, his voice is laced with a subtle threat, "What did I tell you before we went into Sergei's office?"

I lift my chin and purse my lips.

He steps closer, or more like, he stalks, similar to a large cat with a black soul. "What did I say, Lia?"

"I wasn't going to let you talk about me as if I were an object and stay quiet about it. I might have lost my dream, but I haven't lost my pride and self-worth. I won't allow you or your stupid bosses to humiliate me."

"Wrong answer."

He reaches for me and I flinch back out of pure survival instinct. Everything in me tells me to escape this man, to stay as far away from him as possible. But wherever I go, he's standing there like a permanent shadow. It's been like this since the first time I saw him kill a man in cold blood.

Adrian wraps both hands around my waist and flips me, forcing me to lie flat on my stomach with my head on the pillow. He rips the zipper down my back and yanks the dress away, letting the white silk pool by the bed. Since it has a built-in bra, I'm in only my panties and my veil that's now draped by my side.

When Adrian sits next to my good leg, I stare out of the corner of my eye to find him looping the wide leather around his hand a few more times. The sight liquefies my insides, both in utter fear and maddening anticipation.

"You seem to have forgotten how things go, Lia. But I'll be happy to whip it out of you until you learn your place."

"And what am I? Your mute wife? The wife you forced into marrying you?"

"Keep telling yourself lies if you think it'll help you cope better, but you and I both know you want this. You want to be mine to fuck and punish, to own and deprave."

"I never agreed to anything when comes to you, Adrian. You've coerced me into everything since the beginning."

His jaw tightens and a shadow darkens his face. "Coerced you? Did I coerce you into waiting for me every night or coming undone around my cock or tongue or fingers? Did I coerce you into craving the lash of my hand or belt? You're practically shivering in anticipation, Lia, so don't you fucking dare say I coerced you. If anything, I freed your sexual fantasies. You know it, I know it, and your shrink would know it, too, if you weren't ashamed to admit it."

"So now you think of yourself as my savior?"

"I never claimed to be. What I am, however, is your husband and you are mine."

"I'll never be yours. Not willingly."

Adrian grabs my hair and veil, tugging my head back in a merciless grip. "You are mine, Lia. In fact, you always were, so it's best you admit it."

"No."

His hot, threatening breath tickles the side of my face. "Say it. Say you're mine."

"No."

"Lia...you really don't want to anger me more than I already am."

"You'll whip me, anyway, so do it and leave me alone."

"Oh, I won't leave you alone. Not unless you fully admit you're mine."

"Never." I hold his fast-darkening gaze with my determined one. It may not be wise to provoke him, but that's not my aim. I'm only protecting myself so he won't take the small parts I still own. If I give them up, he'll stomp all over them and me, then toss me aside to die in a locked room.

"Very well. It seems you're in a hurry to start your punishment." Adrian lets my head fall on the pillow and runs the tip of his belt down my naked back. I shiver as my body's memory of him kicks into gear.

If there's anything I can't deny about my fucked-up relationship with him, it's definitely the physical connection. We have more chemistry than I could ever imagine, and I hate that right now. I hate that he has this hold on me or how much I crave his touch after weeks of being starved.

I hate that I miss his callous handling of my body.

I hate that I love our difference in size and how easily he can overpower me, throw me down, and own me.

His hand bunches around my panties and he rips them off. I gasp as the ruined material brushes against my folds before he throws it away. It doesn't matter how many times he does it, how many destroyed pairs of panties I have. It doesn't get old and he never fails to turn me on.

"When I order you to do something, you don't think about it, you don't try to defy me, you fucking do it. Is that clear?" His words are as calm as the up and down motions of his belt on the hollow of my back and the curve of my ass.

"Then you should've gotten a toy, not me."

A swish echoes in the air before the belt comes down on my ass. I cry out as the burn settles on my skin and zaps straight to my core. It's been a long time since he took his belt to me or touched me sexually, and my body—that has been revolting against the lack of stimulation for weeks—is now resurrecting from the ashes like a phoenix.

"Don't talk back to me."

"I won't let you break me," I manage between strangled pants. "If you wanted an obedient pet, you should've gotten a different wife."

My self-worth is the last thing I have, and I will fight till death before I let Adrian take that away, too.

"You *are* my wife, Mrs. Volkov, and I will whip and fuck that fact into your body until you act like it."

Swish. Slap.

Swish. Slap.

I gasp, my lips trembling at the ferocity behind the hits. He really is out to punish me and isn't pulling any punches. But the most embarrassing part is that I don't only feel the hit on my ass. It's simmering under my skin and sending pulses to my aching core.

"You will not talk back, whether in front of me or anyone else in the brotherhood." *Slap.* "You'll keep your thoughts to yourself." *Slap.* "You will not go against me in public again."

Slap!

I'm sobbing by the end of his words, my voice hoarse, my heart hammering so loud, I'm scared it'll spill on the mattress and leave me vacant once and for all.

"Is that clear, Lia?"

"Yes...yes..." I'm telling him what he wants to hear so he'll end the torture. It's not only about the welts. It's about the frightening friction in my core that heightens with each of his merciless lashes.

"Good."

I release a breath when his large palm touches my assaulted skin and he slowly kneads my ass. That usually means he's done torturing me—or close to it.

His hand slowly parts my thighs as far as they can go with the cast, and I can't help the moan that escapes as his fingers brush against my soaked folds.

"I see you've missed your punishments, Lia."

I burrow my face into the pillow to muffle my voice. I don't want him to hear me so wanton like this, and most of all, I don't want him to know he has this hold on me.

"Deny it all you like, but your body belongs to me." He cups me harshly. "This cunt belongs to me." He slaps my burning skin and I whimper. "This ass also belongs to me. But if there's still any doubt in your mind, by all means, say it, and I'll punish it out of you."

My breathing is chopped and fractured, and it's not only because of the pain. It's his words. Damn them and damn me for letting them have this effect on me.

"Shouldn't I continue punishing you, Lenochka?"

"No..."

"Then do you belong to me?"

I purse my lips.

He raises his hand and brings it down on my ass. I shriek as my burning skin explodes with pain.

"Do you fucking belong to me?"

"No…never…"

"Lia…don't make me break you."

"You'll break me more if I say those words," I sob, all of my pain receptors pulsing at the same time.

He slaps me again and I wail, my body wiggling sideways, but he holds me down by the hair. "Say you're mine."

"No."

Slap. "Say. It."

My tears soak the pillow and I feel like I might pass out. Like his next strikes will knock me out cold. But they don't. All they manage to do is torture my ass and core. He's using his hand now, but my skin is so tender and stimulated that even the merest hit reverberates through my whole body.

"Stop it…Adrian…please…"

"Not until you say you're mine." His voice is harsh, non-negotiable.

"I can't…" I sob.

"Yes, you can."

"No! You've taken so much from me already. I will not hand you my last pieces. So if you want to whip me to death, do it. I will not say those words, even with my last breath."

I expect him to do what I suggested just to prove a point, but Adrian releases a long exhale and throws the belt away. The sound it makes as it hits the floor sends a small jolt through my chest.

A rustling of clothes comes from behind me and I can imagine him getting rid of his shirt and pants.

He wraps a hand around my jaw and lifts me up using it. The utter possession and the haunting darkness in the gesture leaves me panting. "I'm going to fuck you as my wife and you're going to scream for me."

Adrian plants his knee between my legs and holds me by the hip as his cock forces its way inside, his chest covering my back at the same time so that his head is mere inches away from mine. Despite being wet and more than ready, his entrance into my body always hurts like it's the first time. My backside burns when his groin slaps against it.

"Ahhh…that hurts…"

"Not more than your fucking stubbornness, apparently."

"Adrian…"

"What?"

"Do something."

"Like this?" He reaches underneath me and twists my swollen clit.

"Ohhh…"

"Or this?" He thrusts inside me, and even though his groin still hits against my tortured skin, it adds friction and a carnal type of pleasure.

"Yes…ohhh…yes…"

"That's it," he murmurs against my mouth, his eyes hooded. "Moan for me. Let me hear that throaty sound that's made only for me."

That's when it clicks.

Adrian has always loved it when I release sounds during sex. It seems to get him harder and his pace builds up to a maddening level, like right now. The slap of flesh against flesh and my own arousal echoes in the air as he holds my eyes and everything in me hostage.

But even as he confiscates my body, as he steals it from me, there's just one thing I can steal from him in return.

I'm breathing harshly when he moves at a pace that he knows will get me off. But when the orgasm hits with wrecking force, I bite my lower lip so hard, metal explodes on my tongue.

Adrian's monstrously beautiful face contorts and I hold his gaze as I mute the sounds he loves to hear so much.

He took away my freedom. I'm taking away his pleasure.

Adrian might have started as the only one with power, but I'm slowly finding mine. I might not have guns or an army of guards, but I'll kill him with silence.

His hold tightens on my jaw as he stills at my back and warm liquid fills my walls.

He pulls out of me, but just so he can slam back in with renewed energy.

Oh, God. How could he get hard again this soon? Usually, he gets hard fast, but not this fast.

"We'll have a redo, and this time, you'll fucking scream, Lia."

"Never," I mutter.

"Then we'll go at this all night until you do. You'll bow to me, wife."

Not in this life, husband.

TWENTY-EIGHT

Lia

A MONTH LATER, THE CAST HAS BEEN REMOVED AND Adrian and I are at Dr. Kim's office to start my rehabilitation so that I can walk again.

I don't bother asking the doctor if the verdict about the impossibility of a full recovery is still the same. He's looking at me as if I were a kicked puppy, relaying the words without having to utter them. I'm going to move beyond it, though, because I have another life to worry about now.

Before we left the house this morning, I stood in front of the mirror to get dressed and I was caught in a trance by my stomach. It's still flat, but I can feel the baby more with each passing day.

The life that's been making itself marginally unnoticeable is finally peeking out, reminding me of why I'm here in the first place.

To produce an heir.

And while the objectification, the coercion, and the humiliation still hurt, I don't regret the child. This baby is the one thing that's making me hold on to life, surviving day to day, knowing that I'm not living for myself alone anymore.

I'm going to be a mother. And if mine was any indication, mothers sacrifice for their children. Mothers protect their children from the monstrosities of the world, with their lives if they have to.

We go the OBG-YN, too, and she tells us that the baby is healthy. Adrian places a hand at the small of my back, leading me out of the building and to the car that's waiting outside. I don't miss the possessive gesture whenever we're in public, like he's marking his territory for everyone to see.

I try to ignore his presence, his touch, and his wood and leather scent that's become stronger over the past couple of weeks. But it's impossible to erase Adrian, no matter how much I try. Not only because he forced me to marry him, but also because of everything he does.

The way he cares for me, how he sits beside me on the sofa and places my feet on his lap to massage them. Since the cast was removed, he's been taking care of rubbing oil on my leg. I don't even like to look at the hideous scar right beneath my knee, but he takes over the task with effortless ease.

I hate how he holds my hair and strokes my back whenever I'm hit by morning sickness. Or how he tells the head of his staff, a tenacious woman named Ogla, not to cook food with strong smells.

I hate that he makes me come before he fucks me, how my pleasure is always prioritized before his, and how he's never made me pleasure him. I hate how he cleans me after he's done and then throws a nightgown over my head so I won't get cold.

But most of all, I hate the way he holds me to him, even when I turn away from him, as if having me sleep in his arms is his favorite position. Apparently, it's mine, too, because my nightmares have slowly disappeared since I moved out of my apartment.

It would have been easier to erase Adrian if he were the heartless monster I paint him to be in my head. Though he is heartless, he's not when it comes to his offspring. His care and all these gestures are only his way to ease the birth of his heir. Once that happens, he'll probably demote me to the background.

My feet falter on the sidewalk a short distance away from the car when I see a few homeless people huddled near the corner, begging for money.

My heart aches for them, but at the same time, I envy the freedom they have. They might not wear an enormous diamond ring and live in a palace that's guarded by a hundred men, but they at least have freedom and the ability to go anywhere.

"Is it someone you know?" Adrian asks from my side, his voice low but firm.

Since our wedding night, he's been a bit distant, either issuing orders or sounding frigid like right now. We've lost the somewhat carefree conversations we used to have back in my apartment. But that probably has more to do with the silent treatment I've been using against him.

I shake my head.

"Use your fucking voice, Lia." He leans in to whisper in a threatening tone. "This isn't the bedroom, so you don't need to start a rebellion."

I stare at him square in the face. He didn't win that war. I did.

As promised, he fucked me over and over again that night. It was the longest we've ever gone, and even though I lost count of how many times I orgasmed, I never let him hear my voice until I collapsed.

It's been the same every night—or day, really—since he seeks me out at all hours. Adrian tries to make me moan or scream, but I either bite my lip or the pillow or my hand if I have to.

He lost the right to hear my voice that night.

"I thought I was better as a mute." I push past him and settle in the car, letting the bag fall to my lap.

Adrian joins me soon after, and the sound of his door closing causes a brick to settle at the bottom of my stomach.

"That's one, Lia," he murmurs.

My heart thumps, no matter how much I don't want it to or how much I fight it. My body is attuned to him in ways even I can't understand. I'm addicted to his rough touch and merciless punishments.

I come undone in no time, and that sense of levitating has never changed. If anything, it's been heightening over the weeks.

But it's just a physical connection. A meaningless one.

I'll get over it someday. I *have* to.

Scoffing, I focus ahead as Yan kills his cigarette and slides into the passenger seat. Kolya kicks the car into gear and pulls out into the busy street.

"Two." Adrian takes my hand in his and nibbles down on my pinkie before sucking it into his mouth.

A whole body shiver overtakes me and I try to free myself, but he bites down harder, then speaks against my skin, "I told you not to pull away from me again. Three."

Giving up the futile fight, I stare out the window at the buzzing city. My appointments with the doctors are the only time I get to leave the cage Adrian has built for me, and it's my only chance to see people and the life that's going on around me.

It's odd how I never focused on it when I used to drive to and from rehearsal, but humans don't realize what they're missing until it's snatched away from them.

If I'd known, I would've paid better attention.

Luca hasn't gotten in touch since that time at the lingerie store. I can't call him either, because Adrian not only got me a new phone number, but I'm sure he's also having it tracked.

And since I don't go out alone, I assume it's hard for Luca to find an opening to get in touch.

That's why I need to provide him with that opening, because if there's anyone who can help get me out from under Adrian's steel-like hold, it's Luca.

I spot a tent under which people are serving hot soup to the homeless. The image of the man in front of the hospital comes to mind and an idea strikes me.

It takes me a few minutes to organize my thoughts in a way that won't send Adrian's red flags up. If he gets a whiff of what I'm doing, he'll lock me in a cell until I give birth.

Facing him, I try to ignore that he's still licking and nibbling on my finger, and how his touch is sending tiny bursts of pleasure down my spine and to my belly. "I was talking to the OB-GYN when you went to get the prescription."

"You were?"

"Yes. She said I could be developing depression."

"Is she an OB-GYN or a psychotherapist?"

I lift a shoulder. "It doesn't take a genius to figure it out."

"You've always had depression, Lia. You're not developing it."

My eyes widen. "How did you know that?"

"The pills in your apartment."

Right. I guess it doesn't matter that I've hid them from him. Adrian watches my every move and notices everything, which is one more reason to be careful around him.

"Why have you never asked me about them?" I ask in a quiet tone.

"Would you rather I have?"

"No, but that's what most people do whenever they learn I have mental health issues."

"I'm not most people."

"You...you don't think I'm broken?"

"So what if you are. It's what makes you who you are."

My lips part. It's like he's saying he likes me just as I am. Broken and all.

"You don't have to hide your pills from me, Lia."

"I'm do…not hide them."

"Yes, you do. But you've not been using them since the pregnancy. Not the insomnia pills or the antidepressants. Your nightmares have noticeably toned down, too. You didn't have one during the past week and your pills remain untouched. So how is it noticeable to the OB-GYN that you're developing depression?"

Damn it.

I knew he observed everything, but I didn't realize he was that attuned to me, even to my nightmares.

"I told her I'm feeling confined," I blurt.

He pauses, seeming to be genuinely concerned as he lets my hand fall on his lap but doesn't release it. "You are?"

I scoff. "I'm trapped inside four walls twenty-four-seven with nothing to do. What do you think?"

"You take walks in the garden."

"You make me do it."

"To help your circulation."

"Whatever. It still doesn't count as entertainment."

"You can read."

I scrunch my nose. "No, thanks."

His lips twitch in a small smile. It's not the first time he's suggested I read. He mentioned that it helped getting him through his childhood, but I told him that not all of us are born to be bookworms. Now he smiles whenever the subject is brought up again.

I don't want to get caught up in one of his rare smiles that appears once in a blue moon, but I do. Whenever he shows this side of himself, the slightly carefree and relaxed side, I stop and stare, letting my mind wander to what our relationship would've been like if we were a normal couple. If our first meeting hadn't been when he killed someone in cold blood, and if he hadn't forced me to marry him before announcing ever so cruelly that my only worth is his child that's growing in my womb.

But we're not a normal couple. We never were and never will be.

"What do you want to do, Lenochka?"

I perk up at his question and the use of my nickname. It means he's letting some of his guard down, and I don't take it for granted when Adrian asks me what I want.

So I soften my voice because any stubbornness or high range in it will have the absolute opposite effect on him. "I want to go out."

"We're currently out."

"Not like this. I want to be out in the open."

"Why?"

"To breathe properly."

I realize my mistake when his eyes darken. I just implied that I don't breathe in his company or his house, and while that's somewhat true, I don't want him to get angry and close off any negotiation.

"I mean outside air," I recover quickly. "I want to breathe outside air."

"Security hazard. No."

My heart plummets, but I keep my compliant tone as I implore, "I'll be careful."

"It doesn't matter how careful you are. If someone wants to get to me, they'd do it through you since you're the easiest and weakest spot they can hit. Being my wife has already set you as a target, Lia."

His words slice me open, cutting me in half. I thought he would never hurt me worse than the day in Sergei's office, but he just dug the rusty knife in deeper.

So I'm his weakest spot now.

My lips tremble, but I set them in a line, even as what remains of my heart bleeds. "I need to do some activities or I'll lose it. Your precious baby won't be able to be born if his mother is fucking nuts."

"Lower your voice." His jaw clenches. "And did you hear a word I said about security?"

"I did. Don't care. I need to get out, Adrian. You already clipped my wings. The least you can do is give me something to look forward to."

He clutches me by the chin and I swallow as his merciless eyes clash with mine. "Raise your voice again and I'll put you on my lap and spank that defiance out of you. Is that clear, Lenochka?"

"Give me something," I murmur, tears welling along my lids. "*Please.*"

I wish they were fake tears, that I was just feigning this, but real pain bursts through and my heart and pride ache for ever letting him see me this way.

For letting him hurt me again by calling me his weakness.

"You will go out with my guards. Only once a week and to a location I specify."

My lips part. "Really?"

"Have I lied to you before?"

No. He makes sure all of his promises are executed—whether good or bad.

Actually...

He did when he didn't tell me about his engagement to perfect Kristina. A lie by omission is still a lie, and I'm still not over that. But if I say that, he'll just twist it around, and I'm not in the mood to acknowledge his previous engagement—I don't think I ever will be. I hate the inferiority complex that festers on my soul whenever I think of the pretty blonde on his arm instead of me.

"I'll let you know which location you'll go to."

"I…" I swallow. "I want to do charity work."

He raises a brow. "What?"

"You know, those organizations that serve homeless people food?"

"I know what charity work means, Lia. And you're not doing it."

I place a hand on his chest, my palm expanding on the hard ridges underneath. This is the first time I've initiated an affectionate touch first.

A low growl slips from his lips and his muscles ripple beneath my small hand, then he looks at me as if he wants to devour me.

I bask in the sensation of having this much effect on him. It might only be physical, but it's still empowering all the same.

"I need to have a purpose after my accident, Adrian. And if I'm fighting a noble cause, I won't feel like my days and nights are empty."

He raises a brow. "Your nights are empty?"

My cheeks heat, recalling a recent memory of him tying me up to fuck me until I was spent. "You know what I mean."

"No, I don't. So why don't you explain it to me?"

I sigh, opting to offer him a small fraction of truth even I don't want to admit, but I know he'll like. "After we finish having sex, I know I'll spend the following day alone, and sometimes, I think about that all night long. That's what I meant by empty nights."

He pauses, and I believe he'll shoot me down, but then he nods. "Fine. But I choose which organization."

I smile, feeling the triumph of the win to my bones.

This is it. My chance to escape.

For a life as far away from Adrian as possible.

TWENTY-NINE

Lia

I GET A SLIVER OF FREEDOM THE FOLLOWING MONTH.
It's not much.

But Adrian keeps his word and allows me to be part of a shelter that serves homeless people warm food during the harsh days. We're slowly heading to spring, but the air is still cold.

I look forward to the days I can get out without Adrian. Yan and Boris accompany me, but they mostly keep to themselves in the background.

When it's just Yan and me, we share sandwiches for lunch and then I try to probe him about his boss, questions that he doesn't answer. I should be used to it by now, but I'd rather talk to Yan than not talk at all.

It's sad, but he's basically the only friend I have. The other day, my feet came to a halt in front of a *Giselle* poster. The ballet is still being directed by Philippe and choreographed by Stephanie. Nothing has changed except for the prima ballerina, who's now Hannah Max. Oh, and they changed Ryan for another dancer. No clue if he pulled out, and I have no will to get in touch with that part of my life anymore.

When I stared at that poster, it took everything in me not to cry. To force myself to turn around and not get caught up in how the world moved along and I didn't.

I'm sure Philippe and Steph have tried to reach me, but we don't belong to the same world anymore. They're in the spotlight. I'm in a gilded cage. And if I attempt to get them involved in my life, I'll put them in danger with Adrian.

"If it's of any comfort"—Yan fell in step beside me after I ripped my gaze from the poster—"your Giselle is much prettier and more haunting than hers."

I hated myself at that moment. Not because I disagreed, but because I wanted Adrian to say those words instead of Yan.

Shaking my head from the memory, I smile as I pour more soup for Mrs. Matthews, an old lady who likes her soup.

She grins at me, then escapes to the farthest table, spilling some of her soup on the floor.

The center where I volunteer is probably the biggest in New York, and we have several hundred homeless people who show up for meals.

I make Yan and Boris help, too. Something that Adrian disapproves of because, as he likes to remind me, they're there to protect me, not serve food. Whatever. All they normally do is stand there and smoke. They're better put to use serving food than doing nothing. Though they look a bit out of place with the white and blue aprons strapped around their suits.

They also don't shy away from calling the homeless out on their bullshit when they steal. Especially Yan. I swear he has zero patience sometimes. When I asked him how the hell he gets along with Adrian and Kolya, he said he doesn't most of the time and that they're too 'stoic' for their own good. Then he asked me not to repeat that in front of his boss if his life means anything to me.

I motion at him that I'm taking a bathroom break. He abandons the soup, removes his apron, and throws it at Boris before he falls in step beside me.

"You don't have to follow me everywhere, Yan." I groan as I make my way through the tables with him hot on my heels.

"Yes, I do, or the boss will have my balls."

I chuckle at that image. Adrian is really severe and his calm only adds to his ruthlessness. I've witnessed how he talks to his men, and although it's in Russian, I can sense the authority.

"Glad to see you laugh, even at the expense of my misery," Yan grumbles.

"You're being dramatic. It's not misery."

"Have you seen him? Also, I'm still not okay that Kolya gets all the fun."

"Isn't he the senior guard?"

He scoffs. "Senior grump, maybe."

I smile. Kolya is always giving Yan shit about smoking, and even though I don't mind it, Yan has already stopped smoking in my company, because of the pregnancy, I assume.

He stops outside the bathroom door in his wide, ready stance and goes to open it.

"I can at least open my own door." I motion at his twitching hand. "Go ahead, smoke until I come back."

I can tell he wants to, but his caution is stopping him, so I take the decision away from him. I open the door wide, letting him see the empty bathroom. "See? No one is here."

After Yan's watchful gaze checks every corner, he finally nods.

I shake my head before going inside and closing the door.

As soon as I'm in a stall, a shadow follows behind me. I open my mouth to scream, but a gloved hand wraps around my mouth and uses my body to close the door.

"Miss me, Duchess?"

I breathe harshly against Luca's palm. He's wearing a black leather jacket and a hat that shadows his eyes. He slowly removes his gloved hand. "Whisper or he'll hear."

"What are you doing here? Yan is right outside."

"I can shoot him if he comes in."

"No!"

"I see you're forming attachments. That's the worst thing to do, Lia. He's Adrian's guard, not yours. He's keeping an eye on you on his boss's behalf, and won't hesitate to hurt you if he's ordered to."

I know that, but I still don't want him dead. Yan doesn't deserve such a fate, even if his boss is a major asshole.

"He won't come in here unless I take longer than needed," I bargain.

Luca releases an exasperated breath. "Do you have any idea how fucking hard it is to get you alone? I've been trying for fucking months. First, you were hidden away in his black castle, then he put you in a shelter associated with the Bratva, and his men follow you everywhere. This is the first time that tool guard didn't check every corner of the bathroom first."

Releasing a long sigh, I murmur, "This is my life now."

"I'm sorry, by the way." His brow creases as he makes a vague gesture toward my leg. Luca doesn't offer sympathy. He's more hardened than me and lacks many emotions, so I know not to take it for granted.

"I'm still alive." My voice is clogged as I fight the tears.

"Sometimes staying alive is the worst of it." His features tighten before they relax. "Tell me you have something on Adrian."

I shake my head. "He doesn't talk about his business."

"But you're his wife now. Surely he takes you to those inner Bratva banquets."

"No." Since that day, he's never dragged me to his organization and I'm somewhat thankful for that.

"Fuck, Duchess. I thought we agreed you'd bring me things on him."

"He's guarded."

"Then make him unguarded."

"You think that's easy?"

"You can do it. Being his wife makes you the closest person to him."

No, it doesn't. If anything, we feel further apart than when he used to come to my apartment at night. At least back then, it was about me. Now, everything is about the baby and my despicable role of producing an heir.

While I love my child, I hate how Adrian is using him.

"Tell me what you know," Luca says.

I mention details that I know, about Sergei and Igor and his daughter, Kristina. I also tell him about Adrian calling someone Don and having conversations with him. I don't mention Adrian's family history that he willingly divulged. Luca doesn't need to know that, and it feels too intimate to let someone else be privy to it.

"All of that is old news." Luca checks his watch. "I need more."

"More, like what?"

"His system. What he's working on."

"He would never allow me to get close to that."

"Then force your way in, Lia."

"Do you even know Adrian? Besides, I'm pregnant, Luca." I point at the bump in my belly. "I will not put my child's life in danger."

The more he grows, the smaller that black hole in my chest shrinks. And now, I look forward to staring at my reflection in the mirror every morning, to listening to music and even reading some books so I can form any sort of connection with him.

Luca's lips twist. "Congratulations are in order, I guess."

"Instead of congratulating me, help me leave Adrian."

"No. Not yet."

"Why not?"

"Because I need eyes on him. You can't leave him yet."

"Luca…" My voice breaks. "How could you say that?"

"You'll thank me for it later when you know the truth." He opens the stall door and gives me a quizzical stare over his shoulder. "Take care of yourself, Duchess. No one else is going to do it for you. Not me and definitely not the unfeeling psycho, Adrian."

And with that, he climbs through the window and jumps down.

His words float behind him long after he's gone, settling a weight at the bottom of my stomach.

"Mrs. Volkov?" Yan calls, and when I don't reply, he follows with an urgent, "I'm coming in."

I straighten, stepping out of the stall as Yan nearly yanks the door from its hinges. He steps inside, and his critical eyes study me mechanically. "Are you okay?"

"Why wouldn't I be?" I hide my tremors with a smile.

"I thought I heard voices."

"It...must be from outside." I motion at the window Luca left open.

Yan heads to it with purposeful strides, inspects it, then narrows his eyes before he slams it shut.

When he turns around to face me, all of his nonchalance and playful behavior are gone. "I'm going to ask you a question, and I want your honesty, Lia. Was someone here?"

"No," I say with a conviction I don't feel, hoping he believes me.

He gives a curt nod and precedes me toward the door.

I don't release a breath. Not then, not after we get home, and certainly not when Adrian keeps watching me all night as if I'm his custom-made pet, trapped under his thumb.

Luca was right.

I have to look out for myself, and that includes surviving Adrian until I can escape him.

If that means I need to provide Luca with any scraps of information on my husband, so be it.

THIRTY

Adrian

Six months later

THE SOUND OF CRYING FILLS THE AIR AS THE
midwife fusses around Lia and a few nurses wipe the
sweat off her forehead.

"It's a beautiful boy," the midwife announces with a soft
smile that vanishes upon meeting my gaze, then reappears
when she directs her attention to Lia.

My wife releases the iron grip that she kept on my hand
during the entire birthing process. Her nails broke my skin
from the force of her pain and screams. There's nothing I
wanted to do more than take that pain for myself and relieve
her of it. Having her scratch and claw at my skin is nothing
compared to what she's been through.

She was glowing through the months of her pregnancy,
counting days and crossing them off her calendar until the day
she'd meet *her* son.

I tried ignoring that she never called him *our* son or *our*
baby, or that she never once referred to him as ours. As if, in a

way, she was tolerating me and this marriage only for the child. And while I attempted to let that slide, I don't like it. I don't like that she's been slowly erasing me since the wedding.

Considering the way everything started, I gave her some leeway, content with having her by my side every night and knowing she's safe and fucking mine.

However, no matter how much she comes undone around me, she never lets me hear her voice anymore. As soon as I'm out of her, she gives me her back and moves to the edge of the bed. That doesn't stop me from spooning her from behind, but while she sleeps in my hold, she still squirms every night, still tries to get away from me.

Which will never happen.

And it's not only because of the child. As much as I'm a fucking scum for using my own son, his existence is merely a consequence of keeping her by my side.

How are you any different from your psycho mother? I can hear Yan chastising me, and I push him and his loathsome voice out of my head.

Unlike my mother, I won't hurt my son for my own gains. If anything, I'll burn the world if anyone so much as gets near him or his mother.

All remnants of anguish disappear from Lia's face, replaced by a soft, awed expression. Fresh tears stream down her cheeks, but she looks the happiest I've seen her since before she broke her leg.

Or maybe ever.

The nurse carefully places the baby in her arms and Lia holds him gently, lips falling open, then shut, apparently lost for words.

The child immediately stops crying as his mother pulls him to her bare chest, which is only covered by a sheet. Even though the nurse wiped him down, he's still covered with goo and blood. However, Lia doesn't seem to care about that as she smiles at him through her tears. "Hi there, my beautiful angel."

His small fingers curl into fists, resting on her breastbone, and his eyes move behind his closed lids as if he can recognize her voice. She spent the entirety of her pregnancy talking to him, making him listen to music and dancing slowly because she wanted him to be light on his feet. She even went out of her way and read to him when I know for a fact that she hates it.

"What do you want to name him?" the midwife asks me in a fearful voice.

After I ordered Kolya to close down the entire floor for Lia to give birth, I assume everyone in the hospital knows who I am. This is one of the brotherhood's rare legitimate businesses. Although most know we own it, they don't really get to meet us—except in instances like this. I could've had them deliver the child at home, but I wanted her to get the care she needed as fast as possible in case of any complications.

Since the moment I learned Lia was pregnant, I've been studying pregnancy and birthing more than I've studied anything in my life, so I'm well aware of possible complications. I might have been a tad obsessive about it to the point that Lia once grumbled that I know more about it than even she does.

"What do you want to name him, Lenochka?" I ask.

Her gaze slides from him to me, her teary eyes sparking. "You'll let me name him?"

"Yes."

"Does it have to be a Russian name?"

I brush a stray strand of damp hair behind her ear, and I'm thankful she doesn't flinch away like every time I try to touch her outside of sex. "Not if you don't want that, no."

"Won't…Sergei be mad?" Her breath catches. She's seen him once since that day, during his grandniece's birthday, because he made a big fuss about it and ordered me to bring her.

She was five months pregnant at the time, and she remained quiet as he likes. She was involved in her charity activities so she seemed less trapped and more inclined to be on her best behavior around members of the brotherhood. Besides, she was more interested in leaving that place as soon as I was ready.

"Sergei doesn't tell me what to name my son."

She stares down at him, biting her lower lip, and I hate that gesture. It's how she mutes herself from me, slowly but surely building a wall around herself.

"Jeremy," she murmurs.

"Jeremy?"

"I dreamt about it a few weeks ago. I was dancing in the garden with a little boy who was maybe four or five years old named Jeremy." She smiles, though it's laced with sadness. "He looked so much like you."

And she hates that. She doesn't like the fact that *her* son looks like me.

"Jeremy it is." I keep my frustration out of my voice. While it's hard for most people to hide their emotions, I learned from my deranged parents how to perfect it.

"Thank you." Lia smiles at me, then at him, and he fusses a little before his shrill crying fills the room. She coos at him, but he won't stop throwing a fit.

A nurse with black skin and curly hair peeking from under her cap stands by my wife's side. "Are you going to breastfeed or use formula?"

"She's tired," I say. "She should rest."

"No. I want to breastfeed." Lia lowers the sheet, revealing her full breasts and the engorged pink nipples that have been changing noticeably over the last trimester.

I probably shouldn't think of them as erotic when they're in that state for the baby, but still.

Handling Jeremy carefully, Lia places his mouth at a nipple and nature takes its course as he sucks on it. Lia strokes his head, then kisses it softly, carefully, as if she's afraid to hurt him. "Mommy loves you so much, my angel."

The nurse smiles with apparent awe while she covers Lia.

I feel like an intruder watching the mother and son bonding, and something in my chest aches. It's probably the pathetic boy in me whom I thought I squashed a long time ago.

My own mother never looked at me the way Lia looks at Jeremy. I only had that affection from Aunt Annika, and even she was brutally ripped out of my life.

That's what happens to people like me. We never get anything good. It's payback for all the shit we've done in our lifetime.

We remain like that for a while as the nurse cleans Lia up before covering her in a thicker duvet. Jeremy soon falls asleep, and when the nurse attempts to take him away so she can rest, Lia shakes her head.

I sit on the bed beside Lia and she stiffens when I wrap my arm around the both of them.

"What are you doing?" she whispers.

"What does it look like I'm doing? I'm being a part of this family."

She purses her lips, but instead of talking back to me, she focuses on Jeremy, who has just released her breast, his tiny lips moving in his sleep.

My phone vibrates in my pocket and I retrieve it, absent-mindedly rejecting Kolya's call to focus on my wife and son.

I like that. *My wife and son.*

Kolya calls again, and I know he wouldn't do it twice in a row unless something's up. I answer, "What is it?"

There's a sound of gunshots echoing from his end. "The Rozettis are here, Boss, and they want vengeance for that kill in Lazlo's club."

Fuck.

I jerk up and wrap a thick blanket around Lia. She yelps, her pupils growing into saucers as she holds Jeremy closer to her.

"Which exit is safe?" I ask Kolya.

"A. Yan and Boris are on their way to you."

"How many?"

"A fucking army, Boss. They knew this would be their perfect opportunity."

"How many are with you?"

"Six, but I can manage until backup arrives."

"Keep me updated."

I shove the phone in my pocket and retrieve an earpiece that my guards use for internal communication and strap it to my ear.

After tapping it to connect to Yan, I grab my gun and tighten the blanket around a wide-eyed Lia and Jeremy, then carry them in my arms.

The nurses' faces pale, but they know to remain quiet. It's Lia who gasps. "What's going on?"

"We're under attack. I need you to hold Jeremy close, got it?"

She doesn't need me to tell her twice as she folds around him, shielding him with her body.

"Boss!" Yan barges inside, droplets of red covering his face as he pants. "Now."

I listen in for the safe exits on the intercom as Yan leads the way and Boris covers our back.

Lia trembles in my arms, her lips quivering and her eyes shifty. This is the last thing a woman who just gave birth should go through, and I will make the Rozettis pay for this with blood.

"Don't worry, Lenochka." I try to make my voice as calm as possible as we descend the stairs. "I'll protect you."

She doesn't even show a reaction to hearing me as she holds Jeremy with shaking hands.

Soon after, we reach the parking lot. A few armed men intercept us and Yan shoots one. Lia shrieks, and I fire my gun while still holding her and hit another motherfucker in the chest.

Yan hurries to the car, and we hide behind another one until he brings it around. Boris covers me as I slide to the back with Lia and Jeremy cradled on my lap. Boris slams the door shut and Yan is already taking off before the other guard is properly inside.

Our attention is on high alert as we watch our backs until we get home.

Lia is shaking uncontrollably all the way in, with a steel hold on Jeremy, who surprisingly spent the entire ordeal asleep.

Ogla is at the entrance, and she doesn't need me to say anything before she understands the situation. She's been quick-witted ever since she worked for my parents. "I'll get hot water and warm clothes."

I take the stairs two at a time until I reach our bedroom. I only release a breath when I carefully place Lia and Jeremy on the bed. At least they're safe here. I'll take care of things outside.

My wife scrambles under the blanket and sits up against the headboard. It's then that I notice the trail of blood on the sheets.

Fuck.

I crouch beside her, taking her small hand in mine. "Are you okay? I'll call Dr. Putin."

She squirms free. "I'm fine. It's just normal bleeding from childbirth."

My jaw clenches. "Lia...what the fuck did I say about pulling away from me?"

"I just saw you murder another man in cold blood, so excuse me if I don't want you to touch me with the same hands."

"If I didn't kill him, he would've fucking killed you and Jeremy. Is that what you want?" My voice rises with every word. It's the first time I've bellowed at her like this, and it doesn't go unnoticed as unshed tears rush to her lids.

"Do you expect me to see this as normal? I didn't even get to greet my child properly."

"You know who I am and what I do, so don't pretend all of this is news, Lia."

"I'll never get used to it if that's what you're insinuating." A sob catches in her throat. "A child can't live like this."

"So what are you suggesting?"

A small spark lights the deep blue of her eyes. "We...we can live in another house and you can come visit if you like. We can be normal."

Humorless laughter bursts from me, one that makes her stiffen. "They already know who you are. The moment you walk out that door, you'll be murdered or kidnapped and raped to get to me. You're my wife and that means you belong by my side. So don't you ever—and I mean *fucking ever*—think you can get away from me."

A knock sounds on the door, and it takes everything in me to say in a semi-normal tone, "Come in."

Ogla walks inside with various supplies and I leave without sparing another glance at Lia. If I do, I'll be teaching her where she actually belongs, but I can't do that when other matters are more pressing.

I trust Ogla to take care of her, but I'll make sure to return as soon as possible.

My blood boils with different things altogether. One, Lia's foolish belief that she could live away from me, which means she's been thinking about leaving me all along. Two, the sorry fucks who thought it would be a good idea to attack my wife and child.

Gun in hand, I click the earpiece. "Kolya."

"Yes, Boss."

"Where are you?"

"Doing some pesky cleaning."

"You got rid of them?"

"All but two."

"Bring them to the guest house." I'm going to enjoy torturing the answers out of those fuckers before I kill their boss. If need be, I'll convince Sergei to start an all-out war on them. Lazlo would back me up.

"One of them talked," Kolya says.

"Already?" I don't hide the disappointment at Kolya ruining my fun.

"He's a Spetsnaz fucker."

"Why would the Rozettis hire Spetsnaz?"

"That's the thing, Boss. I don't think the entire hit was orchestrated by the Rozettis. I suspected it at first, but there was too much manpower for their level."

"Then who is it?"

"He says his contractor never showed his identity. They did a transaction over some app."

"Mercenary?"

"I believe so."

Fuck. They really picked the worst day to try and assassinate me.

"Bring him and the other one over."

"On it, Boss."

I don't usually revel in torture, but I'll enjoy every fucking second of making those assholes talk before I kill them.

No one threatens my family and lives.

I pause at that train of thought.

After Aunt Annika's death, I considered myself without a family.

This is the first time I've felt like I have a family again.

Lia and Jeremy.

If I have to destroy the world and everything in it to keep them safe, so be it.

THIRTY-ONE

Lia

I rock Jeremy in his crib, smiling at his sleeping form. His tiny fist is curled around my index finger and the other is resting near his neck.

He's so small and soft and the most beautiful thing I've ever seen. He smells of baby and summer and happy memories.

It's been five weeks since he came into this world, and sometimes, I still can't believe that I gave birth to this little human who looks like the purest of angels.

The events surrounding his birth are the subject of my nightmares, though. Every day, I wake up in a cold sweat, imagining Jeremy drowning in a pool of blood.

The recurring nightmare is similar to the one I used to have about breaking my leg before it happened. My subconscious is telling me something, and I'll be damned if I don't prevent it this time.

Although I had a strong connection to Jeremy when I was pregnant, the moment I held him in my arms for the first time, something inside me shifted. I'm ready to slaughter the world and everyone in it to keep him safe.

This is different from how I felt about ballet. While that was my dream, Jeremy is my flesh and blood. My connection to him is more visceral, and I'd sacrifice myself in a heartbeat to protect his tiny body.

Yan said that the attackers are paying for what they did. I didn't have to ask him how. I saw Adrian kill someone and he wouldn't hesitate to finish off others.

According to Yan, who was obviously trying to placate me, the attack was normal. Adrian is threatened by assassins often, but they never win.

Normal.

None of this is fucking normal. Adrian might consider being hunted down to be killed normal, but it's different for me and Jeremy. We didn't sign up for this life.

Besides, Adrian can only escape death for so long before it catches up to him.

Jeremy's face contorts as if he's hearing the ominous thought I'm having about his father and I coo him back to sleep, my own chest constricting at the idea of Adrian dying.

But isn't that expected with his lifestyle?

Yet, sometimes, I find myself holding on to the hope that he'll somehow defy the rules of nature and remain alive. That, as he promised, he'll protect us.

But the fact remains, there's nothing that will protect us from him. Adrian will always be Adrian, making enemies and forming vendettas. Maybe one day, I'll wake up and find an army of assassins in the front garden.

Jeremy and I will only be collateral damage of one of his assassination attempts.

The door opens softly in sync with my thoughts. I don't have to turn around to know who it is. The loosening of my muscles and the scent of leather is enough to give him away.

It's become so hard to stiffen around him, to pretend that

I'm bothered by his touch when, in fact, his presence awakens a dark, carnal desire inside me.

It doesn't help that he hasn't fucked me since a few weeks prior to Jeremy's birth. He went down on me before the birth and finger-fucked me, but he hasn't touched me since.

At least not sexually. Not even when the OB-GYN told us a few days ago that I'm good to have sex.

I guess he's still mad about how I requested that he let me and Jeremy live separately. But even in his anger, he still spoons me from behind every night. He tells me to get back to sleep when Jeremy wakes up in the middle of the night. He even says I should pump some of my breast milk so I don't have to get up when Jeremy is hungry.

I never expected to see that side of Adrian—being a father. But Jeremy is the reason he married me in the first place. My little angel is the one line that connects us.

But not for long.

My husband wraps his arms around me, his hands flattening on my stomach as he rests his chin on my shoulder. I hold my breath, but the need for air forces me to inhale his masculine scent and welcome his body heat.

"Asleep already?" The rumble of his tired voice shoots straight through my chest and another starved part of me.

Adrian has been working non-stop lately, and he's even been changing the house's security system over the last couple of days.

"He just fell asleep," I murmur, half to not wake Jeremy and half because Adrian's closeness is messing with me far more than I'd like to admit.

"He's only storing his energy to wake up like a wrecking ball later. He takes after you."

I tilt my head to meet his gaze. He looks so rugged and handsome, but the devil is always beautiful, isn't he? "Me?"

"You do that sometimes, stay silent until you explode."

"That's not true. Maybe he takes after you."

"I'll have you know that I was a very obedient child, Mrs. Volkov."

I swallow. Even though we've been married for almost a year, the sound of my married name still gives me a strange sensation I can't pinpoint.

It takes everything in me to rip my gaze from him and release myself from his hypnotic hold. "How come I don't believe that?"

"You can ask Kolya. I was a good boy."

I scoff.

"What?" He sounds almost offended.

"I just find it hard to think of you as a good boy."

"Mmmm. How about you?"

"What about me?"

"Were you a good girl, Lenochka?" The sudden drop in his voice causes my insides to quiver and my limbs to tremble. There will probably never be a day where I will stop responding to him in this carnal way.

"I was wild."

"Wild," he muses. "I like that."

"My mom wouldn't agree with you. She had to chase me all over the property to finally catch me."

"So you were naughty?"

"I guess."

"Are you still naughty?"

"Sometimes." My voice is too sultry, too breathy.

"Mmmm. Maybe I should see for myself." His fingers wrap around my jaw and angle it up. His hot lips drop to my neck, and I shiver as he peppers kisses on the sensitive skin before biting it into his mouth and sucking on it.

I instinctively tilt my head to the side, giving him access.

He nibbles down on my pulse point and I gasp.

Holy shit.

I forgot how much of a turn-on it is when he worships my neck that way, feasting on my life essence as if needing to feel it throb beneath his teeth.

His other hand lifts my skirt and I release a shattered breath when his fingers cup me through my wet panties.

"I see you are naughty, wife."

I hold on to the wrist of his hand that's wandering beneath my skirt, but it's not to stop him as much as it's to control my reaction to him.

He's merely cupping me and I feel like I will explode. Have I been that wanton for him all this time?

"Adrian…" I breathe out.

"Don't even think about rejecting me tonight, Lia."

"It's not that…"

"Good. Because I've waited so long to fuck your cunt and fill it with my cum."

His words send me into a frenzy, both because of the urgency in them and his dirty talk that always twists me in knots.

Adrian bunches my underwear in a fist and I shake my head.

"Adrian…don't rip it…"

"But you like it when I rip them." And with that, he tugs on the cotton material, sending it to shreds.

He's right. I like it, and the small burst of stimulation it creates in my core. He teases my clit, and I don't last two seconds.

I let my head roll back against his shoulder as the sudden but brief wave engulfs me and takes me under.

"There. Good girl."

"It's the hormones," I pant.

A gleam shines in his eyes. "Sure."

"It's true."

"Did I say anything?"

"You don't have to. It's written all over your face that you don't believe me."

"What else is written on my face, Lenochka?"

"I…don't know."

"It must be written all over my face that I'm going to fuck you until you scream my name. Then do it over and over again to get my fill of you. Only…" he murmurs. "I probably won't."

A shiver shakes me to my bones, and my breathing increases until it's chopped off and ragged.

"I'm going to fuck you senseless until the morning. Or more accurately…" he motions at Jeremy's crib. "Until Malysh wakes up."

I yelp when he carries me in his arms and strides through the door leading to our bedroom, kicking it shut behind him. He throws me on the bed and follows soon after like a beast on a mission to conquer his bride.

He doesn't even bother to remove his clothes, only tugging his pants to free his hard cock. It doesn't matter how many times I see it, his dick always spurs a moment of apprehension.

When he parts my legs, my chest heaves so hard, I don't think I've ever felt this way before. Adrian pulls the skirt away so that I'm naked from the waist down, and only a flimsy button-up shirt covers my aching, naked breasts.

He kneels between my legs, grabs both of my ankles, and places my feet on his broad shoulders. "Keep them there."

The stormy gray of his eyes sparks with hunger as he slowly enters me. The change in pattern from his usually rough, unapologetic one causes my back to arch off the bed.

"Fuck." He strains. "You're tighter, Lenochka."

I want to ask if that's a good or a bad thing, but he doesn't give me the chance to speak as his cock sinks inside me with unhurried depth, filling me whole.

Like earlier, the mere penetration is almost enough to send me over the edge. Adrian pushes inside me at a moderate pace, the position giving him a rare depth.

But soon after, his nature takes charge and his thrusts

become harder, rougher, and with a delicious edge. "Fuck, I've missed this. I've missed you, Lia."

His words, coupled with his touch, turn me boneless. My pussy clenches around him and every bundle of nerves is attuned to him.

Adrian releases one of my thighs and holds my legs together with one hand, driving in even deeper. His free hand reaches between us and my eyes widen when he presses his thumb against my back entrance.

He glides it inside and the resistance is real, but so is the exploding of pleasure pooling in my core. The more he pushes in, the tighter I clench around him.

"Adrian..." I moan.

"Say it again."

"Adrian."

"Yes." His eyes are a hot fire as his pace increases in both depth and rhythm.

I guess it shouldn't hurt to let him hear my voice for one final time.

"Adrian..." I moan. "Ahh... Adrian..." Tears pool in my eyes, and I don't know if it's the hormones or the fact that I've also missed him or the knowledge that I won't have this anymore.

I won't have anyone who understands my carnal needs even better than I ever would and makes them all come true.

A low, husky groan rips from his lips as he speaks sharp, short words in Russian, probably cursing.

"Do you have any idea how much I've missed your throaty little moans?" he rasps, his accent thicker than usual, as he pushes his thumb in my tight hole. "You'll scream for me when I claim this ass, won't you, Lenochka?"

My breathing is chopped off by the relentless, delicious way he's fucking me and the intrusion of his finger. My nipples ache so much that two wet spots form on the shirt. I cover them up with a hand, but Adrian has already noticed.

A grunt spills from his lips, sounding almost animalistic in his lust. "Let go."

I slowly do, and his fiery eyes take in the soaked cloth and my protruding nipples through the shirt.

"Fuck," Adrian breathes out, slowing down to watch the evidence of my lactation.

"It's the hormones," I murmur, shame burning my ears.

"I fucking love the hormones."

"Adrian…" I move my hips against him.

"What?"

"Don't…stop…"

A sheen of wild hunger and something else covers his features as he picks up his pace again. I don't know if it's because of that or his finger at my back entrance or his eyes on my breasts, but I come the hardest I have since I can remember.

This orgasm is stronger and longer than earlier and I roll my hips to ride it out. I don't mute my moans either, because selfishly, this is the memory I want to leave him with.

This moment right here—of me moaning his name. I don't want him to ever forget this or me.

Adrian curses in Russian as he empties himself inside me, then falls beside me. We remain there, panting for a moment. Me on my back and Adrian on his side.

He props himself up on his elbow, his hooded eyes zeroing in on my shirt that's soaked with lactation from the orgasm.

Adrian undoes the buttons, and my face heats when he uncovers my nipples, which are still hard, with beads of transparent liquid leaking from them.

"So messy," he teases.

"It's the hormones," I murmur.

"I should take care of the hormones, then."

"W-what?"

"They look painful. Are they?"

"A little."

"Do you want me to relieve that ache, Lia? Want me to rid you of the excess milk?"

His words are a straight zap to my pussy and I clench my thighs as the sole word rips from my lips. "Yes…"

His mouth latches onto a nipple, and I gasp as his teeth nibble on the tip before sucking. Hard.

Holy hell.

I can feel the pulse between my legs. It's so perverse, but I'm strangely turned on by it.

The more he bites, the higher I arch my back. The harder he sucks, the more arousal coats my thighs. Adrian's tongue laps on my areola before he takes my engorged nipple in his hot mouth again and pulls at it with his teeth. His fingers squeeze my other nipple, twisting and pinching until my chest and belly are messy with the evidence of my lactation.

A vibrating sound startles me and I flinch. Adrian groans as he releases my nipple with a pop. My mouth parts and my thighs pulsate with need as I watch his moist lips.

Shit. Why am I so aroused by his perversion?

He retrieves his phone and answers with a grunting, "Volkov. This better be good."

His annoyed expression disappears, replaced by one of pure contemplation as he steps from the bed and tucks himself in. "I'll be there in fifteen."

"Is something wrong?" I ask, sitting up and hoping to hell he doesn't detect the hope in my tone.

"I have an urgent meeting." He kisses my forehead. "I'll be away for a few hours, possibly until the morning. Call me if you need anything."

"Okay…I mean, I will."

He shakes his head but doesn't comment on my use of the word he hates so much.

"Sleep well, Lenochka."

I nod.

I think he's going to leave, but then he lowers his head and captures my lips in a slow kiss. Usually, his kisses are all-consuming, as hard as he fucks and as unforgiving, too, but right now, he's kissing me with passion that reaches my bones.

Like he cares.

I kiss him back, lost in the moment, because it seems that I care, too. Fuck. I more than care.

He pulls away, a small smile grazing his lips. "I've missed you, Lenochka."

And with that, he turns and leaves. I stare at the door after it clicks shut behind him. My mind is bogged down with the realization I had while he was kissing me just now.

I love him.

I fell in love with the devil despite his monstrous nature.

My legs quiver as I slide them down the bed.

No. I must be mistaking lust for love. I need to save myself and my baby from the danger he is.

Whether it's love or lust doesn't matter, because Jeremy and I aren't safe with him.

It takes everything in me to remove my clothes and put on a pair of jeans, a hoodie, and a coat. I stare out the window as I dress. Kolya, Yan, Boris, and Adrian get in the car before it soon speeds away from the mansion.

He took his best guards with him. Good.

After I make sure they're gone, I barge through the door separating the bedroom from Jeremy's nursery and wrap him up in thick clothes and a blanket. I fill my backpack with his necessities and a bottle of my milk that I pumped earlier in preparation for this.

I couldn't possibly have missed out on the opportunity of escaping while the system is being replaced. Usually, Adrian will have every record of my movements at his disposal, but the system change is my only short window of getting out of here unscathed with Jeremy.

It took me a day to come up with this plan. I'll leave

through the back door, from which I've seen Ogla bring in the house's supplies, and then I can take a plane to another state and stay under the radar to raise Jeremy. Since Adrian takes care of all our expenses and I don't have a lease to worry about, my small fortune from ballet has remained untouched. I'll use that to give my son a good life.

It's not the perfect plan, but it's better than nothing.

I was supposed to execute my plan in the morning after Adrian leaves, since he barely spends time at home nowadays, but fate is on my side tonight.

After strapping the baby carrier around me, I carefully place Jeremy in it and cover him with the blanket.

I make sure to leave my phone on the nightstand since it's most likely being tracked, then sneak out of the room.

Usually, I'd be wary of the cameras in the hallways, but due to the system change, they're not working.

I walk silently to the kitchen, watching my surroundings, heart nearly beating out of my chest.

Footsteps sound from around the corner and I flatten my back against the wall, placing a protective hand around Jeremy and slamming the other against my mouth.

The guards aren't allowed inside unless Adrian calls them in, so only one other person could be in the kitchen this late.

Sure enough, Ogla's shadow appears as she pauses in the doorway before she heads down the hall.

I wait for her footsteps to disappear, then I slowly head to the kitchen. Once it's in view, I dash inside, ignoring the thumping of my heart.

Taking a deep breath, I wrap my hand around the doorknob of the door leading outside and turn. I nearly cry with joy when it opens.

The cold November air slaps me in the face, but I couldn't have felt any warmer. I tighten the blanket around Jeremy and quicken my steps away from the house.

From the times I've spied on this place, I already know I'll find myself at a special fence that requires a code. I punch in the numbers I've seen Ogla put in a thousand times and the gate clicks open.

I dash outside, my shoes slapping against the concrete as I run.

A large gulp of air rushes into my lungs when I inhale.

I did it.

I left.

I'm *free*.

No one will pose a danger to me or my son.

My heart clenches at the thought of what I've left behind, but I ignore that sentiment.

In my adrenaline rush, the run from the back of the house to the road wasn't even that long.

I'm surprised to see a cab soon after I'm out and wave my hand at it. I have enough cash with me for a ride and a plane ticket. I'll need to withdraw more from my bank, but thankfully, I can do that in any of their branches. I'll have to be careful about it, and will probably do it in a different place than where I'm residing so Adrian doesn't track me down.

The cab breezes past me and I realize it's occupied. I wave my hand at the next car, hoping it's a cab, too. The vehicle comes to a halt right in front of me, and my heart nearly comes to a halt along with it when the back door opens and my own devil steps out.

Even in the darkness, I can make out his murderous expression. "Going somewhere, Lia?"

As he advances toward me, I know, I just know that I've messed up any chance I had at freedom.

THIRTY-TWO

Lia

I T'S OVER.

Not only did my escape plan fail, but I've also lost any sliver of freedom Adrian might have given me.

It was one thing to ask him to let me go, but acting on it is completely another. He'll make it his mission to tighten the gilded cage around me until I eventually wither and die.

The ride back home is spent in silence. My hand trembles around Jeremy despite my attempts to steady it. I'm thankful he woke up, and I occupied myself by feeding him from the bottle. But he soon goes back to sleep, leaving me in the cruel presence of his father.

Adrian hasn't uttered a word since he grabbed me by the elbow and ushered me inside the car. I didn't even try to fight. What's the point now that he's caught me?

I wish he'd spoken, though. I wish he'd let go of his anger, because if there's anything I've learned about Adrian during all this time, it's that his emotions simmer under the surface, especially his rare anger. When he does release it, the one in his path—*me*—will be ruined beyond repair.

My throat fills with bile due to the sickening type of fear tugging at my stomach.

Even Yan shakes his head at me when we step out of the car. I lift my chin, although my teeth are chattering. I did what I had to do in order to protect myself and my baby. If I had the chance of a redo, I'd do it all over again. I won't let anyone tell me I did something wrong.

Adrian grabs me by the elbow and drags me behind him up the stairs. I flinch when he unstraps the baby carrier and a sleeping Jeremy from my arms, and barks, "Stay there."

Then he strides with his son to his nursery.

My throat constricts more by the second as I remove my backpack and coat with shaky hands. I remain in the middle of the bedroom like a prisoner waiting to be judged. Thoughts of what he'll do to me invade my mind, magnifying by the second.

I can take his punishments, and although I will never admit it aloud, I do enjoy the depravity of them. But what if my punishment this time will surpass anything he's done to me before?

I try arming myself with courageous thoughts, but nothing, absolutely *nothing* could prepare me for the dead look in Adrian's eyes when he returns to the bedroom. The sound of the door closing slices in my chest and sends a whole body shudder through me.

He's wearing a black cashmere coat over his white shirt, but it's not the clothes that make him seem broader and harsher. It's the shadow across his face and the slight twist in his lips, as if he wants to rip someone to shreds with his bare teeth.

Adrian is a tall man, huge compared to me, but now, he seems to have gained more height, filling the room and my air with his unforgiving presence. Even his handsome face looks like the devil's right now.

When he speaks, his dark, threatening voice sends my teeth chattering again. "Now, Lia. Why don't you tell me where you were planning to go?"

I swallow past the solid lump in my throat.

"Where the fuck were you planning to go?" His voice increases in volume.

I flinch even as I lift my chin. "Anywhere but here."

"Anywhere but here," he repeats, musing as he stalks toward me. I'm tempted to step back, to escape his wrath, to put as much distance between us as possible. However, my feet remain glued to the floor.

I did nothing wrong. If anything, he's the one in the wrong by exposing me and his son to this life when he knew we'd be in constant danger.

He stops in front of me, larger than life and scarier, too. "Did you say anywhere but here?"

"We're not safe," I blurt. "I don't want to raise my child in a world where he could be killed any second."

"If I hadn't seen you, I would've found your corpse tomorrow or received a ransom call. Did I or did I not tell you that the moment you step a foot outside, you're fucking dead?!"

I jerk at the building force behind his words. I finally manage to step back, startling when I hit the solid wall.

Adrian is on me in a fraction of a second, his hands slamming on either side of me. I can breathe his rage, his merciless wrath, and it's even scarier than if he were touching me.

"Answer me, Lia," he grinds out.

"You did." I hate how my voice trembles.

"Apparently you didn't listen, or you wouldn't have put yourself and Jeremy in fucking danger. Did you want to witness his death before they kidnap and rape you, is that it?"

"No!" The images make bile rise to my throat once more. "I just…I just wanted to protect him from…from…"

"Me?"

"From your life," I confess slowly, staring at my feet.

He doesn't say anything, but his arms tighten on either side of me, as if the tension will burst free from them. I think he'll punish me now, he'll turn my skin red, and I hope that will be the end of it.

His quiet voice fills the air. "You'll make it a habit, won't you? No matter what I do to make you happy and comfortable, no matter how much I try to make progress with us, you will try to escape every chance you get."

My head snaps up and I shake it slowly. I don't want him to think that or else he'll take away whatever freedom I have left. "Adrian, I...won't."

"Liar. I can see it in your eyes, Lia. You're scared of me and how I'll retaliate, but you won't stop. Not until you accomplish your goal."

"Adrian...please...please..."

"Please what?"

"Don't take it all away. I'll be suffocated to death."

"You should've considered that when you planned to run away."

"Adrian..."

He wraps his hand around my jaw in a firm hold that forbids me any movement. His hands might kill and maim, but they're usually warm and gentle whenever he touches me. Even when he punishes me, his hands are firm, but they're never as freezing cold as right now. "Where did I go wrong, hmm? Was it by allowing you to go out? Allowing you to treat Yan as a friend? I should take care of those two things first."

A tear slides down my cheek as I shake my head again. "Don't...please..."

"After that, I will keep you in a room and use you as my fucking slut. Is that what you want?"

The thought stabs me deeper than his earlier threats. Adrian's caring side is the reason I've been able to get through all these months. While sex has played a big part in our relationship, it isn't what's kept me going or reduced my nightmares. It isn't what saved me from myself after the end of my career.

I didn't think of it much at the time, but I liked how Adrian attentively looked out for me. I loved his aftercare and how he always made sure I was comfortable and satiated. How he held me every night and kissed me before leaving the house.

It was his way of telling me I'm more than just an object of desire to him.

But if he takes all of that away, I'll be no different than a whore with a shiny diamond ring.

And that thought pierces the place in my heart that's come to the realization that I love him. Despite his villainous nature, I love that he took care of me after my injury, that he continues to do so, even after I gave birth. That he devotes time to be there for me and knows my needs before I voice them. I believed he only wanted me because of Jeremy, but his attitude has never changed toward me post-birth. If anything, he's been doing his best to take the load off me.

A fresh stream of tears fall down my cheeks. "No, Adrian, don't do that…"

His harsh features don't ease. Instead, they turn into granite. "I also told you not to entertain the idea of leaving, but you did it, anyway. Who do you think will win if we go down this road?"

I can't control my tears anymore as I stand in the line of his ruthless wrath. It's worse than if it were physical because, while Adrian can be caring, his true nature is monstrous and unforgiving. He won't stop until he crushes everything in his path.

"You will *not* escape again, Lia."

I nod frantically, even if a part of me will always want to.

"If you do, if I find out you're so much as entertaining that idea, I will lock you up in a fucking cell and forbid you from seeing Jeremy ever again. He'll be raised by someone else and you'll lose all access to him."

"No...no..." I sob. "Not that...don't take away Jeremy. He's my only light."

"Then don't fucking pull a stunt like this again."

"Okay—I mean fine. I won't."

He steps back and I suck in a harsh breath, but his anger doesn't lessen. In fact, it seems to have risen to the surface, threatening to destroy everything in his path.

"Are you...going to punish me now?"

"If I do anything in my state, I'll break your fucking skin, so no, I won't touch you when I'm angry, Lia." He releases a long breath, shakes his head as if he's disappointed, then turns and leaves.

The door closes behind him with a finality that echoes through my hollow insides.

I slide to the floor, joining the broken pieces of my heart that are lying there.

I slam a hand on my chest as if that will stop the slow disintegration of my heart. As if it will heal the gaping wound Adrian just left in my soul.

He's always been dark, but there was at least some light when it came to me. Now, that light is gone, and all that remains is his darkness.

A sob tears from my throat, because I know, I just know that I lost a part of Adrian tonight.

The part I fell in love with.

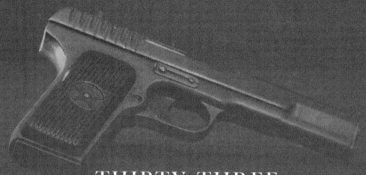

THIRTY-THREE

Adrian

I TAP MY FINGER AGAINST MY THIGH AS I STARE OUT MY office window.

The view in front of me gives me an urge to cut some-one down.

Him, preferably.

Lia is sitting in the garden, holding Jeremy and smiling as she talks to him. Then, she directs that smile at my fucker guard, Yan.

The bastard gives her a toothy grin as he waves at Jeremy.

It's been two months since Lia attempted to escape. Two months of constant paranoia that she'll do it again and succeed this time.

I forbade her from going outside after that stunt, but I can do that for only so long before her depression kicks back in and she'll need a breathing outlet.

Still, I can't help thinking that one day, I won't be careful enough, I won't watch her hard enough, and she'll vanish into thin air.

That's why I allowed Yan to get close to her, even though

that puts me in the constant mood to kill him. I thought that if he watches her all the time and forms some sort of a friendship with her, he'll know when she plans to leave. He might not agree with all of my decisions concerning her, but he also doesn't want her to leave. Unlike her, he knows that what awaits her out there is way worse than what is here.

She's safe under my roof, where no one would dare to touch her, no matter how much the elders in the brotherhood disapprove of her. Being my wife gives her an immunity that she won't be able to find anywhere else on earth.

However, there has been a slight miscalculation on my part concerning Yan. Or rather, a misconception. I thought I could handle seeing them getting close.

That's far from reality.

Every time he's in her vicinity, my head fills with murderous thoughts that keep getting more creative with each passing day. They become more brutal whenever she smiles at him, like right now. The fact that she rarely offers me her smiles anymore but gives them so freely to Yan gets on my very last nerve.

Maybe I should ship the fucker back to Russia.

Some Spetsnaz training would do his personality good. If he dies there, oh well. *What a fucking pity.*

"Sir."

"Hmm?" I release an absentminded noise at Kolya's voice while I continue to stare at Lia and Yan. Even Jeremy, my traitor son, is giggling at him.

"Don't do it."

I halt my tapping and stare at my second-in-command sitting across from me with his laptop resting on his thighs. "Don't do what?"

He pauses, then replies, "Kill Yan."

"What makes you believe I'm thinking about killing him?"

"The way you stare at him."

"I wasn't thinking about killing him."

"No?"

"No. The Spetsnaz will take care of it. What's the most ruthless unit there?"

"You have it in you to get rid of him?"

"If he keeps getting on my nerves, yes."

"He's only befriending her, per your orders, sir."

"I never ordered him to *smile* at her."

"If he's stoic, she'll never open up to him."

"Keep defending the fucker, Kolya, and his Spetsnaz future will become a reality sooner rather than later."

"You can't send him away and you know it, sir."

"Of course I can."

"And leave Mrs. Volkov alone?"

"She's not alone. She has me."

"You work all the time. Besides, you're not talkative enough for her taste."

"I can be talkative."

"No offense, sir, but no, you can't. Let Yan fill that gap. She needs a friend and you're well aware of it."

My lips twist in disapproval. I dislike it when Kolya is right. One of the reasons I allowed her to be close to Yan in the first place is because she's a lonely soul who needs a friend, someone she can feel at ease around.

While I prefer she talks to me, that's not possible lately, after I snapped at her for trying to leave. Though she comes undone around my dick, mouth, and fingers every night, she's still scared and wary of me. She counts her every move and word, and even her damn breaths around me now.

I meet Yan's gaze through the window and beckon at him to come inside. He says something to Lia and she stares back at me, her smile disappearing and her lips parting before she lowers her head and focuses back on Jeremy.

Standing up, I close the shutters. Soon after, Yan knocks on the door before he opens it and comes in. The moment he steps inside, I grab him by the throat and slam him against the wall.

He wheezes, his hands instinctively wrapping around my wrists, but he soon drops them when he meets my murderous expression.

Kolya abandons his laptop on the chair and comes to our side, but he's smart enough not to interfere.

"Aren't you getting too cozy, Yan?" I ask with deceptive calm.

"No, sir," he manages through my strong hold.

"Good. In case you've forgotten, your only mission is to watch her, not to get too cozy with her."

"You're the one who told me to befriend her."

"Did you just fucking talk back to me?"

"Just stating facts."

"Here's a fun fact for you, if I catch you being cozy with her, I'll crush your windpipe. Or better yet, I'll ship you to the Spetsnaz so they can do the honors."

When he nods, I release him with a shove. He catches his breath, massaging his neck as he stares at me. "If you send me to the Spetsnaz, Lia will be sad."

"Shut up, Yan," Kolya scolds.

I tilt my head to the side. "What the fuck did you just say?"

"I'm the only one she opens up to…after you, of course."

I narrow my eyes on him.

"I'm just being there for her. Don't take it away, Boss. I promise to never touch her."

"That's because if you do, I'll break your hand."

"I need my hand, so I'd never do it unless absolutely necessary."

"And don't smile at her."

"That would be impossible. I'm not you, Boss. I can't stop myself from smiling when she does it…" he trails off when I glare at him. "But I will *try*."

"Your future depends on how you behave."

He grumbles a response, and I turn my attention away from him. I should probably call it a day, put Jeremy to sleep, and have Lia all to myself.

I believe that with time, she'll forget about the idea of leaving.

Sooner or later, she'll realize that her place is with me and our son.

THIRTY-FOUR

Lia

Four years later

LIFE HAS NEVER BEEN THE SAME AFTER THAT NIGHT.
I was right. I lost a part of Adrian.

At first, I wanted to fix it, to tell him that it wasn't him I hated, it was what he stood for. That me and my baby's survival came before whatever feelings I'd developed for him.

But my pride forbid me from it. He spent weeks avoiding me, not even eating with me until his anger lessened and he came back to my side.

Our sex life is still as crazy as when we first started out. He still whips, spanks, and ties me up to the bedpost. He still takes me roughly and puts my pleasure first. But there isn't that slightly mischievous tone or dirty talk anymore. He just gives us both what we need, then usually spends the night working.

He's stopped hugging me to sleep when I turn away from him. Once, I was so starved for his affection that I turned around and pretended to snuggle into him during my sleep.

He didn't hug me back. But he didn't push me away either, so whenever I feel like I'll burst, I do that.

Adrian still has the best aftercare and goes out of his way to make sure I'm comfortable, but it's more mechanical now. It used to feel as if he enjoyed taking care of me; however, now, it feels like a duty.

My form of rebellion is muffling my voice. When I did that before Jeremy's birth, Adrian used to demand hearing it. He used to whip me and bring me to the brink of orgasms so I'd say something. Now, he seems content with my being mute.

We hardly talk, and when we do, it's usually about Jeremy. My little angel has become the only reason I wake up every morning.

Okay. That's a lie.

A small part of me, the part that never fell out of love with Adrian, still hopes that today will be better, today Adrian will trust me.

But I wouldn't trust me if I were him. He knows I want to leave, and even though I haven't attempted to escape again for fear of his wrath, Adrian isn't an idiot. He's well aware that if I get the chance, I'll leave.

He stopped me from going to those charity events for months, probably thinking I'd leave, anyway. When I started having nightmares and falling back into a depressive hole a few months later, I told him I wanted to go out, and surprisingly, he didn't fight me on it.

By going back to my charity work, I've been able to meet with Luca in the bathroom, but only for short intervals.

I haven't really had any important information for him, because Adrian is a fort. The few times he's taken me to the brotherhood's meetings, he's treated me as if I'm an annoying rock in his shoe. I hate the Adrian from the Bratva. That Adrian feels like a completely different person, a cold-hearted one who doesn't give two fucks about me.

I hate the brotherhood and everyone in it, too, except for maybe Rai, who's never treated me as if I'm a pest.

They despise me because I took Kristina Petrov's rightful place. They think I tricked Adrian into marrying me by getting pregnant, that I'm a shameless gold digger and without any notable origins. Adrian has never negated that, and I don't have the state of mind to defend myself when no one believes me.

Part of the reason why I continue to meet Luca is because I need some sort of a friend, someone whom I can feel like my old self again around. He knows I probably won't give him anything, but maybe he also likes seeing me.

I don't even think about Mom anymore. I know Luca won't give me that information unless I completely sell out Adrian. That foolish corner in my heart rebels against that idea and it's not just because of my stupid feelings toward him. It's also because he's Jeremy's father.

My baby boy loves his father so much. When my episodes of depression hit and I can't get out of bed, Adrian takes him outside and plays with him.

Besides, if Adrian is gone, Jeremy and I are doomed. I've realized over the years just how much power he holds. Not only in the brotherhood, in which everyone respects him, but also among all the other crime organizations who look at Sergei with envy for having someone like Adrian with him.

Maybe that's why Luca's parting words from the other day are bugging me. After we had our usual meeting in the bathroom, he was shifty, and when I asked him if there was something wrong as he was leaving, he told me, "It's nothing you should worry about. I'll take care of it." Then, he was out of the window before I could ask him what 'it' is.

It could be because of that or the fact that I didn't get to put Jeremy to sleep tonight, but I've been on edge all evening.

Adrian brought me to Mikhail Kozlov's birthday party.

It's being held by Sergei in honor of his 'brother' of almost fifty years. Sergei sure likes to throw parties for those closest to him, and doesn't hold back.

I huddle in a corner, clutching a glass of champagne in my stiff fingers. Usually, Rai keeps me company, but she climbed V Corp's ladder and became a hotshot who doesn't have time for me anymore.

Adrian sure as hell doesn't stand with me, let alone talk to me, when we're in the midst of his own people. But I guess it's better this way. At least no one pays attention to me until it's time to go home and hug my angel.

Gripping my flute of champagne, I stare at my watch, then sigh heavily when I see it's only eight in the evening.

My clutch bag feels heavy in my hand because Adrian now makes me carry a gun. After the attack on the day I gave birth, he trained me to shoot, even when I told him I didn't want to. He said what I want doesn't matter, then made me hold a gun and shoot for weeks until I learned how to use it.

He also trained me to use some self-defense moves.

Adrian said it's for when I need to defend myself when neither he nor his guards are there. I've never encountered such a situation since Yan and Boris are basically my shadows.

I hate that Adrian is forcing me to carry a weapon of destruction, but I've come to know that he's stiff and unmovable on matters like these.

I might win some arguments, like not having the nanny come in every day or being able to teach Jer instead of the Russian teachers. In fact, most of the arguments I win are about Jeremy. He lets me have freedom in raising him, but other than that, he's been guarded since that night.

As if expecting me to run again.

Not that I could with the heavy security. Besides, the thought of him taking Jeremy away gives me damn nightmares.

"If it isn't the lovely hidden beauty?" an amused voice calls from behind me before Damien joins me. Soon after, Kirill appears out of nowhere and stands next to him.

I groan internally, even as I nod in greeting. Their company is the last thing I need. Kirill is always somehow trying to interrogate me about Adrian, and Damien seems happy to throw jabs at me.

At the beginning, I found it hard to keep up with who's who, so I made a long-ass digital document with Ogla's help to specify who is who in the Bratva. Surprisingly, Adrian didn't mind and even told Ogla to assist me. But then again, he fully expects me to stay by his side, so he wouldn't worry about me making an educational file about his organization.

"Adrian said you were sick," Kirill muses, running his cunning gaze over me. "You look pretty good for someone who's sick."

"I got better," I speak in a quiet voice, glad that Adrian lies about my health all the time so I'm not expected to attend.

Even though he does it because I embarrass him, I'm happy that I don't have to meet these people often. When I'm with Jeremy back at home or volunteering at the shelter, I feel like I'm detached from them and their criminal activities.

"Now, Lia." Damien grins. "What's really going on? Is he bruising you, so you can't come out? Tell Rai about it, and she'll help since she's into all of that women standing up for women shit."

"That's not it." I'm slightly offended on Adrian's behalf. He might be cold and aloof, but he's the best family man among all of them. He'd never hurt me or Jeremy.

Kirill adjusts his glasses with his middle and ring fingers. "Then what is it?"

I gulp past the lump in my throat. As much as I've seen them over the years, these two scare me, especially after the stories Yan told me about them. How Kirill was in the special forces and killed more than anyone can count, or how Damien beats people to death if they so much as piss him off.

Sometimes, I think I was lucky to land on Adrian's radar, not theirs. Because spending a minute in their presence has turned me itchy and fidgety.

"He asked you something, beautiful," Damien insists.

"Why don't you ask me?"

I release a breath at Adrian's voice, and I peek at him as he stands beside me, his entire attention on Kirill and Damien who don't seem happy that their fun was halted.

With careful fingers, I bring the glass of champagne to my lips and take a sip to calm my nerves.

Adrian's presence sends a mixture of relief and a stab of chronic agony to my aching chest. One-sided emotions are the work of the devil. Not only do they hurt all the time, but they also keep me hoping, pining. Even when I know that Adrian isn't capable of returning such emotions.

I know he cares. I know Jeremy and I mean something to him, but it'll never be more than that. He'll never look at me the way I secretly look at him when he's not paying attention.

And that hurts more than I care to admit.

Adrian's face is a blank mask, but I can't help admiring the serene look covering his features and the sharp edges of his cheekbones. He's wearing a black suit with a light gray shirt that matches the color of his eyes. He really only ever has those types of dark colors in his wardrobe. And because I volunteer, my taste in clothing is no longer flashy, but more like his, modest and reserved.

"Adrian." Kirill smiles. "We were just telling Lia how lovely it is that she's joining us tonight."

"I thought you said she was sick." Damien raises a brow.

"She obviously isn't tonight." Adrian keeps his cool voice, even though his body is slightly turned toward me.

"Can you tell us more about her sickness that seems to come and go on a whim?" Kirill taps a contemplative thumb on his lips. "I'm curious."

"I don't answer to you, Morozov," Adrian drawls. "In fact, it's the other way around, so why don't you turn around and leave?"

Kirill's expression doesn't change, but a grin is plastered on his lips. "My, my. This is interesting."

"What?" Damien's gaze flits between the three of us. "What's interesting? What did I miss?"

I'm about to down the glass of champagne in an attempt to douse the tension when I catch a glimpse of a shadow moving in the background. It's across from me, diagonally to the hall that leads to the back entrance. I know it because I've often slipped in there to find Yan and hide from the onlookers.

The unease I've felt since a few days ago rushes back in like a merciless hurricane.

I'll take care of it.

My eyes widen in remembrance of Luca's words. No. Don't tell me he…

I don't get the chance to think about it when metal glints in the corner. I drop my glass of champagne and grab Adrian by the sleeve, then pull him down so we're both tumbling against the tables.

A shot rings in the air and a collective gasp follows.

Adrian's large body drops atop of mine and his hard chest covers my front on the ground. He retrieves his gun, and I stare at his face a few inches away from mine.

I feel up his sides, mechanically searching for a wound. That was so close, what if he…what if he…

Adrian grabs my face, his voice harsh as doom. "Are you hurt?"

I shake my head.

"Use your voice, Lia."

"No. Are you?" Both of my hands are digging in the sides of his jacket, but I still want to make sure he's okay.

"I'm fine." He releases a sharp breath. "How did you know?"

"I…I saw a shadow, then a glinting of metal in the corner."

"Fuck, Lia. You should've gotten down first." His eyes clash against mine, and unlike the past four years, there's fire in there, passion, and the utter care I thought I would never see again after that night.

I almost cry with relief, but the sensation is short-lived when he shakes his head, his expression hardening again. "You have your gun on you?"

"Uh…yeah." It's in my bag that's still in my hand.

"Stay here."

Damien and Kirill jump to their feet, running to where the shooter disappeared to.

Adrian pushes off me in one graceful movement, then pulls the table down to hide me underneath it. "Yan will get to you."

He turns to leave, but I clutch his sleeve, my tongue feeling heavy in my throat as I murmur, "Don't…die."

And I mean it, I don't want anything bad to happen to him.

He gives a curt nod before he follows the others.

I don't stay there, though.

As soon as they're gone, I push up from behind the table and flatten myself against the wall as I avoid the chaos in the crowd.

Adrian and the others are headed to where they thought the shooter disappeared, but if my gut is right and Luca is behind this, he won't be so obvious.

I once told him that one of the cameras near the staff's entrance has a delay in recording. I only found out because Rai mentioned it, saying they don't use it that much, anyway, since most staff are live-in.

Luca must've used that information to get in. I don't think the shooter is him, but I have no doubt that he's somewhere near.

The first time I met Luca was in elementary school. He was adopted and hated it, and since his parents were of Italian heritage and I missed Italy, I wanted to be friends with him. I told him I'd lost my parents and he said he'd also lost his mom and dad, and that's how we bonded. However, Luca always played in the background, even then.

He was secretive when we were young, but whenever he pulled a prank or took revenge on the kids who bullied him, he made sure to be present to watch.

That's why I'm positive he's here somewhere, and I need to stop him before he really *takes care* of Adrian.

I remain on the threshold between the back of Sergei's house and the staff entrance, and find that the camera is not blinking at all.

My hand reaches to my gun and I snap the silencer on. Yan gave it to me in case I'm in a situation where the place is full of people and I don't want anyone to hear. No idea why this feels like such a situation.

With careful steps, I walk into the small backyard that's overlooking a wire fence.

I stop when I find Luca whisper-yelling at another man who's bulkier than him with a long scar running down his right cheek. "You fucking fool. You had one mission."

"Luca..." I breathe.

He and the man snap their attention toward me at the same time. Both are dressed in army fatigues and Luca has a mask and a baseball cap on.

"She stopped me." The scarred man points at me with a sneer. "Fucking bitch."

"Duchess." Luca's nostrils flare. "Are you protecting Adrian?"

I widen my stance, staring behind me to make sure no one is there. "I never told you I wanted him killed."

"Well, I do. So don't fucking get in my way again."

I don't know what comes over me as I raise the gun and point it at him. "I will not let you hurt him, Luca."

"My, my, Duchess. You'll kill me for him?"

"I don't want to. Don't make me."

"What if I tell you he's been using you all along? That he's on the side of your parents' murderer."

My hand falters on the gun as his words sink to the bottom of my stomach. "W-what?"

"Here's your truth, Lia. Adrian is only with you because he's an ally to your father. The same father who ordered a hit on your parents in Italy."

"You're...just saying that because I refuse to help you anymore."

"I'm saying that so you'll wake the fuck up. Adrian is not on your side—never was, never will be. He's merely serving his and the Bratva's agenda, and keeping you as a trump card for being Lazlo Luciano's illegitimate daughter."

My head spins and the hand holding the gun trembles.

No. Luca is being spiteful. None of this is true. It *can't* be.

"I'm out of here." The scarred man's voice is like nails scratching against my brain. "I'll kill Volkov next time."

"You fucking better," Luca mutters.

My mind is trapped in a maze and a blow of undecipherable emotions bursts through me. Only one remains, though, as I aim the gun at the scarred man's nape and shoot.

I didn't even have to think about it. Hearing him say that he'd come back for Adrian's life was enough to propel me to action. I had to stop him. To protect my husband and my baby's father, despite Luca's words.

Due to Adrian's strict training, I don't miss. The bullet lodges itself in the back of the man's head, causing him to fall face-first on the ground. The thud is loud in the silence as he stops moving, stops breathing.

Just stops.

Oh, God.

I...killed a man. I just killed someone. A person.

And yet, no feelings wash over me. Maybe I've lost my soul now and there's no way I'll get it back.

I had to protect Adrian. I just had to.

Luca glares at me. "What the fuck, Duchess?"

"Give me evidence." My voice is calm considering the shaking of my hand. "When I make sure your words are true, that I'm merely a pawn in his game, I'll kill Adrian myself."

"I'll hold you to that." Luca jumps on the wall and climbs it before disappearing over the fence.

I don't stare at the man, at the life I've just ended with my own hand, as I approach him and crouch over his unmoving body. I drop the gun to my side and retrieve a nail file from my purse, using it to dig at his bloody gaping wound.

Adrian and the others will be here any minute, but I need to retrieve that bullet or he'll know it was me. Since I have a small gun, it wouldn't be hard to figure out who did it.

Bile rises to my throat and my eyes well with tears as I dig the pointy side in until I finally find the bullet, struggling for a few seconds until I pull it out.

I gather my gun, the nail file, and the bullet, then rush back inside and to one of the bathrooms. I scrub my hands and wash the file and the bullet before I tuck them into my clutch bag. I'll have to get rid of them when I go out to volunteer.

The face that greets me in the mirror is pale, hollow, and there are tears streaming down my cheeks.

The face of a killer.

I finished a life and signed the death sentence of my innocence.

But the possibility of Adrian using me all this time might as well have issued the death sentence to my heart and soul.

THIRTY-FIVE

Adrian

SOMETHING'S CHANGED.

Lia hasn't been the same since the assassination attempt a few weeks ago at Mikhail's birthday party.

I knew I shouldn't have taken her there. Not only is she uncomfortable at the brotherhood's banquets, but I'm also on edge every minute, seeing everyone as a threat and stopping myself from whisking her out of there.

Not to mention that I'm constantly seeing red whenever a man looks at her, let alone talks to her.

But it's different this time.

She often has this dazed expression, where she's staring at nothing, exactly as I found her the day of the attack. Yan said he fetched her from the bathroom. She was pale and had tears in her eyes, but she didn't say a word. Not to him or to me on the way home.

I thought she was in a state of shock, but it hasn't seemed to go away. Instances where I hear her voice are becoming few and far between. Lia isn't just muting herself during sex. She's doing it all the time.

She only speaks to Jeremy now, and I have to sneak in behind everyone's back like a thief in my own fucking house to hear her.

But sometimes, even with Jeremy, she goes into a daze. He calls her name and when she doesn't reply, he comes to me crying because his mom isn't talking to him.

She doesn't even realize when that happens.

After she's out of her trance, she hugs him and tells him she's sorry and that it won't happen again.

But it does happen again and again. Her confused state has been recurring enough that I'm worried. Not only about her, but also about Jeremy. He's young and attached to her, and if she keeps zoning out in his presence, he'll take it as a rejection and it'll traumatize him.

I'll have to gradually get him away from her until she gets back to normal. While I hate separating them, it's for his own good. I know what childhood fucking trauma is and my son will not relive my life. I can at least protect him like my father was unable to.

"Papa!" Jeremy barges through the kitchen, where I'm having a glass of water, his small feet slapping against the floor in his urgency.

It's ten in the evening and way past his bedtime. He must've snuck out of his room to get to the master bedroom. I often find him curled into Lia's side, as if he wants to make up for the time she closes off from him and the world.

However, she doesn't hug him back. Lia returns to sleeping in her corpse-like position, her entire body stiff and endless nightmares plaguing her peace.

I catch Jeremy and lift him in my arms when he slams against my leg. When I look into his tear-soaked eyes, my gut squeezes. "What is it, Malysh?"

"M-Mommy...help... Mommy..."

"What happened?" I'm already heading up the stairs and

to the bedroom. Jeremy is sniffling, his fingers trembling as he wraps his arms around my neck in a tight hug.

My feet come to a halt in the doorway as the scene unfolds in front of me. Lia thrashes in her sleep, fingers digging into the mattress and foam forming on either side of her mouth.

Fuck.

I put Jeremy down and try to speak softly, "Stay here, Malysh."

He nods, sniffling.

I eat up the distance to the bed in a few strides and sit on the mattress. While Lia's nightmares have returned with a vengeance, it's the first time they've been this violent.

I grab her shoulders, shaking her. "Wake up, Lia."

She gurgles, more foam covering her fair skin and her face turning blue.

She's not breathing.

"Lia!" My voice rises as I shake her harsher this time. "Wake up! Come on, open your eyes, Lenochka."

She gulps in a deep intake of air as she startles awake, her eyes open but glazed over. Then she starts weeping like a small child, the sound haunted and guttural as her fingers dig into my forearm. "Mom... I want Mom..."

"Hey," I soothe, pulling her to me and wrapping my arms around her. "It's only a nightmare."

She stills for a bit, sniffling, and her fingers sink into my chest as if she wants to feel me. I stroke her dark strands and inhale her addictive rose scent.

Jeremy slowly approaches us, tears shining in his inquisitive gray eyes. "Are you okay, Mommy?"

She pulls away from me and smiles at him. "Yes, angel. Mommy just had a bad dream."

He points a finger at me. "Papa will make them all go away."

Her expression falls, but she nods anyway. After he kisses

her goodnight, I carry Jeremy to his room and stay with him until he falls asleep.

By the time I go back to the master bedroom, Lia is sitting up in bed.

I close the door and get rid of my jacket as I stand in front of the vanity and meet her gaze through the mirror. "What's going on, Lia?"

"Huh?" Her glassy eyes slowly meet mine. I hate seeing her in this state, hate that's she's out of it more than not lately.

"Is it shock from the shooting? Should I get you a psychotherapist?"

She shakes her head, scoffing softly. "It should've been that."

"Should've been?"

"Nothing."

"It's obviously not nothing. What's going on?"

"You never asked about my parents again," she says out of nowhere. "But then again, you never really cared about me, anyway."

I turn around to face her, a muscle working in my jaw. Does she really believe that? Does she fucking think I'd put myself in an unfavorable position within the brotherhood if I didn't fucking care?

Sure, it might not be the type of care she wants, but I'm keeping her and our son safe.

I've been searching for the fucker who tried to shoot me that day, to no avail. The man we found dead with a bullet plucked out of his nape was an Eastern European mercenary who could be working for anyone.

In order to find who hired him, I've been calling in favors and searching day and night, but have had no luck. He must've been killed by whoever hired him, but why dig out the bullet? Did they fear the possibility of it being traced back to them? Although mercenaries usually have their own ammunition suppliers and wouldn't be able to be tracked.

At any rate, finding the bastard who threatened Lia's life has been the only thing I can focus on, and yet, she says that I don't fucking care.

I hold on to my calm as I speak, "If you'd wanted to talk about your parents, you would've."

She lays her hands on her lap, palms up, and studies them with that same glassy look. "Mom, Dad, and I weren't well off, but we were happy. I knew he wasn't my real father, but he was the only father I had. We lived in a small house by the Sicilian fields in which Dad managed a big farmer's workers. It was beautiful, with huge olive trees and clear summer skies. I got to play with some of the farmer's kids and Mom got me hooked on dancing. We were a cozy little family who prepared for the harsh winter and thrived in the summer. We had festivals during the harvest season and danced all night long. We were...normal."

Her voice lowers, but it doesn't break as she continues, "When I was five, something was wrong. I could feel it, even though I was young and clueless. I could tell something wasn't sitting quite right in the house. Mom wasn't playing the loud American music that Dad shook his head to, and he wasn't there to kiss me or hold me. I was hiding behind the door when I heard them. Men were yelling at Dad in Italian, telling him he should give them the girl, and my composed dad was shouting back that he wouldn't.

"Someone grabbed me and I squealed, but Mom wrapped a hand around my mouth and shook her head to quiet me. We ran outside toward a separate cottage, and she ushered me into a small box and put her finger to her mouth. She had tears in her eyes when she kissed me. She said she was sorry that Dad wasn't my real father and that she wished she could change it. Then she told me not to get out under any circumstances until someone called me by her maiden name, Gueller."

Lia's hands shake, her delicate throat working with a

swallow. "I spent a long time in that box, sweaty and scared. That box was so dark and tight, but I didn't dare leave it. I could hear loud bangs from the house before it was silent. I don't know how long I remained in the box until someone came to fetch me by calling me Little Gueller. I was starved and cold and I wet myself, but all I wanted was Mom and Dad. The man who took me to the airport told me they had died from gas asphyxiation and that I'd be living with my grandmother. He didn't even let me see them one last time. Back then, I believed they died because of gas, it made me feel more at ease. But the older I grew, the surer I was that there was something else. Otherwise, why would Mom have hidden me?

"I asked Grandma about it and she refused to tell me anything until she was on her deathbed. She said that my mom got involved with the wrong man, a mobster, and became pregnant with me. She was forced to marry my dad so that my illegitimate existence wouldn't reflect badly on my biological father. Grandma never told me who that was and I never wanted to get involved with him." She meets my gaze. "But you know all of this, don't you? You're well aware of my whole background. That's why you never asked."

I tap my finger against my thigh but say nothing, waiting for her to give me what I need.

"Is it true, Adrian?"

"Is what true?"

Her chin trembles and her eyes fill with unshed tears. "Have you been keeping me all this time to get close to my father?"

"Maybe."

Her expression falters, hurt and something else filtering in. *I need those strong emotions. Let them all out, Lia.*

"But why? Why would you go to all this trouble to use me against Lazlo Luciano? He doesn't even know I exist!"

There.

My muscles stiffen as she offers me what I've been waiting for. "I thought you didn't know who your real father is."

She swallows, realizing her mistake. "Grandma told me."

"You just said she didn't give you a name."

"She…did."

I'm in front of her in a second, holding her chin up with my fingers. "I torture grown men for answers, and I know exactly when humans lie. So why don't you tell me who the fuck really told you your father's name?"

Her lips tremble, cementing the fact that she does indeed have outside help. *Fuck.* How could I not have seen it before?

Her sparkling eyes flood with fear as she shudders. "No… one."

"Lie."

"I heard you," she blurts.

"You heard me," I repeat slowly with clear menace.

"You were talking with Kolya, and he told you to use Luciano's offspring against him and you said you'd think about it. I also thought back on when you used to ask me about my Italian origins and connected the dots."

"You're good, Lia. You've become so good at spewing lies that you can make up an entire story out of scraps, but you're not good enough to fool me." I tighten my hold on her jaw. "You have one more try."

"That was really it."

"Wrong answer." I release her with a shove and retrieve my phone. "We'll start with Yan. After I torture him, I'll know if it's him. He might lose his dominant hand or maybe his neck, you never know. If it's not him, we'll move on to Boris, then to everyone else who's been near you in the past few years."

"No!" She lunges forward, holding onto my hand that's grabbing the phone. "How could you hurt your own guards?"

"They told you or they let you meet with an outsider. Either way, they weren't doing their tasks and deserve everything that befalls them. You'll watch every second of it, so when I tell you to talk, you'll fucking *talk*."

A sob tears from her throat. "It's someone else. Please don't hurt them."

Someone else? Someone fucking else? I don't know why I hoped it was Yan or Boris. If they'd betrayed me, I could've dealt with it. It would've been even better if she'd overheard them and I could chalk all this up to something trivial.

But someone else is involved? My mind speeds up in a different direction as the worst comes to mind.

Someone. Else.

As in Lia has been meeting someone behind my fucking back.

"Who?"

She shakes her head. "I won't tell you who he is so you can kill him."

He.

It's a fucking *he.*

Lia has been meeting a motherfucking 'he' behind my back.

A red mist covers my vision until it's nearly impossible to see her through it.

My voice turns deadly calm, hinting at nothing of the raging volcano erupting inside. "Are you protecting him because he's your lover? Are you cheating on me, Lia?"

She blinks twice, her lips trembling. "If I deny it, you'll never believe me. You'll just lock me up and suffocate me more. You'll kill me slowly, so think what you want, Adrian. Do whatever the fuck you want! You're using me, anyway, so get on with it."

"I said, is he your fucking lover?"

She lifts her chin, and all emotions vanish from her face when she says the one word that shatters my world to smithereens, "Yes."

I slam my fist into the headboard beside her head and

shatter it to pieces. Lia remains in place, her face paling and her bright eyes going back to their glassy state.

My hand wraps around her throat, tilting it back and squeezing. "I should kill you right now."

"Do. It," she manages. "Dying is better than living with you."

Her words crash into the marrow of my bones, turning me into a damn fucking beast. A growl slips from my throat, and I'm acting on pure fucking instinct as I rip the nightgown off her. The material turns to shreds and her pink nipples harden while her thighs clench together.

"Did he look at this body, Lia? Did he look at what's fucking mine?"

She doesn't say anything, struggling for air as I use my other hand to unbuckle my pants and free my cock.

I'm hard, but it's with rage, with the need to murder him and punish her. The need to own her whole so she's mine in every sense of the word.

I'm not an idiot, I know Lia's never really loved me. It's evident in the way she's pulled away from me any chance she gets, how she tried to escape, but I believed she was as devoted to me as I am to her. That she cared enough about the semblance of the family we have.

But she was fucking someone behind my back.

Lia was giving what's mine to someone else.

Where? How?

The one place I don't have direct access to Lia is at the shelter. I'm going to find the motherfucker and kill him with a slow death.

"Did you open these legs to another man?" I slap her thighs apart and she gasps in air. "Did you let him look at my cunt?"

Lia is trembling all over, even as her pupils dilate. I give her enough of an opening so she can breathe and she sucks in a long breath through her mouth.

I cup her pussy harshly. "Whose cunt is this?"

"Yours..." she lets out in a small voice as her arousal coats my fingers.

"That's right, mine. So how fucking dare you give what's mine to someone else?"

Her mouth is parted, but she says nothing.

"Who's the only one who gets to fuck you, Lia?"

She stays silent.

"I said, who's the only one who fucks your cunt?"

"You..."

I hold her thighs down and drive inside her wet heat in one ruthless go. Usually, I'll let her adjust to my size, but I'm in no state of mind as I pound into her with a wild rhythm that's meant to punish her, to let her feel how much she's cut me fucking open.

"This cunt is mine." I lift her thigh and slap her ass, hard, and she gasps. "This ass is also mine. You belong to me, and I will fuck that fact into you until it's the only thing you breathe and think about. Next time you even consider letting another man look at you, let alone touch you, you'll recall this moment when every inch of you is owned by me."

Her walls tighten around my dick, strangling me as she shatters around me. I pull out of her and smear her own juices on her back hole.

Lia's eyes widen as I push the crown of my dick inside. "I said, every fucking inch of you, wife."

"Adrian..."

"What?" I growl.

"You're angry."

"Who made me angry? Who made me lose my fucking mind?"

"But you're going to hurt me."

"Don't you love it when I hurt you? Or am I not doing it hard enough?"

She shakes her head frantically.

"Tell me to fuck you in the ass, Lia. Tell me to own every inch of you."

"Fuck me. Own me…" she whimpers.

That's all the words I need.

Lia sucks in a deep breath, more of her arousal dripping down her cunt and onto my dick as I push farther inside. Her head rolls back and I groan at how tight she is. Even though I've fingered her here before, I've never taken it, because I wanted to leave it until she came to me, until she fucking wanted me enough to initiate sex.

But fuck that.

Fuck my sappy notions about her.

She went ahead and ruined us, so I'll ruin her in return.

I shove all the way in, causing her eyes to shut and her pulse to quicken.

"Look at me."

She slowly opens her lids, staring at me through hooded eyes.

"See this?" I thrust in her ass as I pound three rough fingers into her cunt.

She nods slowly, her face flushed with both pleasure and pain.

"Does your body welcome him as it welcomes me? Did you let his limp dick in your ass?"

Lia shakes her head.

"Hmm. So it was only the cunt? *My* fucking cunt?"

I drive harder into her, my groin slapping against her ass cheeks and my fingers powering into her pussy with renewed energy that leaves her panting. "Did you like it? Do you tighten around him as you tighten around me?"

"Noooo!" she screams as her orgasm rips through her, and her entire body bucks off the bed. I pump into her some more and then pull out and come all over her face, my cum dripping down her parted lips and chin.

It's the first time I've done it, but it seemed fitting since she probably let him fucking come inside her.

I'm so paranoid that if Jeremy didn't look like a younger version of me, I'd do a DNA test.

My beast takes complete control, and I feel like the hurt and anger will detonate me from the inside.

"Understand this, Lia. I might not hurt you, might not fucking kill you, even though you deserve it, but I'll find that bastard, and when I do, I'll fuck you in front of him before I slice his fucking throat. Then I'll fuck you again in the pool of his blood." I release her neck and she sucks in deep breaths, tears sliding down her cheeks. "Protect him while you can."

THIRTY-SIX

Lia

I THINK I'M GOING INSANE.

In the beginning, I chalked it up to my nightmares getting the better of me. I was dreaming about memories of Mom and Dad in Sicily, and most of them were about being trapped in a box with no way out.

But then I started having those nightmares while I was awake. My mind broke my spirit, my soul, and my fucking heart.

I realized something was definitely wrong when Jeremy became scared of me. He called me a ghost and said he hates Ghost Mommy.

Adrian has his nanny working full-time now and he's been distancing Jeremy from me like he always intended to. He's been taking away my angel.

Since the night I broke whatever is between us, Adrian hates me. He doesn't say it in words, but he proves it in actions more than enough. He hate-fucks me every night, in the pussy, then in the ass, and sometimes he'll take me to the shower just to do it all over again. I loathe how much I like it, how much

I tingle with anticipation for his rough handling and unapologetic owning. In a way, that's the only time I'm forced to be alive, to snap out of my daytime nightmares and the demons lurking in my head.

But whenever he's not touching me, the vicious circle resumes. I'm plagued by memories of the man I killed, the life I finished, the innocence I slaughtered.

I overestimated my mind and believed that I'd survive killing someone. I haven't. Ever since that day, I've been going downhill with no way to stop the slide.

I always thought myself above Adrian's lifestyle, but I'm as much of a killer as he is now. The notion that I'll become just as soulless brings tears to my eyes.

I'm losing touch with reality and with Jeremy. It's worse when I take my antidepressants. I turn into a zombie, too numb to move or talk or even think.

Adrian took me back to my shrink, the same one I used to see. I didn't bother asking how he knew about her, because Adrian knows whatever he wants to.

Even though he waited outside while I had my visit, I couldn't find the words to talk to her. Before, I used to tell her about my parents and the black box, about how ballet wrenched me out of that box. After my career ended, I was stuffed into it again, but only for a brief while until Jeremy came along. However, now that I've killed someone, the box's walls are tightening around my soul.

How could I tell the shrink that? How could I tell her that I murdered a person to protect my killer husband who married me just to use me?

It's been months since I told Adrian I was cheating on him. At that moment, when he didn't deny that he'd gotten close to me because of who my father is, he hurt me so badly, it was like the tip of his sharp blade tore through my heart and the feelings I had for him. I should've expected it, considering he doesn't know how to feel, but I thought after five years of being together, he would've somehow gotten used to me like I've gotten used to him. He could've built a place for me in his black heart, even if it's not as big as the area he occupies in mine.

I believed that maybe he cares a little.

Maybe he loves me a little.

But that was all naivety of my part. I'm the foolish one who fell in love. Adrian only ever saw me as a possession, as property. Someone he could fuck and keep under his thumb.

So I wanted to hurt him deeply. I wanted to stab him in his emotionless heart over and over so he'd feel a sliver of what I did. The only way to do so was by telling him that he was second, that the object he loved to possess wanted someone else.

But while I liked that night's sex and the sex that followed after, I miss the other side of Adrian. The one who took care of me.

The one who hugged me to sleep and placed my feet on his lap, massaging away the tension.

Sometimes, I pretend to fall asleep in Jeremy's room just so I'll feel him lift me up, hold me to his strong body, and tuck me gently in bed.

Because in my waking moments, all I see on his face is hatred.

Sheer, utter hatred.

Adrian might have slightly gotten over my escape attempt, but he'll never forgive me for cheating on him. He might not leave me, because I'm Jeremy's mother and his 'property,' but he'll never look at me as he did in the past.

He'll never show me his rare smile or his caring side. He'll never stroke my hair and kiss me before he goes out again.

I have to sneak around to watch him do those things with Jeremy.

That's when I realize I've ruined everything.

Sometimes, I want to tell him it's not true, that I lied

because I was hurt, but his clipped words discourage me. He'd never believe me, anyway. Not when I held on to the lie for so long.

He still allows me to volunteer, but he sends at least five guards with me now, probably searching for my lover.

Thankfully, Luca has probably read the atmosphere and hasn't gotten in touch again.

I have no doubt that if Adrian finds my childhood friend, he will skin him alive. People like him don't like others to touch their property and will go the extra mile to prove a point.

Yan goes before me into the bathroom and checks every stall. When he tries to open one, a woman screams profanities at him from inside it, and he merely shrugs a shoulder. He can be so apathetic sometimes, both Adrian's and Kolya's personalities rubbing off on him.

After he makes sure no one is at the window and closes it, he checks the stalls—aside from the occupied one—one last time.

"Is this necessary?" I sigh.

"I'm just following orders," he says apologetically. He's been addressing me with more frowns than usual, probably sensing that things aren't the same.

Before he leaves me in peace, he pauses and shuts the door, trapping us—and the screaming woman, who's still in the stall—inside.

"What?" I ask with alarm.

"You're not doing well, are you?"

"No offense, but I haven't been doing well since I made your acquaintance."

"None taken"—he lowers his voice—"but it's different since after the assassination attempt."

"Different?"

He rubs the back of his neck. "Look, I know you didn't cheat on Boss."

"How can you be so sure?"

"You're not that type of person."

I scoff. "Obviously, your precious boss thinks I am."

"He's blinded by you, Lia."

"By me?"

"Yes. His obsession with you is forbidding him from thinking logically. And you did tell him you cheated. Did you think he'd pat you on the back?"

"I said that after I found out that he's using me because of who my father is!"

"Still, do you think painting his most precious person, you, as a cheater was a wise idea?"

No, it wasn't. "I'm not his most precious person."

"Yes, you are, Lia. I've known Boss since I was younger than Jeremy and I've never seen him treat anyone the way he treats you."

"With disdain, you mean?"

"You must me be joking. Listen, he's not the type who allows anyone to cause him pain, but you were able to. You hurt him."

"No more than he hurt me." Tears well in my eyes. "Besides, he'd need to feel for me to ever be able to be hurt by me."

"You're just as blinded as he is, I swear. Just talk to him and I assure you that he'll see your honesty. You're torturing each other and it's painful to watch."

"How can I torture him when he doesn't care?"

Yan opens his mouth to say something, but a bang from outside, probably from Boris, stops him.

"Just talk," he insists before he gets out.

Arguing in Russian reaches me from outside. Boris is like Kolya's twin brother when it comes to stoic behavior. He doesn't like it when Yan talks to me and never fails to remind Yan of that fact.

After I quickly finish my business in the toilet, I stand at the sink to wash my hands.

The woman who screamed at Yan earlier shoves her stall door open. "The fuck is this? Family drama isn't supposed to happen in a damn toilet…" she trails off. Then she whispers, "Fuck."

I raise my head and my mouth hangs open as the water keeps running from the faucet onto my stiff fingers.

I'm staring at a replica of me.

She's dressed in a faux fur pink coat, torn blue gloves, and her hair is a mixture of blonde tips and darker roots.

Her face is smudged with dirt and a few other things, but we're still so similar that both of us stop and stare for a second.

"Wow," I murmur.

"Fucking wow, indeed." She circles me as if I'm an animal at the zoo. "If I didn't know I was an only child, I'd think I have a twin sister. How old are you, girl?"

"Thirty."

"Eh, I'm twenty-seven, so we can't be twins." She stops in front of me and grins. "Fucking life kicking a lookalike my way, ey?"

"You're…" I trail off searching for the right words. "Do you come to this shelter often?"

"Nah, first time. But what a first time it is." She stares at my hand and her eyes bug out. "Look at that fucking rock! Bet it could feed me for a year."

I'm about to tell her that this wedding ring is the key to my cage, but while I study her, a crazy idea slowly forms in my head as the cold water soaks my skin. I must've really gone insane if I'm thinking about executing it.

"I'm Lia. What's your name?"

"Winter," she says, still looking at my ring. "Winter Cavanaugh."

"How did you become homeless, Winter?"

She throws her hands in the air. "It started a few months ago. I became an alcoholic after my baby girl was stillborn and my mom died."

"I'm so sorry."

"So am I, but I'd be less sorry if I was married to a man who gave me such rocks. Goddamn, girl, look at your necklace. It must've cost a fortune."

"Do you really want that?"

Her head snaps in my direction. "What type of question is that? 'Course I want it."

"What if I can make it happen?" My voice is monotone and scary, even to myself.

"How?"

I step closer to her and speak low so Yan and Boris don't hear. The running water also serves as a camouflage. "Take my place, my husband, my fortune. Everything."

"Are you kidding?" She laughs, then stops when I don't join her. "You're serious?"

"Dead serious." This feels like a movie, a reckless one, but I would be stupid if I pass on the chance that fate is finally offering me.

Her small features crease. "Why in the flying fuck would you give up all of that?"

"Because it's suffocating."

"I'll choke by money any day."

"It's not that easy. My husband is a mobster."

"Even cooler. Means he has more money."

"You really don't care about what he does? He's in the Russian mafia."

"That's badass."

I frown. How could she be this acceptant of it? But homeless people have a different way of thinking than I do, so she probably sees Adrian's profession as an advantage, not an inconvenience.

She nudges me with her elbow. "You really gonna give me your husband and money?"

"If you agree. All I want is my son."

"Of course I agree. Who wouldn't want to live like a queen?"

Footsteps echo behind the door and I whisper, "Listen, do you have something I can write on?"

She opens her coat and lifts her sweater, revealing her fair belly with stretch marks. "Do it here."

I retrieve my super matte lipstick pencil from my bag and scribble on her stomach. "This is my email address and password. Tonight at eight, I'll self-send a document that has all the information you need to learn about my husband and his organization. I'll also include notes about my mannerisms and way of talking so you can mimic me. I'll delete the email in three minutes, so make sure you download it immediately and print it out. I'll give you money. Hide your face with your hoodie when you leave, and don't come here again except to meet me in this bathroom next week at the same time if you still want to swap places."

"Sure thing." Her eyes gleam as she stares at my email and password on her stomach as if they're sacred.

I drop my lipstick back in my bag. "See you then."

"Wait." She grins, showing surprisingly white teeth, but that's probably because she hasn't been homeless for long. "You said you'd give me money to print out the document. Can you include change for some alcohol?"

I give her all of the cash Adrian tells me to keep on me in case of emergencies. "Dye your hair the same color as mine and buy shampoo with a rose fragrance."

"Got it!"

I straighten as I exit the bathroom with my heart hammering.

This is my last chance to escape before I either kill myself or Adrian hands me over to my biological father to do the honors.

THIRTY-SEVEN

Lia

A WEEK LATER, WINTER IS HERE.

She's washed up and dyed her hair the same color as mine. She smells of roses, the scent Adrian recognizes me by.

I don't waste time as I strip from my coat and one of my dresses. I wore two, one on top of the other, so I don't have to spend long here.

Winter does the same, humming joyfully. I feel sorry for her, for the life I'm thrusting her into, to the point that I thought about backing out of the plan this entire past week.

But Adrian's cold shoulder kept me going. When Rai and I were shot at during a gathering she planned a few weeks ago, he didn't show a sliver of concern, as if I didn't almost die. All he did was bark orders and completely ignore me. If that isn't a sign that he'll soon hand me over to my father, who's possibly worse than him, I don't know what is.

Besides, Winter said she read the file and doesn't mind. That file has all of the information about the Bratva monstrosity and should've been a serious red flag.

Winter actually seems more ready for this than I am.

"I learned that doc by heart like I never learned anything during school," she says, getting rid of her pink coat. "I'm so envious that you're a ballerina."

"Ex-ballerina." My throat closes.

"Oh, right. It said you broke your leg. Pity. I always wanted to be a ballerina, you know."

"Never being one is better than having to give it up." That pain will never go away, but it's not worse than learning I'm only a means to an end to Adrian.

It's not worse than falling for the wrong man and allowing him to suck my soul from my body.

"I guess."

We change in a haste and then I fix her up and lift her shoulders so that her posture is straight like mine.

"Remember, stay in a daze. They're used to that from me in the house."

"Okay."

"Don't forget not to say that word in front of Adrian. He hates it."

"Oh, yeah. I remember reading that."

"And be careful of Ogla. She knows everything about everything." And I'm more and more sure that she's the one who snitched to Adrian about my escape attempt soon after Jeremy's birth.

"Got it."

"Next week, bring Jeremy with you and I'll get someone to help me so I can take him with me. If Adrian says no, tell him you miss being with Jer and want to spend some time with him."

"Yup."

It's going to kill me to live a week without Jeremy, but it's a small sacrifice to make for escaping this life. One in which my fate is hanging on a word from Adrian.

The moment he decides he hates me more than he wants me, he won't hesitate to get rid of me.

"If you survive another week after that, I can ask the person helping me to get you out," I offer.

"Nah, I'm gonna be a boss bitch. Why would I want to leave?"

I grab her shoulders. "Listen to me, Winter, Adrian is dangerous."

"So you keep telling me. Are you having second thoughts?"

"Of course not."

She shrugs. "All is cool then."

"Are you sure?"

"Are *you*? Because it seems like you're really having cold feet, girl."

"I'm not, I'm just warning you."

"Maybe you just don't want to give up your man."

"That's not true."

She hums joyfully. "Then is it okay if I fuck him? He looked smoking hot in the pictures."

Her words stab me in the chest and bile rises in my throat. I want to scream no, that he's mine and always will be, that no one but me is allowed to touch him, but is that true when I'm escaping him?

"I don't care what you do after I'm gone," I mutter.

"Cool. You can't take it back now." She gives me a Cheshire cat grin. "No changing your mind either. I mean it."

I give Winter my bag with all my belongings and tell her to spray my perfume. She does that with glee and waves two fingers at me.

Hiding in the bathroom, I keep the door open the slightest bit to watch her go to Yan and Boris. My heart hammers loudly, expecting them to find out and come in for me, but they just walk in front of her, talking animatedly in Russian.

I release a breath, but the relief is short-lived. How could they not realize it's not me? I know we look alike, but still. I'm disappointed in Boris and Yan—especially the latter.

Adrian will see her as me, too. He'll touch her like he touches me, fuck her the way he fucks me.

Nausea assaults me and I want to throw up my guts in the toilet. However, I force myself to straighten and hold my head high.

This is for my survival.

I might love Adrian, but I won't stick around until he's bored of me, until he makes me go really crazy.

Now, to the next part of my plan.

Rai said she'd help me, and I believe her because she's strong enough in the brotherhood to go behind Adrian's back. Unlike Luca, she wants nothing in return.

I'll tell her to hide me from Adrian, then help me escape from him once and for all.

THIRTY-EIGHT

Adrian

BEING SOMEONE WHO TRUSTS HIS SYSTEM TO THE point of blindness, I can tell when something is wrong. I've been racking my brain trying to figure out where everything hit rock bottom. When the fuck did I start to lose the top-notch efficiency my system provided?

One thing's for certain, Lia has something to do with it. Or, more accurately, my obsession with her does.

At one point, it became carnal and dark. I tried to lighten it at the beginning, to make up for my lack of feelings with my actions, to show her that she's special to me, even if I'm wired differently and didn't know how to feel as she secretly wished.

I thought she'd eventually see the effort I was making. It'd take time, but it would happen. Lia would come to me, not work against me. She'd trust me and talk to me.

But she chose another man.

One who has been in hiding since she confessed her adultery, because there's no way in fuck she would've met him since then. I've been assigning an army to stay on her case and installing cameras everywhere she goes.

The more I smother her into my closed off system, the closer I am to losing control, because I know, I just know, this is heading for the worst, not the better.

I had a talk with her shrink—or more like threatened her shrink—and she said that her hallucinations are getting worse. She's escalating from when she started to have this condition as a kid. In the past, antidepressants and sleeping pills managed to gradually rid her of her neurotic episodes, but lately, she's been talking to Ogla about things that never happened.

She told me that Lia recently crossed paths with Hannah, her previous colleague and the current New York City Ballet's prima ballerina. However, that never happened.

The psychotherapist is worried because this could be the beginning of a dissociation episode. Her condition has gotten worse since she was shot at during the women's gathering organized by Rai. She had a PTSD episode and said she saw red eyes coming for her.

When the doctor said that she shouldn't be put in stressful situations or surrounded by people who make her anxious, I distanced myself further. Even though it kills me to stay away from her, I can at least recognize that I'm the major cause of her depression and anxiety. Even Ogla, whom she didn't get along with at the beginning, has gotten closer to her.

The only person in this house whom she loses her smile upon seeing is me.

Even my fucking guards get her smiles. But never me.

There's a permanent frown etched upon her features when she meets my gaze. Her delicate face pulls down with deep, tangible sadness.

Fuck that.

I still believe that I'll be able to draw out the Lia from the past. The Lia who sat down with me for dinners and talked about everything and nothing, trying every trick under the sun to get me to talk as well.

But first, I need to find the fucker she cheated on me with, figure out his relation to her and Lazlo. Only after I kill him in a slow death will I be able to breathe again.

Maybe it won't get clean air into my lungs, maybe I'll never forget what she did, but I'll never let her leave either.

Tonight, I'm going to talk to her one last time about it. I'm going to ask her and I will listen as Kolya and Yan have been urging me to.

I find her in the kitchen rummaging in the fridge, wearing one of her fluffy nightgowns with a robe that has layers upon layers of faux fur. She wore that once, then threw it in the back of the closet because it was too eccentric for her tastes.

Narrowing my eyes, I watch her movements. They're too fast, lacking her usual finesse and elegance.

"What are you doing?"

She turns around, yelping, and I'm staring at a replica of my wife. Someone who has the exact same looks and build. Even the eyes are almost identical.

Almost.

Because those eyes? They don't have the deep sadness in Lia's. The permanent sheen of gray.

"Who are you?" I ask.

She gulps, the packet of frozen meat dangling from her hand. "W-what do you mean who am I? I'm Lia."

I reach her in two steps and she runs around the counter. I pull out my gun and point it at her. "You're not Lia. Who are you?"

She freezes, eyes wide as she puts her hands in the air, letting the frozen meat fall to the floor. "Please don't shoot! She said nothing about being shot at. I'm so sorry, *please*, I only want money. I don't want to die."

"This is the final time I ask this question. Who the fuck are you?"

"My name is Winter. I met your wife at the shelter, and

she asked me to take her place because she wanted to escape or something. I meant no disrespect, I swear."

Fuck.

I stare at the woman again, hoping I'm wrong, but when I don't find Lia in there, my chest constricts with something so similar to…fear.

This is not Lia. So, where's my wife?

"Kolya," I call.

He comes inside in a second, frowning when he takes in the scene. He probably thinks she's Lia. This Winter may be able to fool the world, but not me. She doesn't have the permanently haunted expression Lia has. She might smell like her, but she doesn't have that natural soft body scent that no one but my Lenochka has.

"Find Lia's location through her dental tracker and send it to my phone," I order. "This one is an imposter."

"What should we do with her?" Kolya narrows his eyes on her and she takes a step back.

"Keep her locked up until I figure out what to do with her."

"No! I did nothing wrong." She steps back further and turns to run, but trips over her long robe and shrieks as she falls, her head hitting the counter. Blood splashes on the tile as her body slips down with a thud, her lips open and her eyes blinking slowly.

Kolya reaches for her, but I stop him. "Track Lia. Let Ogla take care of the imposter."

Then I'm out the door, Kolya following behind me.

The red mist that I only see when Lia is involved covers my vision and all I can think about is that she left.

She fucking ran.

I never thought she'd leave Jeremy behind, but she went ahead and did it. She had enough of pretending and escaped.

Probably to be with her lover.

She not only cheated on me, but she also went to him.

They're probably both laughing at my expense, thinking they've gotten away with it.

Fuck that.

If anything, they should both be ready for my wrath. As I promised her, I will kill him in a slow death in front of her eyes and fuck her in his blood.

Then I'm bringing her home.

THIRTY-NINE

Lia

RAI HAS AGREED TO HELP ME.

At first, she was hesitant about going against Adrian since, like the entire brotherhood—or the whole crime world, actually—no one wants to get on his bad side. My husband has the ability to inflict irrevocable damage that no one can escape. He may be silent, but his wrath is lethal.

He's the type who learns someone's weakness, exploits it, then suffocates them with it until they wish for death.

I guess that's what he did to me.

The only difference is that he showed me a side of him I fell in love with, then he took it away, leaving me with painful emotions and hope for nothing.

My gaze strays through the window, watching the empty road go by as Rai's guard, Ruslan, drives me to a safe house.

I miss Jeremy and his beautiful smile. I miss how he draws me and his father together as if we're some sort of a happy family. Not seeing him since this morning is messing with my already screwed-up head. I don't know how the hell I'll survive a week without his bright energy and contagious smile.

He's probably asleep by now, having joyful dreams.

I wonder if Winter is sleeping in my bed, fucking Adrian because he looks 'smoking hot.' I wonder if he's already replaced me with her—touching her, driving into her, and cradling her body into his.

Moisture stings my eyes at the image and I shake my head. I will not think about it. Everything has been said and done, and now I have to focus on the future.

But that doesn't mean those thoughts don't slice my heart open deep enough to leave a hole.

"Fuck." Ruslan's low curse pulls me out of my reverie.

"What?"

"I think we're being followed, Mrs. Volkov." He stares at the rear-view mirror.

I shift in the seat to look behind me and my eyes are met with bright, almost blinding headlights.

No.

Adrian couldn't have found me after all the trouble I went through.

He should be with Winter.

A small part of my heart revels at the idea that her identical appearance didn't fool him, that he knew it wasn't me.

But the bigger part wants to break free of my shackles, to just be free of him and his cold shoulder and the way he's killing me slowly.

"Can't you go faster?" I urge him.

"Mrs. Sokolov can't be implicated in this. If Adrian finds out she helped you…"

He will ruin her.

I know he will, and because of that, Ruslan can't let me implicate Rai. All the doors are closing in my face, and I know I can't go far, nor can I endanger Rai when she went out of her way to help me.

"Do you have a weapon you can lend me?" I ask.

Ruslan's brow furrows. "My spare knife."

"That'll do." I'd prefer a gun, but it's better than nothing.

He reaches into his glove box, pulls out a hunting knife, and hands it to me.

I suck in a deep breath. "Drop me off at a location where they can't see you."

"Are you sure, Mrs. Volkov?"

"It's the only way to protect you and Rai. Please leave before he catches you, or all of you will be in danger."

He gives a curt nod and accelerates, taking a swift turn toward the forest. Gravel and dirt crunch under the car's tires, and then it comes to a halt.

"Thank Rai on my behalf," I say and dash out of the car with the knife nestled in my palm.

Darkness has staked its claim on the forest, making it eerily quiet with the occasional haunting sounds coming from the night owls. The tall trees shape the distance and everything looks black, aside from the moon shining above, partially camouflaged by clouds.

I don't think as I run in the opposite direction to Ruslan. I barely see a path in the forest and I follow it, all my fears about the unknown vanishing in the background.

"Lia!" The very familiar voice bellows from not too far behind me, sending tendrils of fear down to my soul.

Run.

I have to run.

My heart thumps harder, slamming against my ribcage as I charge through the forest.

"Lia, stop!"

No!

If I do, everything will be over. This time, I won't be able to survive his wrath and I will splinter into irredeemable pieces.

This time, it'll be the end.

"Lia!" His voice is nearer, moving in closer, as if he's pulling me back by the marionette strings attached to my nape.

The knife is heavy in my hand as I slice it through branches and anything else that gets in my way.

A rustling of footsteps comes from behind me and I halt, spinning around and waving the knife. I gasp when it hits a warm body.

Adrian.

He barely winces as I release the knife, letting it fall to the ground, but the damage is already done. The blade has penetrated his bicep. Under the moonlight, I can make out the blood dripping from his jacket. His face is shadowed by both the darkness and the anger that's tightening his jaw.

Something tells me it's not because of the wound.

That's all I can focus on, though.

The injury.

His life essence oozes out of his bicep in a steady rhythm. I wrap both hands around it and squeeze, willing it to stop.

However, blood slips between my fingers, coating them, warm and almost black in the darkness as it drips to the ground.

"You need to make it stop." My voice is a haunted murmur.

"What about you? Are you ever going to stop escaping me?"

I flinch at his words, releasing him and stepping backward.

The reason I unintentionally stabbed him in the first place slams back into me.

I have to run.

I turn and sprint away, but my gaze keeps flitting to my bloodied hands, to Adrian's life on my hands.

I finished it today. I think I finally signed the death certificate of our relationship. As fucked-up as it was, what we had was a relationship and I just killed it.

Thudding footsteps sound behind me and I know he'll

catch up to me in no time. He'll take me back and it'll all be over.

Jumbled thoughts and emotions coil inside me with a wrecking force. They mount and scatter in different directions, stealing my breaths.

My sanity.

My everything.

Reality blurs with something a lot more potent—hallucinations.

My demons start whispering in my head, words that I can't even discern.

Oh, God, no.

Please don't torture me with my own mind.

I dig my nails into my wrist and a tear slides down my cheek as pain explodes on my skin. If I hoped for this to be a nightmare, my wish doesn't come true.

My feet come to a halt at the top of a cliff. I stare down at the violent waves hitting the harsh angular rocks with trembling limbs.

I don't think I've ever been attracted to something so frightening.

No, I actually have.

Adrian.

Seems I'm broken beyond repair, because since the beginning, I think I was attracted to the danger he promised. And that only consumed me until there was nothing left.

He said he'd ruin me, and he did that with flying colors.

"Lia."

My name leaves his mouth in a whisper, and I turn around to meet his gaze, my feet on the edge.

Adrian is a few steps away from me, deep lines etched in his forehead. "Come down."

"So you'll take me back and lock me up?" I taste salt, and it's then that I realize tears are soaking my cheeks.

"No."

"You will! You'll also take Jeremy away from me for good. You'll torture me with your silent treatment until I go mad or kill myself."

"I will not do that."

"You've been doing it already! Can't you see that you've been slowly killing me? Killing us? You don't even kiss me anymore." I hate how my voice breaks with pain.

"That's because you fucking cheated on me! I have only ever been faithful to you, but you met another man behind my back."

"And you've been just using me!"

He sucks in a long breath, calming his voice. "Come down and we'll talk about this."

"What's there to talk about?"

"Everything, Lenochka."

"I want to know something first." My chin trembles as I speak so low, I'm surprised he hears me, "Have you ever loved me, Adrian?"

He pauses as if the question is alien to him, but he doesn't reply. Fresh tears stream harder at the answer he indirectly gives me. He hasn't. Or, more accurately, he doesn't know what love means.

Never has and never will.

"Because I loved you." I lay a palm over my heart and fist the material of my dress. "And it's killing me every day."

He extends the hand of his uninjured arm. "Come down, Lenochka. *Please.*"

"I took your hand before, Adrian, and you smothered me with it." I smile a little. "I'd rather die quickly than slowly."

"Lia, no!"

I close my eyes and let the wind take me down.

TO BE CONTINUED

Adrian and Lia's story concludes in the last book of the Deception trilogy, *Consumed by Deception*.

Curious about Rai and Kyle who appeared in this book? You can read their completed story in *Throne of Power*.

For a sneak peek into Adrian's past, you can download the free prequel, *Dark Deception*.

WHAT'S NEXT?

Thank you so much for reading *Tempted by Deception*! If you liked it, please leave a review.
Your support means the world to me.

If you're thirsty for more discussions with other readers of the series, you can join the Facebook group, Rina's Spoilers Room.

Next up is the conclusion of the Deception Trilogy, *Consumed by Deception.*

<u>Blurb</u>

My husband. My monster.

The truth isn't always what it seems.
Lia doesn't realize that, but she will. Soon.
I chose this life. This road. This twisted arrangement.
For her, I made a deal with the devil.
For her, I toyed with fate and death.
There's no going back.
I stole her and like any thief, I won't return her.
Lia is my addiction. My obsession. My love.
Mine.

ALSO BY RINA KENT

For more titles by the author and an
explicit reading order, please visit:
www.rinakent.com/books

ABOUT THE AUTHOR

Rina Kent is a *USA Today*, international, and #1 Amazon bestselling author of everything enemies to lovers romance.

She's known to write unapologetic anti-heroes and villains because she often fell in love with men no one roots for. Her books are sprinkled with a touch of darkness, a pinch of angst, and an unhealthy dose of intensity.

She spends her private days in London laughing like an evil mastermind about adding mayhem to her expanding universe. When she's not writing, Rina travels, hikes, and spoils cats in a pure Cat Lady fashion.

Find Rina Below:

Website: www.rinakent.com

Newsletter: www.subscribepage.com/rinakent

BookBub: www.bookbub.com/profile/rina-kent

Amazon: www.amazon.com/Rina-Kent/e/B07MM54G22

Goodreads: www.goodreads.com/author/show/18697906.
Rina_Kent

Instagram: www.instagram.com/author_rina

Facebook: www.facebook.com/rinaakent

Reader Group: www.facebook.com/groups/rinakent.club

Pinterest: www.pinterest.co.uk/AuthorRina/boards

Tiktok: www.tiktok.com/@rina.kent

Twitter: twitter.com/AuthorRina